A New England Romance

By the Author

The Shape of Man: A Novella and Five Stories

The Mutilation Gypsy and Other Stories

Where the Streets Are Paved With Gold: A Novel in the Compton Cycle

Jay And The Bounty Of Books

A New England Romance

&

Other Southern Stories

Randall Ivey

GREEN ALTAR BOOKS
SHOTWELL PUBLISHING
Columbia, S.C.

Produced in the Republic of South Carolina by

SHOTWELL PUBLISHING LLC
Post Office Box 2592
Columbia, South Carolina 29202

www.ShotwellPublishing.com

Cover Design: Boo Jackson TCB
Adapted from « Railway station, York » by Joseph Pennell (1857-1926).
Courtesy LOC

ISBN-13: 978-0997939309
ISBN-10: 0997939303

10 9 8 7 6 5 4 3 2 1

This book is for Susan and Jamy Cunningham
With love and gratitude

Acknowledgement is made to the following publications in which some of these stories first appeared: *The Abbeville Review* ("Second Sight"), *The Charleston Post and Courier* ("A Soldier for God" and "Still Life With Solitary Lady") and *The Dead Mule School of Southern Literature* ("The Cold Front" and "Snake in the Grass").

All other stories are published here for the first time.

—R.I.

Publisher's Note

SOUTHERN LITERATURE is the glory of American culture. Faulkner, O'Connor, Warren, Lytle, Davidson, Gordon, Percy, Chappell, Berry will be known as long as Western civilization survives and long after today's politicians, "experts," and celebrity writers are forgotten. Another of the greats, George Garrett, wrote that "all signs indicate that Southern literature, far from being on its last legs and far from representing a falling off from earlier and better days, seems very much alive." We support Garrett's witness by launching GREEN ALTAR BOOKS—a collection of Southern fiction and poetry. The first entry is Randall Ivey's latest collection of short stories. Shotwell will be in the not very distant future presenting other writers, some celebrated and others soon to be so.

Shotwell Publishing
Columbia, South Carolina 2016

Contents

A New England Romance

For William Price-Fox

"IF IT WAS MINE, I THINK I'd take better care of it," Doreen Henderson announced to her old schoolmate Georgina Caul as the two women stood with the white, frilly-necked gown swaying gently between them. Each of them had grabbed hold of a musty shoulder and had raised the dress above them as though trying to intimidate it. The action left a faint pile of dust at their feet.

"Well," Georgina said, "Even if it is a bit unkempt, I think it's elegant. Don't you?" She gave a short tug to the faded blue ribbon tied at the waist.

"Strange and sad," Doreen continued, as though she were alone, "that it never was used."

"Yes," Georgina answered, "especially when you consider the figure it was meant for." She patted the broad, lacy bosom, and dust rose from the neckline like smoke. "I'm beginning to think it's going to hang in that closet for good, neglected."

"Strange and sad," Doreen repeated. They exchanged

glances. Doreen's mouth parted some. The dress fluttered between them as their arms grew tired.

"Don't do it!" Georgina exploded, letting her half of the gown crumble to the floor and moving to the door. "Don't you dare do it!"

"Do what? What in the world are you talking about, girl?" Doreen asked, and while the question hung in the air she lifted the dress from the floor and laid it in a nearby Morris chair then turned and stood looking demurely at her friend, waiting for an answer.

Georgina heaved and her eyes flashed, but it did not look like true anger to Doreen.

"You want me to tell it, don't you? You want me to tell the whole story of why that gown wasn't used. Don't you?"

"I didn't say such a thing."

"You didn't have to. The request was apparent in your voice and the way you looked at me."

"Well, my goodness, would it hurt any for you to tell it?"

"See there!"

"I've never heard it, long as I've known you. And from what I understand from others you used to tell that story with a certain relish, as though you enjoyed it yourself."

"I was a younger woman then and more bitter. People's foolishness used to amuse me then. Now it makes me sad. Especially when it is the foolishness of my own blood kin."

"I'm not sure I've ever heard the whole thing. It seems

to me you might have left some things out."

Georgina gazed lopsidedly at her friend. It was a steady glare, delivered from one side of her face, that had intimidated many a man, woman, and child over the years. "Is that the only reason you agreed to come up here and help me clean, so you could hear that old story again?"

Doreen only smiled.

"Lord, Lord. If I had only charged admission every time I used to tell that tale, I'd be a rich woman today." She settled herself in the chair opposite the one in which the dress lay. "You sure you haven't heard it, Doreen?"

"Only in bits and pieces. Never the whole thing. There was always some interruption. Or you just stopped yourself."

They were not in Georgina's home. They were in the home of Georgina's aunt, Myrna Poage, who was in a Spartanburg hospital recovering from surgery on her back and had asked her niece to look in on things.

Georgina sat deliberating, touching her index finger to her lips. "Well," she said slowly. "I suppose if you have to hear it.... After all, you have shared so many of your own painful family stories with me."

"Yes ma'am. That I have."

"And I wouldn't want you spending the rest of your life not knowing the *right* version of this story."

"I knew you wouldn't. You have a lot of integrity that way."

3

"For there have been many erroneous versions of it floating around through the years, with many false and monstrous additions from those who did not live it or even hear it first hand."

"Yessum."

"All right. But I do it only for the sake of truth and nothing else, and you must promise me that if this story ever passes out of your lips to others, it will be this version, the correct one, which comes out and not some fabrication of your own making."

At once Doreen nodded and yanked the stool out from under a vanity table and drew it up to where her friend sat. She sat down, fixing her skirt around the stool, anxious as a child to hear a good yarn.

"But I want to make one thing perfectly clear to you before I begin: my cousin was not and is not crazy. No, no. She was a victim of that snub-nosed, stump-limbed little demon that catches hold of all of us at one time or another."

"Love, you mean," Doreen filled in and continued watching her friend on the verge of the story. Georgina glared again. "Well," Doreen explained, "that's how Jesse McMillan says you start this thing, by talking about how cruel and harmful love can be and how we have all experienced its heartbreaks."

"Well, why don't you get Jesse McMillan to tell you the rest of it?" Georgina snapped, chin raised, and Doreen went silent.

"Jane Poage's problem is she has a sentimental streak in her a mile long. And her head is in the clouds much of the time. If anybody's to blame, I would say it was her mother, Myrna. Myrna never treated Jane like a regular little girl. Whenever Jane got upset or lonesome, Myrna wouldn't give her cookies or dolls. She gave her books. Fanciful books about fanciful people and people who live in the kind of world you and I know. For a long time we lived a few blocks from them, and I remember many times glancing out the window and seeing that child come struggling up the road with an armload of books then shaking my head and thinking something someday was going to go terribly wrong for her. I'm twelve years older than Jane, so I felt I had some insight into these things. I've never known a bookworm that didn't have some bad run-in with reality. And I've seen too many people hook themselves up to one thing or another and pretty soon be driven to distraction by it and to catastrophe. I don't care if it was money, drink, religion, books…."

"Love," Doreen interceded wistfully, as though recalling an old paramour to herself in all the clear detail of his attractiveness.

"*Love*," Georgina repeated, her voice like a harshly-pressed organ note. "Doesn't matter what it is. It's just not good for somebody to let her whole life rotate around one thing. It's not healthy."

"Is that what happened to Jane?" Doreen asked with some caution, fully aware how a foolish question could set her friend off. "She let her life rotate around books?"

"Not so much the books themselves as what was in them. Now, please don't get me wrong. I've got nothing against books. I wish I had time to read more books myself. Anyway, whenever she and Myrna came to the house, she would rush right to the bookcase in the den and after a few minutes come right back with the most pitiful look on her face. She was disappointed because all we had were cookbooks and paperback romances. She asked us, almost with tears in her eyes, why we didn't have Nancy Drew or *Treasure Island*. *Treasure Island* now! For a girl! Or if I was visiting them and went up to Jane and asked her if she knew anything new, she'd recite a poem or tell me she had decided to be an aviator like Amelia Earhart or go to Africa and chase lions and tigers."

"She was a child, Georgina. Children are creatures of fancy. Didn't you dream like that when you were a little girl?"

"Yes, but she kept on talking like that when she was well into her teens and older, although her ambitions got a bit more sophisticated though not much more realistic.

"Well, all this began to worry my mother, who is Myrna's sister, you know, and one day, and this was when Jane was a senior in high school, she asked Myrna if she didn't think it was time to turn the girl's thoughts to more practical things.

"'Oh no, Esther,' Myrna answered her. 'I'm not like

you. I'm not going to tell my children how to live their lives and put them in some sort of strait jacket of my own making and have them hate me for it. I'm going to let them follow their dreams.'

"'Well,' Mama went on, 'I sure hope their dreams don't lead them into a ditch.'

"Myrna just laughed and said, 'Oh no. That's not going to happen. I believe in my children and I believe in my children's dreams.'"

"Georgina, why did Myrna keep referring to her 'children?' I thought she only had Jane."

"Myrna was a dreamer herself, Doreen. She always hoped she'd have others, even though the doctor told her otherwise and she was past forty by then."

"Oh. Well."

"And Myrna meant what she said too, about not telling her children how to live. She was practically a conspirator in all the craziness that followed, if not the chief engineer. She indulged that girl's every whim, no matter what it was. Once Jane got the notion to wear scarves, so Myrna took her all over town, to dime stores and thrift shops and everything in between, looking for scarves, red scarves, black scarves, embroidered scarves, plain scarves, any kind of scarves you could imagine. I believe by then Jane had the notion to be Isadora Duncan. Good thing she never wore any of those long scarves in a convertible. But the love of scarves soon wore off, and guess where all those scarves are now? That's right." Georgina pointed to the closet. "They're sitting in a hatbox in that very closet.

"And when Jane was fifteen she decided she wanted to take a trip to Boston on some educational tour, something for high school students. Nobody I'd ever known had been to Boston or ever wanted to go. It was a vat of Yankees and still is. But Jane was determined, and Myrna thought it was a grand notion, and they got up the money and had her packed and ready to go, and then her daddy died, and that was that. It was off. The trip, I mean. Not the notion. She held on to the notion years later. 'Why Boston?' I asked her once after she had gone on and on about it. And she said – and you better hold on tight to that stool, Doreen – she said, 'Because, Cousin Georgy, I want to breathe in the air of all that history.' *Breathe in the air of history*? Now what kind of level-headed, down-to-earth South Carolina woman would say a thing like that? *Breathe in the air of history*!" Georgina made a huffing noise hard enough to raise her own shoulders. "My goodness, she could have gone right down to Charleston, three hours away, and breathed in all the history she wanted, but no, there was this fascination with Boston. It had to be Boston."

"Well, before he died, Georgina, didn't your Uncle Ford have anything to say about all this?"

"No ma'am. Not much. He just sat back and let the circus roll in and out of town. Bless his heart. Well, you know he never did enjoy good health, even when he was young, and it was not a good idea for him to get too excited over anything, and he didn't. Besides, he adored Aunt Myrna, thought she was sinless, an absolute saint, and treated her like a little girl herself. I guess after a while he must have thought he had two daughters, cooking up their adventures, running around, treating the world like a sandbox."

The two women sat in a silence for a few moments, both of them staring at the dress, which, in the lazy, late-afternoon sunlight, resembled a fuzzy tarpaulin thrown over the chair.

"Myrna and Jane got into the habit of going to plays once Jane started college. You remember that little community theatre, don't you, right next to Mount of Glory Baptist Church? Oh you remember it! It was only there a couple of years before it closed. The young fellow who ran it couldn't keep up with the bills. Then it became a cattle feed warehouse. Then the church bought it and turned it into a parsonage. Anyway, Myrna and Jane went to the shows there all the time, no matter what was playing and how many times they had seen it. Every Saturday night for two years. Usually it was local people who acted in the shows, but now and then they'd get companies from out of town to perform, and one time this acting company with a real funny name that no longer registers with me came down from *Boston* of all places. That's right. *Boston*. Oh, Doreen, the world's a great big circle. Everything comes right back around, doesn't it? And, well, the fact they came from *that* place made Jane bubble like a pot of grits. She didn't care what they were acting in. It could have been Jack and Jill or Goldilocks for all she cared. They were from *there*, where the air was filled with history and needed so much breathing in by South Carolina girls. She was determined to be in the front row every night they were there. I don't remember what they were acting. I didn't go. It sounded right gloomy to me, whatever it was, and I don't like depressing things. I like happy things. If I leave a movie or a play, I want to come out smiling, even tapping my toes a little bit. And that play sure didn't sound like a toe-tapper. Oh I don't know. It had *elm tree* somewhere in the title is all I can remember. But Jane was there, every night it played for the two weeks the company was in town. Of course I didn't understand why she was so crazy about this play, why she had to see it every night, so I asked Myrna, thinking Myrna would have a good insight on the matter.

"'Well, Georgina,' she answered me, and there was a little laugh in her voice, 'I don't think it's just the play she's interested in anymore.'

"'What do you mean?'

"'Jane has met a young man.'

"'Is that right?'

"'Um-hum. And he's not just any young man either. He's a member of the acting company. He plays –' And she went on to tell about the character this young man played, who he was and what his motivation was, but I didn't care about that. All I cared about was that Jane had met someone. As pretty as she was, as full-figured and bright-eyed, she refused to get involved with dating and going out. She was too interested in…well, I don't want to go through all *that* again. And of course Myrna wouldn't push her in that direction.

"'How did she meet him?' I asked Myrna.

"'She went backstage after the performance. She went right up to him and struck up a conversation with him. And she went up to him three nights in a row, until he asked her out.'

"I asked her if *she*, Myrna, had met him.

"'Of course. I saw him in the play. I went backstage with Jane the first time. And, well, he had dinner over here the other night.'

"''Is that right?'

"''Um-hum.'

"'Why haven't you told me about all this sooner, Myrna?'

"'You didn't ask me about it sooner, dear. Would you care to meet him?'

"'What's his name? You haven't told me his name.'

"'Why, you didn't ask, dear. His name is Jonathan Howell. He is from Boston. He is twenty-six years old and' – and she went on about this Jonathan Howell, sounding like some sort of advertisement, even giving me a list of his other acting credits.

"'Myrna. Twenty-six?'

"'He is very courteous, very nice, a real gentleman. And, Georgina' – her voice dropped to a whisper – 'he's very good-looking. Would you care to meet him?'

"'Of course.'

"'Would you like to go to the play? See Mr. Howell "in action," so to speak?'

"'Oh no. No thank you. I don't want to go to the play. I want to meet the boy, but I do not want to go to the play. Do not tell that boy that I will be willing to attend his play. Do you understand?'

"'Yes, dear.'

"'I'll come to dinner, but I will not go to the play.'

"'All right. You have done a splendid job making your point, my dear.'

"This was on a Monday, and I told Myrna it would be nice if she could have this dinner on Wednesday, since Wednesday was my day off at the hospital. She said she would see what she could do, and two days later, on that Wednesday morning, called back and told me everything had been arranged, that Mr. Howell was pleased to hear that I was so anxious to meet him. Now, Doreen, she got it wrong! After I told her! It wasn't Mr. Howell I gave two hoots about! It was Jane. My cousin Jane. I was concerned about what type person she was getting herself involved with. I don't trust actors. I think they've got something to hide, and they do it with make-up and costumes and funny accents and wide gestures that throw you off. They can't handle their own feelings, so they dodge behind somebody else's. And that type person Jane did not need to associate herself with.

"To make sure Mr. Howell knew that I wasn't going out of my way to impress him, I didn't put on a dress or anything else too formal. I wore a plain white blouse and a plain brown skirt. The kind of thing I might go to the grocery market in to buy a loaf of bread. I didn't put on make-up or dab myself with perfume. I was as plain as a paper sack. And to top it off, I made sure I was twenty minutes late, so that by the time I got there they were fixing to sit down at the table and eat.

"Jane and Myrna made a fuss as usual, cooing and calling in voices two octaves over their regular ones, telling me how nice I looked, and both of them led me into the dining room by the arms, with real tight grips at my elbows, as though they feared I might try to make a get-away the first chance I got. 'Oh, Georgina! Dear Georgina!' they chirped like birds. Mr. Howell stood upon my entrance, but I wouldn't look at him right away, even as I shook his hand. Indeed I acted as though he wasn't there. Studying him would be an after dinner exercise.

"Myrna may not be known for her good sense, but she is known for her pot roast, and she made a lovely one that night, one of her best, all smothered in onions and carrots and potatoes, and she complemented it with English peas with pearl onions and a plate of warm, buttered rolls, and we enjoyed it all so much and were so much caught up in our eating we almost forgot to have a conversation. I took the moments of silence as opportunity to assess the guest of honor.

"Myrna was right: he was good-looking. Doreen, I have never in my life said this before about a man, but I will now: Mr. Howell was *beautiful*. He should have been hanging in some museum in Paris or perched on the Acropolis for the oracles to worship and divine. He was tall and had dark blond hair and a broad, smooth face and full mouth and eyes so blue it hurt to look straight into them, and his powerful muscles were clear even under his suit jacket. His voice was so deep you could feel it rumble in your own chest when he spoke. You know, I have always respected a strong voice in a man, and I believe Mr. Howell's topped any other I've ever heard. Listening to him talk was like slipping into warm water, all peaceful and soothing, but I wasn't going to let myself get too soothed. No, I pulled out of that creek before I went under. I know his type. All slick and well-mannered, just waiting to slip through any opening a person makes for him.

"Poor Jane, I thought to myself as she giggled at something he whispered in her ear. Poor thing had let herself be swallowed up in her fantasy world. Any slickster could yank the wool over her eyes; all he had to do was be a character from a play or one of the books she read; all he had to do was smile and promise her an adventure, and it would be all over for that girl.

"And I thought the same thing about Myrna. Really I felt like crying for the both of them right then. Here they were, two grown women still sashaying through storybook land, still believing in fairies, still wishing on a star, still hunting for four-leaf clovers. You know, people like that are the sweetest people alive, but they're also the saddest. The world is cruel to everybody, but it's especially cruel to the dreamers. But the dreamers don't care. They love it. They love the world so much and believe in the world so much, they don't care if it tramples all over them. They just dream away the insults and injuries the world gives them and go right on.

"Well, Doreen, I'm sorry. I drifted way off what I was supposed to be telling you, didn't I?

"Jane got the talk started along. I was helping myself to another slice of Myrna's exceptional pot roast when Jane cleared her throat and spoke.

"'Cousin Georgina,' she said and seemed nervous, 'did you know that Mr. Howell here comes from a very prominent family in New England?'

"'Why no, dear,' I answered. 'How could I? I just met the gentleman. How could I possibly know a thing like that?'

"'I thought Mother might have spoken of it to you.'

And she told me that Mr. Howell's father was the heir to and president of a company in Massachusetts which manufactured cod-liver oil. It was the fourth largest such company in New England. The

senior Mr. Howell had served as mayor of a Boston suburb, a little town called Wicker, Massachusetts, and was on the board of trustees of several colleges, including the big one (this she said with a theatrical whisper), *Harvard.* He was so well-regarded and beloved in Wicker that a wing of the public library had been named in his honor.

"'That's all very admirable,' I said once Jane was done. I stared straight at Mr. Howell, who smiled and nodded his thanks to me. 'It strikes me as odd though, Mr. Howell, that you aren't back there in Wicker, Massachusetts, helping your daddy out. I mean, there aren't too many men I know who wouldn't make a running dash to be part of a business that sounds as successful as your father's. Now, I don't know much about acting or about cod-liver oil, but it seems to me that cod-liver oil would be a much more stable profession than acting. After all, people are always going to have afflictions for which cod-liver oil is the best remedy, but actors, well, no actor I've ever heard of has cured the rickets.' Everyone laughed nervously. 'I mean, Mr. Howell, I can just picture you behind a desk as the brains and the muscle behind a thriving company like your father's. You certainly do have the air of the executive about you.'

"Mr. Howell laughed another laugh so deep and

resonant it nearly rattled the plates. 'Mrs. Caul - '

"'*Miss* Caul!" I corrected, a bit quicker than I should have maybe, but I wanted there to be no misunderstandings.

"'I'm sorry. No one told me.'

"'I'm the one who should be sorry,' Myrna said shyly. 'I failed to inform you that Georgina is not married.' She turned to me with embarrassment.

"'It's all right, Aunt Myrna. No harm has been done. You were about to say something, Mr. Howell?'

"'Well, I was just going to say that you're not the first person who has asked me this question, why I haven't gone into the family business. By now I'd feel strange if I wasn't asked the question by someone to whom I'd just been introduced. The truth is, and please don't take offense, but I find the business world boring, stifling, debilitating, and beset by crippling routine.'

"'Heavens!' I replied after a gulp of water.

"'Yes. While I've never worked for my father on any kind of regular basis, I've had a close view of what it means to run a company, to be part of a big, thriving business, as you call it, because my father is the type man who brings his work home with him, who cannot live without his work. There isn't one minute of the day when he isn't doing something connected to the company, when he isn't on the phone making some transaction or scheduling a trip somewhere in hopes of snagging a deal. Meals are often left uneaten at my father's house. Holidays are postponed. Life stands still when it comes to the company."

"He went on to tell how his father brought home folks to entertain, executives or prospective partners, and how after dinner the grown-ups would gather in the living room with their cigars and their brandies and talk for long hours about the company, about what should be done to improve the company's image, what should be done to pull in out of state investors, what should be done to catapult the company to national, even world-world prominence. 'They company, the company, the company!' he shouted, as though he were on stage. 'They spoke of it as though it were a teething infant, a prodigy, a frail old woman in need of constant vigilance. Sometimes I used to sneak down from my room and listen to them and feel knotted up and troubled. I wondered why such things concerned men, why they would go to such lengths for some smelly old oil that we never even used in our house.'

"He said he got one thing from those dinners, though: an introduction to art. Sometimes the wives of his father's guests would bring presents to the house. Often they were record albums. Beethoven symphonies, Brahms concertos, Bach cantatas, or, most wonderful to him, recordings of Shakespeare: Olivier doing Hamlet and Edith Evans doing Lady MacBeth. These recordings were put on any time – before dinner, after dinner, during dinner – they served as background noise and none of the adults seemed to pay much attention to them. It was just the idea of being surrounded by culture that appealed to them, not the actual works themselves. Young Mr. Howell, however, was mesmerized and strained his ears above the dull grown-up talk to hear every perfectly-pronounced word. He became obsessed with those records. He said he used to sneak out of bed early in the morning or late at night, when nobody else was around, and go down to the living room and listen to them with the volume turned low. Even muted they were magnificent to him. He went to the family library, he said, and hunted for the word 'Shakespeare,' and when he found it he lugged down the fat volume to the floor and sat with it for hours and tried to understand all this language, this wonderful, difficult flood of words, these long, strange sentences, and at the end he would pound his fist on the text, determined to read those words and to pronounce them just as Larry Olivier pronounced them, so that they sang and flew, in rolling, piercing syllables. In other words, he finished up, 'I'd been bitten by the acting bug.'

"During the whole time he talked, Mr. Howell kept his head tilted toward the ceiling, as though he had spotted something, and the rest of us watched him. Jane was quivering near tears, and Myrna was smiling so wide I thought her face had frozen that way. He was impressive, I must admit, but I couldn't get over the feeling it was all an act, a display. After all, he was an actor.

"'Well, Mr. Howell,' I said, and this seemed to break the general spell, 'did your father at any time want you to join him, or was he supportive of your intentions from the start?'

"'Oh no. He objected from the start to the idea of my acting. He is a practical New England gentleman, highly suspicious of anything that doesn't produce tangible results. No, no, we still don't see eye to eye about my choice. In fact we have had many titanic clashes over the matter and are not presently speaking to each other.' He described one such encounter to us in the most dramatic fashion and even shadow boxed the air to illustrate the time he and his daddy had come to fisticuffs over the matter. It was all quite impressive, Doreen.

"Myrna suddenly burst in. 'I believe it would be nice to have our coffee in the parlor.'

"We all agreed that was a nice idea, so we got up from the table and moved to the living room, and pretty soon Myrna came back holding a tray weighed down with a coffee carafe and the cups and saucers my mother and father had scraped and saved to get Myrna and Ford for their wedding present. We complimented Myrna on the meal. She took the praise with modest pleasure. Mr. Howell said he usually didn't like to eat a heavy meal before he went onstage – there was always the possibility of renegade digestion at inappropriate moments - but, he said, Myrna's cooking was so agreeable, he didn't think it would be any problem. Then he cleared his throat and said, 'Miss Caul, do you have any interest in the theater?'

"I was unnerved by the question; it was thrown at me so directly, without warning, but I wasn't going to back down from it, no matter how deep and velvety the voice that asked it or how blue the eyes that sparkled behind it.

"'Well, Mr. Howell, to be frank, no I don't. Of course I've got nothing against it, mind you. I'm sure it takes lots of heart and soul and gut to get up and do what you do. Of course it does. But I'm afraid the spell of art and theater and things of that nature just doesn't catch hold of people like me. I'm afraid I'm too practical a person to be dazzled by pretty words the way you were when you were young. My mind just isn't geared in that direction. I've been taught, ever since I was a little girl, to think about what I can do to get from one day to the next, to make things easier for the people I love. For better or for worse, daydreaming just hasn't fit into the overall pattern of my life.'

"'Miss Caul,' Mr. Howell returned with a chuckle. 'Are you sure you aren't a New Englander? You sound an awful lot like my father.'

"'No, I'm a born and bred South Carolinian. Never been anywhere else.'

"'And I assure you that art is more than daydreaming. Much more.'

"'Oh I'm sure! I'm sure!'

"'Well,' Myrna broke in, 'it isn't my fault Georgina doesn't like the theater!' She laughed a long, embarrassed laugh. 'Goodness knows I've tried to get her to go. Jane and I both, but she won't budge.'

"'But, Myrna, the things you have invited me to. When you told me about them, I just shuddered. I would find more amusement at the mortuary.'

"'Can you believe it, Mr. Howell? She refused to see *A Doll's House*. She turned down *Three Sisters*. All the masterworks of the stage.' Myrna threw up her hands with another laugh.

"'Well, what do you like, Miss Caul?' I was glad to see him maintaining the formalities.

"'I like musicals, Mr. Howell. I like happy music and bright costumes and bright lights. I like something that steals you away from the hard world for a while but then brings you right back. Something that won't leave you gummy feeling and depressed once it's over.'

"'Gummy feeling and depressed,' Myrna repeated with rolling eyes.

"'Cousin Georgina works at the hospital here in town,' Jane explained. 'As a receptionist. She sees a lot of the world's misery, don't you, dear?'

"'What are your favorite musicals, Miss Caul?'

"'Well,' I began, having to think a minute, 'when I was twelve years old Aunt Myrna and Uncle Ford took me to Greenville to see *Showboat*. It was my birthday.'

"'Of course. *Showboat*. A standard. I sang it for a month in a community production back home.'

"'Is that right?'

"'Yes. I've appeared in several musicals. Love to sing!'

"Myrna sighed. 'I just love "Old Man River." Mr. Howell, of course you know "Old Man River"?'

"'Certainly. I never got a chance to sing it on stage, of course, but I learned it. I learned all the lines and all the songs from everything I've ever been in.'

"Jane giggled and said, 'Why don't you make Cousin Georgina happy and sing it for her?'

"'Make me happy?' I said, as though Jane had just spoken in Cantonese.

"'Well, if you would like me to.'

"And before I could say yea or nay, Doreen, that young man had risen from his chair and gone to the middle of the floor, clearing his throat with enough volume to wake the dead and brushing his hand down the front of his crisp linen shirt. His face grew very tense, as though all his thoughts were gathering up at his mouth and between his eyes, and before I knew it he had started up and went from line to line of 'Old Man River' without missing anything. It was as though he'd been rehearsing it all day. It stood still through most of it, but once in a while he'd raise up his arm beside him or let it glide out in front of him to indicate the movement of the mighty Mississippi. He meant for it to be dramatic, I know, but for me it was a distraction, that and the fact that when he hit real low notes his voice tended to shake like a foghorn and sound more comic than dramatic. Still, it was quite a performance, that could not be denied, and when he was done we all gave him his proper due of lively applause. Myrna stood up, as I was afraid she would do.

"Almost as soon as our applause died down, Mr. Howell announced that, as much as he didn't want to, he had to leave, since he was due at the theater in an hour. Myrna and Jane protested, but he was firm, so we all gathered at the front door for a last little chat. I wished him luck on the stage, something I shouldn't have done: first, because it is bad luck to wish an actor such a thing and better to say "Break a leg"; secondly it prompted him to invite me to the play. I told him I was sorry but that I couldn't and gave no further explanation. He gave me another handshake, and that was that; he was out the door. Myra turned and asked me if I wouldn't mind helping her do the dishes. She said she had decided to accompany Jane to that night's performance. I said of course I wouldn't mind. I would do all of them if that would free her up to get prepared for the evening.

"I didn't see or hear from Myrna or Jane for the next few days, which surprised me, as I expected them to call the first thing that next morning looking for my opinion of Mr. Howell. I was so surprised I started to call them, but I stopped myself. First off, I didn't want to seem anxious to give my opinion of the man, and secondly I was so preoccupied at the hospital, pulling my own shift and filling in some for Mrs. Spessard, that dear old industrious soul who had not had time off from the receptionist desk in twenty-seven years and was going down to Charleston for the weekend with her husband.

"Anyway, I was frustrated over the fact that I hadn't heard from my aunt or my cousin. It wasn't like either of them to contain their enthusiasm so well. Usually they had to know right away and as soon as possible what you thought of something they had just presented to you. Yet at the same time, it wasn't like me to offer up my opinions so freely, so I didn't call them, just wouldn't do it. It wasn't easy holding back though. I kept my eye fixed to the telephone, either the one at home or the one on my desk at work. Every time the phone rang, I had to hold back from lunging for it, remembering that cool calmness befits a lady better than heat, but when I picked up the line and neither Myrna's nor Jane's voice greeted me, I felt let down.

"When it did happen, when Myrna did call nearly a week later, she didn't mention Mr. Howell's name. She asked if I would come over and help her fix up the guest room upstairs. Ford's widowed sister was coming down from Gaffney to stay a few days. It was Guynelle's birthday, and they didn't want her spending it all alone, since they were the only family she had left. Myrna said Jane would help, but she wasn't feeling well and was laid up in bed.

"During the time we turned over the mattress and changed the sheets and washed the curtains and scrubbed the adjoining bathroom and filled the vase on the chest of drawers with hydrangeas, Guynelle's favorite flower, Myrna not once breathed the name

Jonathan Howell. It was as though the man didn't exist or had not caught her daughter's fancy or had not sat down and eaten her well-liked pot roast while fielding questions from her very skeptical niece. And she didn't mention it later, when we sat down to coffee and sandwiches on the front porch to enjoy the Indian summer. She didn't say much at all until we were taking our dishes to the sink.

"'Georgina, I think Jane would like to speak to you before you go.'

"'Oh? You have any idea what about?'

"'Yes, but why don't we let her tell you?'

"Jane was suffering the twenty-four hour stomach flu, and when I walked in, she sat propped up in bed covered in what looked like letters.

"She smiled and reached towards me and said, 'Georgy, how are you?'

"Jane had the tendency to add silly endings to people's names. I wouldn't have tolerated anybody else's calling me by a boy's name.

"'Your mother said you wanted to speak to me.'

"'Did she? How sweet.'

"'Sweet? You mean you didn't know she was going to send me up here?'

"'Well, yes, but I still think it's sweet all the same.'

"'Who are all these from?' I asked, pointing to the

envelopes in her lap.

"She smiled, and I could see the virus drain from her face, to be refilled by happiness. 'From Jon.'

"'Oh.' I took the chair closest to the bed. 'Is that right?'

"'Yes. He writes me all the time. From everywhere he goes. Chicago. Boise. Cheyenne. Everywhere. He writes me all the time. He goes to the most interesting places and meets the most interesting people and he tells me about them all. Today he wrote me and told me his company's been asked to perform at a fall dramatics fair in Vermont. Oh, let me see. Where is it?' Her forehead divided in thought until she caught what she was looking for. 'Mount Pelier! Yes. That's it. Mount Pelier.' Her smile dimmed. 'Mount Pelier's the capital, isn't it?'

"'Jane, have you been taking any kind of medication? Anything that would make you swimmy headed?'

"'And, Georgy,' she started, and despite being sick she giggled a little, 'Georgy, Jon wrote me another letter a little while ago, a couple days after the dinner you attended. He put it in the mailbox himself before he left....'

"'Yes?'

"'This is the thing I called you up to tell you. We're engaged.'

"There are times when you know something's coming, when you see it on its way. Still you try to stop it, to keep it from coming, even though you know you are going to fail.

That's how I felt upon Jane's announcement.'

"'Georgy? Say something, Cousin!'

"'You're engaged?'

"'Yes. Isn't it exciting?'

"'Have you set a date?'

"'Oh no. It's indefinite.'

"I let out my first sigh of relief. 'Jane, you haven't known this man more than a month.'

"'That's not true. I mean, it seems that way. But not in the way that counts.'

"I didn't have to ask her to tell me the way it counted. I knew she would tell me. I had unbelievable faith in that.'

"'You see, even though we haven't known each other long, we've known each other forever. I mean, I feel like he's been out there looking for me all this time, and I've been looking for him. And that common search is a bond we've had, and it's been there as long as we have. Does that make sense?'

"'Not much, dear. But that's okay. Jane, have you been giving this man money?'

"'What?'

"'Money? In those letters...has he been soliciting funds from you?'

"'Why, no! Goodness.'

"'Jane, you haven't promised this man your trust fund or anything, have you?'

"'Georgina!' she nearly screamed, leaping up. The

letters jumped from her lap and landed at the foot of the bed and on the floor. Her anger must have trumped the stomach bug, because she had a sudden healthy red glow to her cheeks. 'I can't believe you're saying what you're saying. It's a terrible thing to imply. Terrible. I wish I did have money to give him. I'd give him all of it. Every last cent. He has lots of things he'd like to do.'

"'Like what?'

"'Well, he has a friend in Boston who has written a play Jon says is terrific, and Jon thinks if he can get the money for it, it will be a terrific hit.'

"'Why can't he just get his daddy to give him the money?'

"'Georgina, he's very much like his daddy. He has enormous pride. He wants to do things for himself. It's that Yankee New England stubbornness. You know? And don't you remember, Georgina? He and his father aren't speaking. Haven't for a while. The father is adamantly opposed to Jon's acting. Oh it makes me so angry to think of anyone trying to stifle him!'

"'Oh Jane, Jane, Jane,' I repeated in mournful dirge.

"What is it, Georgy? Dear, dear Georgy? Aren't you happy for me?'

"I asked her why couldn't have fallen in love with a banker or lawyer or a reasonably attractive mechanic, someone whose future was well-assured. She replied that she was happy, truly happy, really for the very first time in her life. I was genuinely shocked to hear her say that, and I asked, 'The first time? I never knew you to be unhappy. Do you mean, until now, until the arrival of this man into your life, you have not been happy? All these years, Jane?' And it was her turn to be taken aback, because here she had built herself up to be miserable, had convinced herself of the dissatisfaction of her life up to then, and now someone came along to challenge her. I spent a moment reminding her that she had lived a life relatively free of want and more fortunate than the lives of those around us. 'When, Jane?' I said after several minutes of silence. She stammered and her face balled up like a fist.

"'Well, I don't want to talk about it,' she said finally. 'It doesn't matter. It's all in the past. The present is what matters. And the future. The wonderful future.' She walked over to me slowly with the most serene smile and took my hand and kissed one of the knuckles. 'It doesn't matter now, Georgy. Just be happy for me.'

"And about that time Myrna burst into the room, bright as a flare, and said, 'Did you tell her?' When Jane nodded with a wide smile, Myrna turned to me, girlish giddiness sustained, heightened, and said, 'And what do you think?'

"'Aunt Myrna, I haven't had time to think.'

"'And guess what? We're having Mildred Klink make Jane's dress. That's right. We're having a dress made. We thought it would give the whole proceeding a personal touch if Jane had her own dress.'

"Doreen," Georgina said, looking at her friend directly for the first time in several minutes. "You remember Mildred Klink, don't you? You know she had a stroke not too long after her husband died. Left her paralyzed some on her left side, but that didn't keep her from making the prettiest dresses in town, even prettier than the ones in the store fronts."

"Oh yes," replied Doreen. "I remember Mildred. She made my sister's coming-out gown." Doreen was happy to be, at last, acquainted with a cast member of the unfolding drama.

"Well, Jane and Myrna said they went to Mildred almost as soon as they got Mr. Howell's proposing letter. They brought her patterns and homemade sketches and materials. They told her they wanted something unique, something that would fit only *one* woman, so to speak, and would be appropriate for *one* occasion. They said Mildred, despite her infirmities, was excited about the project and took all they had brought with them and assured them that soon it would all be turned into something very special and disappeared into her workroom without even a goodbye to either of them.

"When Jane and Myrna made their announcement to me, they were, in their own way, making me a part of the whole thing. From that day on, I got reports on the progress of The Gown. They filled me in on all the dimensions of the dress. They told me what Mildred Klink put in and what

Mildred Klink took out. They told me about the alterations and the frills. And they called me anywhere to file their reports. At home. At work. After a while I was almost scared to be in the vicinity of a telephone, anywhere, even a payphone on the street corner, for fear it would ring and out would pour, as though by recorded message, news of some miracle or disaster in the raising or the lowering of the hemline.

"Mildred's average working time on a dress was usually four to six weeks, that is if she had all the things she needed and didn't have to order much from out of town. Now this is what I have heard, Doreen. Of course, she never sewed for me. All I know is it took her six and a half weeks to finish this gown, even though she had a girl to help her.

"I was at home when Jane called to say The Gown was done.

"'Well, almost done,' Jane corrected herself. 'Mrs. Klink says she needs to do a little touching up here and there, around the shoulders and such, but that for all intents and purposes, it is complete.' She paused, I guess to get some sense that my happiness matched her own. Then she said, 'The reason I called was to tell you about the dress and to ask you if you would like to come with Mother and me when we go to look at it this afternoon. Mrs. Klink is letting us have a peek.'

"Of course I did not want to go, seeing my capitulation to such a request as a kind of compliance in this whole fantasy Jane and Myrna had wrought. I hunted for excuses to beg off. I told Jane I would get back to her and let her know for sure. But Jane and

Myrna made the decision for me, and a half hour later they pulled up in front of the house.

"Mildred Klink lived in Beaslap then, on the Newberry County line, far away from other folks. Her shop was at the back of her house, you know, and it's no wonder her business declined near the end. It was blamed hard finding her. Even Myrna, driving, forgot a couple of turns on the way. When we found the place and went to the front door

to knock, nobody answered for the longest time. 'Maybe she died,' I said quietly. 'Her masterpiece now completed.' Myrna and Jane shushed me together, laughing nervously, shooing away the bad luck, and then the three of us went round the back, and it was there where Mildred Klink stood on the screened-in porch, bent and brown and gnarled but still standing, like an old dog-wood tree that's been hit by lightning but will not give up life.

"Nobody said a word till we got inside the house. Then Myrna and Jane broke into a little fit, just a-hugging Mrs. Klink round her papery neck and kissing her worn-out old face and telling her how good she looked – as though that really mattered at *that* point – and how much they appreciated all the hard work she had done. They made me feel inadequate and stone-cold, like I should have at least gone up and patted the old gal on the top of the head. But I didn't. I just stood aside and let the love feast proceed and stared at the recipient of the affection. She was a powerful-looking old woman, short and bent but still strong. Maybe I should have upgraded her from a dogwood to an oak. It was hard to tell at first she'd been the victim of a stroke. She showed no signs of lameness. She stood leaning the whole time on a cane, but somehow that only made her seem stronger, not weaker.

"In their celebration, the three of them forgot about me – I wasn't even introduced – and went on talking about the gown. Suddenly Mrs. Klink turned from Jane and Myrna and in the direction of an open door yelled 'May-ry! Mayyyyyyy-ry!' with such sustained loudness I thought she had just burst into an aria, that maybe happiness at completion of the Great Project had led her finally and triumphantly into song.

"A shadow appeared on the open door, followed by a young girl, a blond girl, plainly dressed though pretty, who came right up to the group with a serious look on her face, as though she had been interrupted while preparing to perform surgery. Mrs. Klink said, "This is May-ry West from out at Selden. She's my assistant. Been with me a year and a half. High school girl now. Says she wants to go to Con-verse College and study psychology. Ain't that right, honey?'

"The girl nodded. 'Yes ma'am.'

"'Told her her real talent was in dress-making, that you

can tell best about folks' psychology by the way they dress theirselfs and you can help them best by making them look the best they can, and that way they won't have no psychological problems from worrying about what other folks thinks of 'em. But she's got her mind made up. Won't listen to me. But, Lord, I sure do hate to see the talent go to waste. May-ry helps me do what I ain't able to do no more. Sometimes I stand to the side and give her instructions, and she follows 'em to the T. Other times I keep my mouth shut and let her do on her own, and I'll be durned if what she comes up with ain't better than what I had in mind.' The old woman shook her head, mourning the death of the prodigy. 'Well, May-ry, these is the Poages, Miss Jane and Miss Myrna. These is the people we've been making that dress for, that wedding dress.'

"Mary nodded and said, 'Yes ma'am.' She stared hard at Jane and Myrna, as though already practicing her future profession. Best of luck to her, I thought, fathoming the minds of *those* two, and felt immediately ashamed, Doreen, for even having thought it. 'I remember them,' she went on, 'from the first time they were here. I've spoken to them on the phone too.'

"I was looking at Mrs. Klink the whole time, so it startled me when she spun round, spun right around so neat and quick, as though she were on castors, and said 'And what was your name, hon?'

"I told her.

"'I don't believe I've never sewed for you, have I?'

"'No ma'am. I do all my own sewing.'

"She squinted at me a moment, and I wondered if she would raise her cane at me for my smart mouth. Instead, she said, 'I figured as much. I would have remembered your face. I remember the faces and names of all the folks I've sewed for.'

"Myrna just wiggled in, excited. Couldn't help herself. 'Mrs. Klink, I've always heard that you treat all your customers as though they were your next of kin. I think that's admirable.'

"'Thank you, Ms. Poage, for saying such, but the fact of the matter is I'd never treat my customers like my next of kin, because I can't stand my next of kin. Pile of drunkards, liars, and cheats. Every one of them.'

"And that ended the round of compliments. It was quiet a minute, and then the old woman said, 'Well, if we're done talking, let's go look at the thing.'

"I'd warmed up to her some, so I got in behind her as we left the parlor and made our way to the stairs, and when we got to them, I said, 'Would you like me to help up, Ms. Klink?'

"'No ma'am,' she said. 'I like to climb my own steps. Thank you just the same.'

"Mary led the way up and Mrs. Klink followed behind her, maneuvering herself up and along quite well. The work-room was on the right at the top of the stairs, and when we got to it, Mrs. Klink seemed to step aside and relinquish the role of hostess to the girl. Except for some pieces of scrap cloth and a large thing in the middle of the floor covered in a sheet, it didn't look like a work room. The floors were carpeted and the windows were draped and there was a beautiful old hickory hutch closet in one corner and a hardwood love seat in the other, but Mrs. Klink said it was the work room, so I couldn't do anything but take her word in the matter.

"Mary, her assistant, went over to the covered mystery in the middle of the floor and yanked the sheet off, pulling it so hard and so quick it let off a little snap. It turned out to be a bald-headed mannequin wearing *this* dress.

Georgina stood and went over to the opposing chair where the dress lay. She lifted it up as though showing it to Doreen for the first time.

"The three of us, Jane, Myrna, and I, had to adjust ourselves to the sight of it before we finally realized what it was. And when that happened...when wisdom came...oh, mercy, I wish you could have seen Jane and Myrna. They circled the dress slowly a couple of times, slowly and reverently, reached out very carefully and touched it, laid their hands over it as though it had once dressed the Ark of the Covenant. Then they looked at each other and smiled. It was mostly as it is now, except it didn't have this blue ribbon around the waist. Jane added that as an afterthought.

"Mary, the girl, stepped up to Jane and said, 'Like we

said, Miss Poage, it's pretty much done, except Mrs. Klink and I think the shoulders need tightening a bit. But that won't take more than another day or so.'

"'Wonderful. Just wonderful.' Myrna put her hand on the mannequin's hip. Then she and Jane and the girl started in talking about the particulars of the gown.

"I was left to myself once more, alone, isolated, and suddenly, while I stood there, I felt something nudge my elbow. I turned. Mrs. Klink stood there with something like a smile on her face, the left corner of her face twisted just so; she had tapped me with her cane: it had just touched the ground again when I looked back.

"'Maybe we can make a wedding dress for you someday,' she said. Then neither one of us smiled, half-ways or otherwise.

"After that visit, things quieted between Myrna and Jane and me, and as much as I love them, and I truly do, I was somewhat glad. I got to where I didn't wholly trust myself around them, didn't know what might drop out of my mouth before I could catch it, didn't know what I might say. So I left Jane and Myrna to themselves, let them continue their blissful stroll through Wonderland, still loving them of course, loving them to the point of pain. I guess when you love somebody it's best just to let them go on and walk to the end of their folly, let them see how much you love them and that you are still here for them when they come back up from the valley.

"The way I turned away from them was to get more involved in the hospital, the way other folks give themselves up to a church. I put in as much overtime as possible. I filled in for other women at the receptionist desk and elsewhere when that was possible. I took to other jobs I wasn't necessarily being paid for. I read Mother Goose to a little girl with a two degree burn on her back. I read Song of Solomon to an old man with cancer and cataracts. Sometimes, when I was still full of energy and my mind began to rebel, when it began to turn back to the foolishness of my kin, I stayed up with Mr. Runnels, the night watchman at Marshall Bates at the time, stayed up the whole night with him, and he would teach me old drinking songs he learned in the navy and old nursery songs his granny sang him when he was a boy and couldn't sleep at night.

"And if I was ever at home, I made sure I stayed busy there too. I learned new recipes and brushed off old ones. I took up sewing, maybe with the aspiration of one day impressing Old Lady Klink. I wrote letters to school mates who'd left South Carolina years ago and with whom I hadn't been in touch since we graduated Compton High. I did everything there was to do in that house, and if there wasn't anything to do, I went to neighbors' houses and volunteered my services to them. And while I was home, I kept the phone off the hook. Yes. Knowing it was a dangerous thing to do, and a call for help might come.

"I was so worked up and preoccupied with all my new

hobbies and chores and responsibilities, I didn't have time to dwell on marriage and wedding dresses and New England and acting companies and 'Old Man River' and elopements. I had wound a tight web around myself, a web of forgetfulness, you might say, so tight and strong all I could see was myself. I knew I was protected; I knew that web couldn't be torn.

"And it wasn't torn, it was yanked, yanked so hard and so quick I didn't even know it was gone and that I was once more exposed to the uncertainties of the world. Oh, the yanking hand didn't come through the telephone. No ma'am. It came through the United States Post Office and a letter addressed to me in a hand I knew to belong to one person and one person only, my Aunt Myrna Poage. It hit me like a punch in the stomach. It spun me round. It got such a hold on me I had to sit down at the kitchen table and just stare at it a few minutes to get used to its reality. Then I was able to open it and read it. Oh Doreen, let me see if I can recall Myrna's words from memory." Georgina paused a moment, standing still and quiet, like an actress contemplating her most important speech. "'Dear Georgina,' she wrote. 'We have decided to follow our instincts, to throw caution to the wind, to go with our feelings. By the time you read this we will more than likely be on our way north, to New England, to Boston, site of the Tea Party and other significant historical events you have read of. Please do not think ill of us, for we know we have made the right decision and are doing the right thing; we have never been more sure. Jane is in love. I am her mother and cannot deny her, for her pain is my pain and her joy my joy, and if I am able I must see her through both. Don't think us impulsive. Think us free, for we have finally done what our hearts have instructed us to do.

"'We will be in Boston long enough to see the young man, to become acquainted with his family. Do not think us presumptuous. He will soon be a member of our family. Should we not get to know his? Think of it as an experience, an education, an adventure. Wicker, Massachusetts, should be beautiful in the middle of October. New England is famous for its scenery. I am anxious to see the red and gold in the trees.

"'We will not contact you further, dear Georgina, not because we want you to worry but because we do not want you to try to persuade us to come back before we have done

what we have to do. We love you and will think of you often as we proceed in this most momentous chapter of our lives.' The letter was signed with Myrna's and Jane's names and had a P.S. attached. 'We have taken the dress just in case the young ones are inspired to do something wonderful.'

"Doreen, I am not one to be overcome by many things. You know that. I have seen too much in my years at the hospital to be bothered or surprised at what human beings manage to come up with. But here was an exception. Here

I was truly taken aback, speechless, thoughtless, winded in every way possible. So what could I do? Why, go straight to bed. Which is what I did. And as I lay there, listening to the two-thirty train from Spartanburg creep quickly and quietly north, I wondered how those two women were getting along up yonder. Wondered what trouble they had messed themselves up in. How Boston society might be taking to them. Of course I trusted them as far as manners and such went. They were experts in all that. They would know the right time to curtsy, the right words to say in the right situations, the right spoon to eat their soup with; all that would come naturally to them. Then, too, the wonderful Mr. Howell would be there to

guide them in all the other niceties of New England living. He would not let them stumble. I suppose what should have worried me most was whether or not they might decide to go ahead and tie the knot, right then and there. But it didn't worry me, I guess because it simply did not seem possible."

Georgina walked to the window. The afternoon was dissolving, the sun edged from the room, and shadows sprouted from everything – gown, furniture, human arms and legs and profiles – like dark flowers.

"And right before I fell asleep that night," she went on, peering at nothing, "I thought about one other thing, Doreen, that hurt worse than anything else. I thought about myself in comparison with Jane, and Myna too, for that matter, but mostly Jane, and it was like I had set myself on a high cliff and was rocking on it from side to side, from safety to danger, from truth to fancy. I wondered why it was that Jane and her half of the family were so prone to dreaming and why my half, specifically Mama and me, made sure always to walk on a straight, clear road, a dreamless road, you might say; and then I wondered what it might be like all switched around, with Jane and Myrna clear-headed, and Mama and me all cloudy. I'm not sure if you can call that a form of sympathy, but you see, Doreen, I wasn't without some understanding of Jane's feelings toward Mr. Howell. I, too, had once had a great passion." Ms. Caul paused as though waiting for an objection from her friend at this detour; hearing none, she proceeded.

"His name was Eugene. His family was from Broadusville, and like most folks of my acquaintance from Broadusville, they were good-for-nothings who thought they were

better than anybody else. Oh, you know the type. White trash that thinks it's royalty. But not Eugene. No, no! Eugene was the exception to the Broadusville disease. He was \different. He wanted to work. Wanted to put his shoulder to the wheel. He knew what the fruits of honest labor were and how good they tasted. Oh, there was no glamour to the boy. Not at all. He wasn't pretty like our acting friend from up north. My daddy used to say the best thing anybody could do for Eugene Dowdy was to introduce him to a razor blade. And he stooped a little on one side, like he was always carrying his laborer's load. But he was practical and strong-minded and direct, like me. His talk wasn't pretty either, but when he spoke to you, you had no doubt where you stood with him. He wanted land of his own. He wanted a chance to do the things his daddy and granddaddy had been too lazy to do. You see, he had dreams too, but his dreams were useful ones. He dreamed about the sun and ploughs shearing soil and cattle and fat, healthy children helping him make something good out of the land he owned. This put him in favor with my mama and daddy, although my mama got upset once when she heard him say 'g.d.' in the backyard when he cut his finger with his pocket knife while trimming weeds, but she forgot about it soon enough. Or at least she forgave him for it.

"We didn't have formal dates like other couples. We didn't go to the movies or to dances. We drove out to the country where there weren't many houses or stores or people around. Eugene would stop at a certain place, get out, and stand awhile and ruminate. Then he would tear himself from his thoughts and stalk the ground, brushing his hand over the broom straw and the rabbit grass, feeling the bark on the trees, pinching up bits of dirt and letting it slide back to the ground gently from his fingers. Then he'd drop to his knees and take up two handfuls of dirt and study it, look at it closely, inspect it, just like he might find the answer to some terribly important question about his life in the grains. It was as close to a mystical experience as I've ever witnessed. Certainly I'd never seen anything like it in church. I'd sit in his truck and watch him. When he was done he would walk back smacking his hands clean and shaking his head. 'I don't think hit'd do,' he'd say, and we'd go on.

"His favorite place, the place we'd go most, was about five miles from Compton, close to his hometown, but it was nothing like Broadusville. No, no, it was rich and green and looked like it was just anxious to be plowed into something fertile. But it was owned by a gentleman who planned to sell so it could be cleared and made a place for a gas station. Eugene would stand in the middle of it, in the middle of all that high grass and bright blond sedge and say, 'It wasn't meant to be no gas station! Hit was meant to be somebody's home!' It sounded like his heart was snapping into a thousand pieces. And he'd say, 'Hit was meant to be *our* home, Georgina.' I loved him for saying that. I was proud of him, proud of what he wanted.

"One summer night, a year or so before I moved out of Mama and Daddy's house and got on my own, I was lying in bed, about to drop off to sleep, when I heard this tiny clicking noise, so small and faraway I thought maybe it had been part of a dream that was coming over me. But I was wide awake and heard it again, and again, louder each time. It came from the window. I got up and went to the window and lifted it. Down below, in the dark, was Eugene with his arm drawn back to throw another rock. He lowered his arm and motioned towards the back door, stepping over to it himself. I pulled on a housecoat and went downstairs. I invited him into the kitchen, but he shook his head.

"I said to him, 'Well, Eugene, what is it you want so late at night?'

"'I come to get you,' he said quietly.

"'Get me for what?' I said.

"'I want you to come with me.'

"'Where?'

"'Listen, Georgina, there's a man in Augusta, Georgia, who's hiring folks to work on his peach farm.'

"'Augusta?' I said, like I'd never before heard of the place. Eugene went on.

"'He's paying them a decent wage and giving them a place to stay. I'm going down yonder, and I want you with me, as my wife.'

"'But why Augusta?'

"'Because that's where the farm is. That's where the opportunity is.'

"'In Augusta?' I laughed.

"'What's so dadblamed funny about it, Georgina?' he asked me.

"'I can't go.'

"'How come you can't go?'

"'You're talking about right now? Leaving this very minute?'

"'Yes, ma'am. Tonight.'

"'What about my mama and daddy?'

"'To hell with your mama and daddy!'

"'Eugene!'

"'Get you some clothes and let's be on our way.'

"'No sir. I will not!'

"'Listen here, Georgina, there's no way I'm letting a chance like this slip through my hands. Not with the kind of money that man's offering.'

"'But Augusta, Eugene? Now? Tonight? How come you want to work for somebody else all of a sudden, when it's always been your dream to be independent?'

"'For piss sake, Georgina, I can't wave my hand over a patch of crabgrass and turn it into a farm! Got to start someplace. Make money. Make my name. This is the start. Can't you understand that?'

"'All I know is I'm not running away in the middle of the night to marry you.'

"'You so durned cautious, Georgina. And so careful. Don't you know that ain't no way to be if you're going to make something out of yourself?'

"'I'm not running off to Georgia with you tonight. It's unseemly. It's...it's trashy.'

"'Ah hell, Georgina!'

"'I'm not going.'

"'You sure about that?'

"'I am.'

"'You sure you sure?'

"'Yes.'

"He was gone from my door, disappeared like a ghost.

"Later I heard he went into the army, which is what happens to boys who don't have the money or the interest for education and don't have the perseverance for regular work."

Georgina wheeled away from the window, was quiet a moment, then threw back her head with a long, loud laugh. "What have I done? What have I done?" She giggled. "I've wandered so far off the subject that – " She stopped, thought a moment, then smiled. "Why did you let me go on, Doreen? Talking about myself that way. You didn't come to hear that. You came to hear about my cousin Jane and my aunt Myrna a-way up in Boston, didn't you? You should have spoken up so I wouldn't have wasted so much time. Lordy, lordy!"

She gave another short laugh, this one weaker, then pulled herself away from the window, strolled past the chair holding the gown, and settled into the opposite chair. Doreen, embarrassed, looked away and fidgeted with the hem of her skirt.

"Well, now, where was I?" Georgina asked and cleared her throat. "Let's see. Oh yes. Jane and Myrna away. In Boston. And me, with no way at all of getting in touch with them. Well, what could I do, but let things play out as they would? And when they returned home, there was no fanfare about the fact or even an announcement by phone. I wouldn't have known they were back had I not been driving by the house that night in October and seen the lights on in the front room. I stopped the car as though to decide whether to go to the house, the light, the people inside. I didn't know how I would do such. There was such an enormous, mysterious thing waiting inside that might not should be disturbed. Didn't know how I would knock to come in or what I'd say – couldn't say the usual things: they wouldn't do under the circumstances. So I pulled into the driveway and got out of my car and put one foot in front of the other. Oh this was a strange feeling! Unknown to me really, who has always been so forthright. But I just put

one foot in front of the other and kept on moving, feeling at any point like I might be snagged and held back, and went on into the house with my key and stood in the entry hall. There was a light from the parlor that fell on the suitcases and bags piled up by the closet in the hall. Five bags. One, I knew, contained The Dress.

"I turned the corner. Myrna stood in the middle of the parlor with her back turned, as though in the middle of conversation with a person only she could see.

"'Aunt Myrna?' I called softly.

"She stood still a second longer before turning.

"'Why it's Georgina! How are you, Georgina?'

"I walked over to her, led her to the couch, and took the upholstered hardback chair beside her.

"'Aunt Myrna, you just got back from Boston.'

"'Why, yes, yes, as a matter of fact I did. I was going to call you, eventually, and let you know of the fact.'

"'Aunt, you were gone eleven days. What happened up there?'

"'Oh, let's don't talk about all that.' As though the whole matter were some unpleasant news story, something that had happened to other people.

"'You've been in *Boston* eleven days! What else is there to talk about?'

"'Well, only three days in Boston itself. The train trip itself took eight days coming and going.'

"'Myrna! Please! This is not a time to be facetious!'

"'I'm tired, Georgina. I finally realized why I don't travel as much anymore. I don't have the back for it.' She giggled.

"'Myrna, did you and Jane see Mr. Howell?'

"Her face darkened. 'New England isn't what it is all cracked up to be, I'm afraid. I don't think so anyway. I expected more trees. It's the middle of October, and I expected to see all the leaves changed. I read all the brochures and the magazine articles, and I get so built up, expecting the beautiful colors in the trees and they're not there, and....' She sighed heavily and shook her head.

"'Myrna, what in the world possessed you to get on that train and go up there?'

"'What possessed me?' She gave me the most straightforward, clear-eyed, *adult* look she'd ever given me before or since. 'Why, it was love. Love possessed me. I love Jane.'

"'Eleven days, Myrna, and you didn't write or call me.'

"'But I was fair, wasn't I, and honest? I wrote in that letter we left for you that I wouldn't contact you until things had been resolved, and I didn't. I was honest.' She stood and went to the window. 'Honesty,' she continued, 'is something I hope I can maintain till my dying day. Anything less hurts people so much. So very much.' She turned back to me. 'Oh the things I've learned about honesty! First hand lessons. Painful but necessary. And I learned quite a lesson up north.'

"'Aunt, I would like you to go over this whole thing with me. I feel as though you're obligated.'

"'Obligated? Oh yes. Obligation. Honesty. Things to ponder. Perhaps before they are violated. But, I suppose you are right, Georgina. I guess I do owe you the story of the last eleven days. It would be nice to tell it over coffee, though.'

"Right away I rushed into the kitchen to make coffee, and when I had it done and had carried it and cups and saucers on a tray back into the parlor, I remembered *Jane* all of a sudden and asked about her.

"'She's upstairs. Resting. She's had such a trying time, Georgina. You can't imagine.'

"I poured her a cup of coffee then one for myself and sat back down across from her and waited for her. She took her time. I had the time to give her. Then she began.

"'What can you say about a train ride?' she asked, more to herself than me, I think. And then she began the story of their journey on a long grey train from Compton to Richmond, from Richmond to Boston. A train packed with strangers. They didn't know a soul. Didn't speak to anybody else but themselves. Except this nice young albino salesman. A Fuller Brush man, in a tweed jacket. He came and sat down beside them like he'd known them for years. Just started up talking. Said he was going to Richmond to see his sister. Wasn't looking forward to it though. She was like the rest of the family: always trying to get him to give up being a traveling salesman and come home. Jane reached over to him and touched his sleeve and said, "We know just how you feel."

Myrna said she nodded in agreement. He rode all the way to Richmond with them then got off there. They didn't speak to anybody else. Not till they got to Boston.

"Saturday morning they arrived in Boston and got outside the train station and set their bags on the sidewalk, and Jane said, 'Let's go sightsee, Mother! Right now!' Myrna said Jane had experienced an epiphany. A revelation. This was a place she'd been seeking out and dreaming about and so on ever since she was a little girl. And the dream came true. Myrna had never seen her prettier than that, that moment she realized she had reached the place of her dreams. Not in her whole life. Just radiant. Myrna laughed and told her all that would come in time. That would *unfold* later. Myrna pronounced the word as though stretching it out with her tongue and teeth, as though it were dough. *Unfoooooooooold.* And she moved her hands in such a way to indicate the motion. Jane laughed in agreement. And then they flagged down a taxi cab.

"Before they got in the taxi, though, they told the driver where they were from and asked him if he knew any small, homely places where they could stay, since they weren't interested in going to a big city hotel. He said he sure did, that there was a place called Cumberland's, which was a combination of boardinghouse and hostel. A woman ran it, and they had hot meals there. It was only a few blocks from the station. They said fine and hopped in. When they got out in front of Cumberland's, the driver said he would wait, with no extra charge, for them to decide whether they wanted to stay or not. They thanked him and headed for the door. It was a two-story wooden house with a brick front and long porch. The lawn spread around it like an emerald-green lake. A morning chill swept off the porch and made them shiver. As they got closer Myrna heard this soft screeching noise from the right front window, and when they stepped up onto the porch they realized it was music. Someone was playing a phonograph. 'Mendelssohn,' Myrna informed me as though I would feel the same awe she had felt. 'The violin concerto. I was delighted, not necessarily because it was happy music – I have always found that piece rather sad, as a matter of fact – but here was something I was familiar with, something I *loved*, in a strange place. That made it a little less strange.' She said she moved to grab Jane's sleeve and inform her of the fact, but at the same time the front door opened and a middle-aged woman stood there and said, 'Why, hello!'

"Jane turned to Myrna and said, 'Let's tell the driver we're staying.'

"'We haven't even seen the place yet,' Myrna told her.

"'I've got a good feeling about it, Mother. It just *feels* right. Let's tell him we're staying.' And she ran back to the cab without waiting for Myrna to agree."

Georgina paused a moment, as though this point in her narrative was a milestone worth contemplating, a moment of terrible, enormous significance.

"Myrna said she turned back to the front door. The woman - in her middle fifties or thereabouts – had moved out some from the door with her hand extended. 'I'm Felicia Cumberland.' Myrna took her hand. Together they looked back to the car. Jane was fishing in her pocket for fare and the driver was setting their bags on the sidewalk. 'I'll have someone bring them in,' Mrs. Cumberland said. 'Come on in here, out of the chill.' 'Funny,' Myrna told me, 'how everything seemed to be settled without our saying a word – well, hardly a word.'

"Once they were inside the house, the Mendelssohn came at them full force. Myrna touched the woman, Mrs.

Cumberland, on the shoulder and informed her of the name of the composer. With a smile the woman said she knew who it was.

"Three rooms stood visible to them there inside the door: the shut room from which the music came, the parlor, and the dining room. A long hallway led back to the kitchen. Almost everything was hardwood and very tasteful, Myrna was quick to add, with circular rugs placed here and there of mute and dignified colors and low talk coming from the parlor. A staircase stood to the right of the front door, and down it came a tall, white-haired gentleman, whom Mrs. Cumberland asked to go fetch Jane's and Myrna's bags. He obliged with a wide, white smile. Dentures, I would think. No man that age has a 'wide, white smile' unless the dentist has supplied him with it. In Myrna's world, however, such a thing is possible. She referred to this man as 'very, very handsome.' In the meantime Mrs. Cumberland led Jane and Myrna past the kitchen to the desk, behind which stood a flat panel with tiers of keys and hexagonal cubbyholes for mail. Mrs. Cumberland charged twenty dollars a night for a room. The handsome old man reappeared with the bags and let them go to the floor. 'Oh, the only thing I dislike about the female species is they pack their bags way too heavy,' Myrna said he said, and when she did, for some reason I thought of W.C. Fields, except this gentleman was handsome with a full head of glittering white teeth. But I could hear him saying what he said in that kind of voice that

Fields had. He was directed by the woman to take them upstairs. Jane and Myrna followed him up. When he left them, they unpacked their things into pinewood drawers then returned to the stairs. Mrs. Cumberland was waiting for them.

"'Ladies, this would be a splendid time to meet some of our other friends.' She held out her hands for them, and they joined her downstairs, where they crossed the hall, past the stairwell, and stopped in front of a partially-cracked door. A recording played something operatic. Mrs. Cumberland tapped gently on the door as she opened it. Four elderly people looked up from a round, dark-oak table covered in playing cards.

"One of them, a shrunken little old lady, said, pointing to a shrunken little old man, 'Ms. Cumberland, Lewis spilled the deck on purpose. On purpose, I tell you, to confuse the rest of us!'

"Myrna said Lewis was short and chubby with big white eyebrows and an ugly mouth.

"'She turned down m' music,' Lewis returned. 'Turned it down so's I can barely hear it. *Aida*! The most beautiful work of music ever composed! It helps me concentrate. She knows that. And she turned it down!'

"'Beautiful or not, it distracts the rest of us. You are merely being spiteful.'

"Ms. Cumberland intervened most diplomatically. 'Actually, ladies and gentlemen, this is probably an excellent moment to reduce the volume. I have with me two new guests I would like to introduce to you.' And she introduced Jane and Myrna, making much of their South Carolina origins.

"'Hello!' the old folks said in unison, even Lewis and the shrunken woman. Their voices sounded so cheery it was hard for Myrna and Jane to believe they had been bickering with each other the moment before.

"'I have always loved the name Jane,' Myrna said a stout woman in a pink nightgown offered. 'When I was thirteen years old I had a kitten that was the apple of my eye, and I named her Jane. After my very favorite author: Miss Jane Austen.'

"The others immediately plied Jane and Myrna with questions. The other man at the table wanted to know how long they would be staying at Ms. Cumberland's esteemed establishment. Myrna took especial notice of this one. He wore a black formal suit with a blood red necktie descending from his throat and had even prettier teeth than the gentleman on the stairs. Real ones, she said, when I expressed my doubts. Somewhat mesmerized, Myrna told him that she and Jane would be on their way in a day or so.

"'Oh, that's too bad,' the gentleman answered, his smile flashing like saber blades. 'I could listen to that accent the rest of the night and into the next morning.'

"Myrna said a small gasp went up from the group at that statement. She had to catch hold of the doorjamb to stay afoot.

"To assuage the awkwardness of the moment, Ms. Cumberland took the opportunity to make more formal introductions and named the card-players: Lewis, the lover of *Aida*, was Lewis Chesmire. He was joined by his nemesis Marie Foster and by Giselle Chauncey, who loved Jane Austen enough to name her cat after her. The dapper Dan with the silver tongue was Mr. Emeric Samuels, esquire, a retired attorney, which surely did not surprise Myrna, although I have my doubts about that too. Afterwards Jane and Myrna went back to their room to rest before dinner. Jane however kept staring at the gown, which she had hung up on the back of the door for a better, and symbolic, view.

"As they made their way back downstairs for dinner, Mr. Samuels appeared at the bottom of the steps, smiling, and threw up his hand. 'Hello,' he said cheerily. He reminded them of his name and his profession and asked them please not to hold it against him. He made himself laugh, and Myrna said his laugh came out so soft it sounded like bird wings flapping – the coming together of doves' wings. 'And you are Miss Poage and Miss Poage. Correct? Oh but no! No! One of you is *Mrs*. Poage!'

"Myrna said she was Mrs. Poage.

"'Oh drat!' Mr. Samuels went on. 'Just drat my luck.' He threw back his head and let out another of his feathered laughs. Myrna didn't tell him she was widowed. 'Well, in any event, what brings you ladies to Boston? Why are we so privileged to have the two of you amongst us?'

"Jane explained that they were on their way to Wicker and had just stopped to rest and see the city.

"'Wicker?' Mr. Samuels asked, as though he had never heard of it before. 'That's cod-liver country, isn't it?'

"Jane and Myrna laughed together and answered yes together. The gentleman shyly asked them why.

"'Jane,' Myrna answered proudly, 'is engaged to a young man there.'

"Mr. Samuels clapped his hands lightly and laughed. It must have sounded like a covey unleashed. Then he said, 'Delightful news! But, tell me, why did you laugh just a minute before?'

"'You mentioned cod-liver.'

"Mr. Samuels's look remained, in Myrna's estimation, and I quote her directly now, 'charmingly perplexed.'

"Myrna informed Mr. Samuels that Jane's fiancé was connected with cod-liver oil.'

"The gentleman could not help but keep being 'charmingly perplexed.' His smile didn't move.

"'Her fiancé is Mr. Howell's son!'

"Mr. Samuels thawed out. His smile grew wider. He clapped his hands again. 'You're joking!'

"Jane informed him that the Howell family was re-uniting that weekend and that she and Myrna had come up to surprise him.

"'You mean he doesn't know you're here?'

"They nodded together.

"'Delightful! Oh, I do wish I had such a lovely surprise waiting for me!'

"Jane and Myrna laughed. Mr. Samuels held out his arms. 'Let's go in right this minute and announce the wonderful news to all the others.'

"They took each of his arms and he escorted them into the dining room. It was not, Myrna pointed out, a large room, and she had to wonder what happened when a good number of people stayed there and they all wanted to eat in. I reminded her that there was such a thing as shifts, that the Lord God had not yet declared that *everybody* must eat at a certain point. She mumbled, 'Yes, yes, you're right' and went on to describe what a lovely room it was – tastefully appointed like the rest of the house, with the decorating idea being that less is more. Candles were lit, and their flames showed in the glass doors

of the china closet and made everything very soft and peaceful. Everyone they had met previously was there, and they all greeted each other again in high, happy voices, as though *they* were the reuniting kinfolk. They especially made a fuss over Jane, as though meeting her for the first time, and Myrna admitted with pride that Jane certainly looked beautiful in all that reflected, glowing candlelight.

"It was a fine, big meal they ate, Myrna said, maybe a little too much for so few people, but everybody turned out to be hearty eaters, so nothing went to waste. The table talk was all jumbled and touched on a little of everything. Miss Foster talked about rug-hooking. Mr. McHenry, he of the helpful hands and dazzling dentures, said he'd heard on the radio that there was a chance of some snow flurries for the next three mornings. Mr. Chesmire and Miss Chaucey got into another argument over music. Miss Chaucey said she had read somewhere that jazz was the only truly indigenous American musical style, an art form that had been born and reared here, in these United States, and Mr. Chesmire slapped his knife down on his plate and said that if that were true, then America be damned to hell! Jazz was lewd and lascivious and produced responses only in the body. The great music, the *real* classics, he said, were ennobling, as they produced great responses in the head and heart.

"Myrna noticed that Mr. Samuels sat above the fray and kept a smile on his face throughout all the talk, and after dessert he stood, cleared his throat very loudly, and said, 'I have a wonderful announcement to make.' He looked in Jane's and Myrna's direction and beamed. 'There is in our midst a lovely young woman who, in matter of days, will enter the wonderful and holy bond of matrimony.'

"'Well, it sure ain't me!' said rug-hooking Miss Foster, and her big belly just shook with laughter.

"'No, it most certainly is not,' Mr. Samuels continued with no loss of gentlemanly pace. 'It is the lovely Miss Poage here. Miss Jane Poage.' He bowed in Jane's direction.

"'Oh that's marvelous!' Mrs. Cumberland exclaimed with her hands clapped together, and the others joined in, all except Mr. Chesmire, who sat glaring, still heated from his bout with Miss Chaucey.

"'Who is the lucky man?' asked Mr. McHenry.

"Jane, all blushed and embarrassed, looked to her mother, and Myrna urged her on with a nod and a smile.

"'Jonathan Howell,' she said simply.

"Myrna said that she and Jane, and Mr. Samuels too, sat and waited for a second chorus of oooh's and ahhh's from the assembled group upon hearing the famous name of Jane's betrothed to be. But all they got were polite smiles and uncertain nods of old heads.

"Mr. Samuels' smile dropped; he leaned over the table and shouted, 'Jonathan Howell! Howell! HOWELL! Doesn't that name mean anything to any of you?' There came no answer, so he went on. 'Mrs. Foster, you claimed to have raised five children, correct?' Myrna said he suddenly appeared and sounded as though he were questioning a witness. It had been quite unexpected and quite impressive. 'When any of those children complained of the belly ache to you, what did you administer to them as remedy?'

"Mrs. Foster's heavy face stayed dim a moment and then, all at once, lit up. 'Why, cod-liver oil, I suppose.'

"Mr. Samuels nodded his head vigorously, as though a hidden piece of evidence had just been revealed to his jury.

"'Cod-liver oil?' Mrs. Cumberland asked. She thought a moment. 'Cod-liver oil. Howell. Cod-liver oil. Howell.' She slowly raised her head. 'You're joking!'

"This time Mr. Samuels shook his head vigorously. 'I am not. Miss Poage here is engaged to marry young Jonathan Howell, son of Fennis Howell, founder and president of Howell's Cod-Liver Oil right here in our very own backyard, in the quaint and charming hamlet of Wicker!'

"'Son? Is that what you said?' asked Mr. McHenry. 'I thought you were going to tell us our young friend here is about to marry Old Man Fennis Howell himself!'

"'I didn't know Fennis Howell had a son,' Mrs. Foster added.

"'Yes, yes,' Mr. Samuels went on. 'The young man is an actor by profession. Tours the country. That is how he and Miss Poage here met in her native South Carolina. And you know what the delicious part is?' Mr. Samuels' voice suddenly dropped to a whisper. 'Young Mr. Howell doesn't even know Miss Poage is here to see him!'

"'Oh that's right. The Howells *are* having their reunion this weekend. It was in the papers and everything.'

"'I didn't know Fennis Howell had a son!' Mrs. Foster repeated very loudly. 'I thought he only had daughters. Their pictures are all the time in the paper.'

"'There is a lot about Fennis Howell you don't know.' Finally Mr. Chesmire had spoken up. It was so unexpected

Myrna said they couldn't do anything but stop and listen. 'I worked for him for twenty-five years, and even I don't know how many children he had or whether they were girls or boys. Because that is the kind of man Fennis Howell is. Very private. Very secretive. He doesn't want anything else about himself emphasized except his company. That company is his real baby!'

"Myrna said Jane, like herself, was a bit perplexed and didn't know how to respond to any of that. All Jane said was, 'We're headed to Wicker tomorrow.'

"'Ah, so that's why you're not staying longer.'

"'Yes.'

"They all wanted to know if Jane and Myrna knew their way around Wicker, and Myrna was smart enough to say, 'I'm afraid we don't know our way around anywhere up here.' Right away the kindly, white-toothed Mr. McHenry volunteered to drive them into

Wicker. It was, he said, only an hour and a half drive. Myrna accepted the offer with many thanks and told him they would like to get started as soon as possible in the morning, to which Mr. McHenry said fine.

"They listened to records for a little while after dinner. Some classical music then light jazz, which prompted Mr. Chesmire to stamp mumbling and angry from the parlor. Shortly after that everyone turned in for the night.

"Myrna, however, could not sleep and went back downstairs to the kitchen. She took the liberty of making herself a glass of warm milk, which she took into the parlor to drink. She sat in the dark, thinking of all that was to take place the next day, feeling probably as excited as her daughter, when all of a sudden, a rustle came to the door. A shadow lingering. She called hello. The shadow sighed then laughed gently. It was a man.

"'Mrs. Poage,' it said, as though relieved. Myrna reached over for the lamp nearest the chair where she sat and switched it on. Mr. Samuels was revealed standing in the doorway, still wearing his suit and tie. He smiled. 'May I join you?' he asked, his hands raised to show himself defenseless. Myrna said of course, and he took a seat on the couch adjacent to the chair where Myrna sat. He didn't say anything for a few minutes. She didn't either. It was terribly awkward. Then Myrna began some small talk but Mr. Samuels, contrary to his gentlemanly nature, cut her off. 'I find you utterly fascinating, Mrs. Poage.' For the first time Myrna said she detected the lilt of alcohol in his voice.

"'Why thank you' was all she could say. She wanted very much to be out of the parlor and back in her room with her daughter. Mr. Samuels would not stop staring at her.

"'It's an injustice,' he went on, 'a cruelty, that you would come here for so brief a time and then be gone the next day. But I know you have to go. You're a woman of purpose, of principle. You're here for a reason, the happiness of your own child. You're sacrificing everything for her. I find it so noble, and I wouldn't do a thing in the world to try to stop you. There's so little nobility left in human relations these days. You are to be honored. And I do honor you. And when you leave the steps of this establishment, know you take away with you the heart of one very old, very sad, very smitten man.'

"All Myrna could do was look away.

"'I'm being forward, I know. I'm sorry. Very sorry. But it's been so many years since a woman has charmed me the way you have. Since the death of my own dear Agatha. And may I venture to say, Mrs. Poage, that you may very well outdo that dear woman in charm. Oh, I hate to say it. It sounds like betrayal. But....'

"Myrna stood quickly, barely able to hold on to her glass of milk. 'Mr. Samuels – '

"'I'm sorry, Mrs. Poage. Terribly sorry. This was a lapse of manners, an inexcusable breach of good taste for a man who holds himself to be a gentleman. But I felt if I didn't express this, and you gone tomorrow, well it would be just one more regret added to a string of many. If we just had time! Time! That scoundrel! Always robbing us of our dreams!'

"Myrna said she merely wished the gentleman a good night and left him. Of course she couldn't sleep. Not a wink, and when she needed sleep so much too. Had that whole conversation been a dream? No. She checked, with her eyes and ears and hands. It was all real. She was not asleep. She pulled the covers up over herself, almost afraid of the emotion she had obviously awakened in Mr. Samuels. She had never…no not ever…been the object of such a vulnerable kind of 'admiration.' That's what she called it, Doreen. 'Admiration.' She pushed it away, everything, his voice, his face, his words, her own stirred-up feelings. No, not even Uncle Ford had declared that kind of passion to her so…nakedly. She pushed it away. It was an unwelcome thing in the face of her mission, with her daughter beside her the focal point of their trip. It would be unwelcome in any circumstance. *She was too old for it!* Why had he come to her and said those things? What a foolish distraction. What a crazy thing! She couldn't force herself to sleep, not even with hot milk in her.

"The next morning was bright blue and chilly. Mrs. Cumberland, so sympathetic to what Jane and Myrna were doing, got up early along with them and made them breakfast, while the kind and smiling Mr. McHenry gassed and checked his pick-up truck. They then packed their things into the truck and were off. Mr. Samuels did not come to bid them farewell, which suited Myrna just fine. If he had, then all those confusing feelings she had fought the night before would just have popped right back out of her to be a nuisance.

"It was a quiet trip to Wicker. Mr. McHenry tried to talk. He told them about Wicker and what an agricultural center of Massachusetts it had once been, that it had some of the richest growing soil he had ever seen in his life. Nobody there cared about that, though. Everybody wanted industrial power. They'd have sacrificed their young for it, he said in ominous and angry tones. That was why Mr. Howell was revered. He was a god to some of the people in Wicker. Jane and Myrna sat and tuned him in and out. They had other things on their minds, of course. Jane strained to look out the window, hoping to see something *historical*. She was disappointed. So was Myrna. All they caught on their way out of Boston were the same lawns and traffic and houses they could have seen in any good sized city in South Carolina.

"Mr. McHenry didn't give up though. At some point he cleared his throat and asked them what time they were expected at the Howell residence. Jane informed him that there were not going to the Howell residence. They were going to see her fiancé. She had his address tucked away in a special corner of her purse.

"'But you still don't have a place to stay?' the gentleman asked and stated at the same time.

"The both of them said no together.

"'If you don't mind, I know a fine place in town to stay. Philmont's. It's in the heart of Wicker. Nice and homely, with nice shops and restaurants around.'

"'Sounds lovely.'

"'I'll be glad to drive you there.'

"'Please!' they answered together.

"So he drove them to Philmont's, right in the center of

town, as he promised, and unloaded their bags, and when they were registered, he shooed aside the bellboy and took the bags up to their room himself. When he got back downstairs, Jane and Myrna could not thank him enough. In fact when he left, they said it felt like saying goodbye to kin. At lunchtime they decided to try one of the nearby restaurants. When Jane asked the waitress what the most *New Englandy* thing on their menu was, the lady replied, 'The bacon-lettuce-tomato. They ship the bacon in from Maine.' Jane and Myrna got watercress sandwiches and ice water. Afterwards they decided to stroll across the block, not too far from their room, hoping they could catch the flavor of *something* in Wicker. The poor dears. They seemed to be under some kind of notion that the air in New England would be so different, so filled up with the scent of pilgrims and musket powder and witches burning and goodness knows what all. I've always wondered if they never realized how historical their own home state is and how if they walked or rode a little bit down the road, they could be where some great battle was fought or some important paper was signed.

"Back in the room Jane was fidgety. Couldn't sit down. Couldn't keep still. She went to the window, stuck her head out a moment, and came back in. 'Oh Mother!' Myrna said she called out. 'I've never been so excited in all my life! Ever!' Then she went to the bathroom door, on which the dress was hung, and said, 'I think I'll put it on.'

"'Myrna said her mouth dropped, and Jane said, 'Oh Mother, it seems so right. I haven't had it on for a week.' And before Myrna could say another word, she had the gown off the hook and dashed into the bathroom. She came back out slowly, bloomed from the bathroom door, Myrna said, like some white flower being born into the room, an enormous rose. 'Georgina,' Myrna said to me, 'she was the most beautiful girl I ever laid my eyes on. So happy. So beautifully, wonderfully happy that I couldn't help but be happy too. That's why we live, Georgina, to see our children happy.' Myrna said she felt a love then that almost burst out of her body, it was so big, so encompassing. 'I loved Jane,' she said. 'I loved Mr. Howell. I loved the world that held the two of them together in the same place. I loved the world then more than ever, felt as though my whole heart were closing over it, holding it. The world, that is. The wide, gigantic world of love.' You can imagine, Doreen, how dramatic she looked saying such as that, with her arms out and floating over her head and her face turning up to the ceiling. She should have been on the stage herself, right up there with little Johnny Howell.

"The two of them stood at the hotel mirror. Jane leaned against her mother. 'Let's go find Jon right now,' she whispered into Myrna's ear.

"'Silly thing!' Myrna replied.

"'Oh Mama, let's go find him!'

"'Like that? With you in your dress?'

"'Now you're being silly.'

"'Can't wait for anything.'

"The cab driver frowned when they gave him Jon Howell's address then shrugged. As they rode through Wicker, Massachusetts, past its laundromats and shops and movie houses, Myrna thought of Jane again in that dress, and all fears and doubts and trepidation just melted away. Wicker, Massachusetts, became the center of all goodness and love. The streets rolled golden beneath them. The air was tinged with perfume. The sun broke through the trees in big, white, glorious flames. Wicker was calm and kind. Wicker was filled with all that is good. 'Oh, how I loved the world then!' Myrna told me as she recounted.

"Suddenly the driver announced the address he'd been given and stopped.

"'2626 Ambrose Road?' Myrna asked him. He said yes. The two of them scrambled to the window to look out. There were two buildings on the block. One was a dilapidated old warehouse, the other a padlocked hardware store. In between the two structures stood nothing at all – just an ugly gap of weeds and crabgrass covered in a sheet of corrugated iron rusting in the sun and an automobile tire sticking partway up from the dirty, dead, dry ground. They looked around them to see if they could spot anything that remotely resembled an apartment building or tenant house. But there wasn't a thing. They asked the driver again if he was sure that was 2626 Ambrose. The driver looked at them in a way that let them know he didn't like being asked again, as though his sense of direction were being questioned. Jane opened the door and hopped out. Myrna followed. The driver followed her, hand out, brow furrowed. Myrna found fare. The driver took it and went back to the car. He slammed the door petulantly and drove off. Myrna went to Jane, who stood looking at the street with a sense of bewilderment.

"'2626 Ambrose Road, Mama,' Jane said. 'It was on all his letters.' She had one of the envelopes in her hand and lifted it and jabbed the return address as though there might be any doubt. She lifted her arms up and drifted into the high grass, and when she reached the center, near the protruding tire, she turned around and around, and when she stopped turning she stood still and looked at Myrna.

"'Dear, anything could have happened,' Myrna said she told her. 'It's been two weeks since he last wrote you.'

"But Jane shook her head. '2626 Ambrose Road.'

"Back in the room they sat and let the late afternoon come on. Jane was staring at the dress hard. It hung over the window and the sun filled it up and made it glow like a candle.

"'I don't understand, Mama, why couldn't he have written and told me his building had been condemned and he had been evicted?'— for that was the conclusion her imagination had reached; no other existed for her. The old warehouse, as far as Jane was concerned, had been a residence of some sort for young men like Jon Howell, which, for whatever reason, had in a matter of no time at all shut its doors and spit out its tenants.

"'He's a busy man, Jane. He can't write you about his every move. I am sure he *meant* to write and tell you that he had moved. And he probably has. Why, I bet the letter's in the mail right now, on its way to South Carolina as we speak, with his new address included.'

"Jane had shrugged.

"'And imagine how it's going to feel when he sees us! When he sees *you*! Imagine the joy.'

"'Mama, right now I'm just trying to imagine where he lives. How are we going to surprise him when we don't know where he is?'

"Myrna said at that point she just raised her chin and puffed out her chest. 'If need be, daughter, we will go to the Howell residency and announce ourselves. We'll *barge* in if we have to. At this point, my dear, boldness may be our only option.'

"'Oh Mama!' Jane exclaimed and threw her arms around Myrna's neck.

"Myrna had promised Jane dinner at a smart looking restaurant they had passed that afternoon. Jane walked with a new purpose in her step, Myrna said, a new energy. There was a chill in the air. They strolled to the restaurant leisurely, Jane holding her mama's arm. The restaurant, called Borne's Plenty, sat two blocks down from their room.

Lanterns sat in each of the two front French windows, and a pine wreath stood on the front wooden door, which the girls took as some sort of lucky sign of things to come.

Inside the lights were dimmed. Candles sat on the small, intimate tables and glowed from the mirrors surrounding the dining room. Hardly anyone else was there at that hour, a family or couple here and there. Myrna told Jane they had plenty of money and to get whatever it was she wanted. Jane bunched up her shoulders in happiness and said, 'Let's try lobster. Finally, something *New Englandy*!'

"'Mother,' Jane said, 'if and when we see Jon, let's don't get carried away. I mean, let's don't do anything silly when we first see him. Not that I don't trust you. Well, I don't trust myself. Lord, I hope I don't embarrass him in front of his big, rich, important daddy!'

"'Don't be silly, dear,' Myrna answered. She craned her neck a little. 'I do wish they would turn on some lights. It's hard to see who to flag down for service.'

"'Oh Mama, if Jon does ask me to marry him, I'll go all to pieces. All to pieces. I'm just not used to this sort of thing. Maybe I should have dated more. Just for practice. You know?'

"'No, dear. No. That would have spoiled you. You're meant for one man. You've been growing and blooming all this time, waiting for Mr. Howell to come pluck you. Where is the waiter?'

"'Mama, I don't want to leave you. He'll ask me to live

here, I just know it. New England is wonderful, but...but....Or he may want to go on the road with him. Or, even worse, he may go on the road and leave me here!'

"All the while they were talking, Myrna said, she had her eyes set on a tall, white, broad figure moving through the dark, making tiny white flames shake in their stems as it passed, walking toward them, coming into shape, sharp and beautiful, familiar and bright.

"'May I start you ladies out with a beverage?' the dark angel asked them, in a voice dark and lovely and deep as the ocean.

"Myrna's eyes had dropped at this point in the telling, Doreen. She joined her hands in her lap. She let out a sigh and said, 'I remember putting my elbow on the table and wincing, opening and closing my eyes to adjust them. I even managed to run my hand over my mouth during that time. You see, Georgina, I was staring up at Jonathan Howell. He was that handsome ghost who strolled among the candles to our table. And the candle light must have been strong on our table, because as soon as he set eyes on me and took a second glance, his smile dropped.

"'Mother, order,' Jane said, like she was embarrassed. She was still straining to study the menu, but when she finally glanced up and saw who stood in front of her, her smile dropped as quickly as Mr. Howell's.

"'Jon?' she said. Mr. Howell didn't say anything. Then Jane lifted the candle from the table and held it aloft, high enough to be absolutely sure about who it was. And she repeated 'Jon?' just like a child who's been told there's no Santa Claus and cannot get over the news.

"'Mr. Howell?' Myrna said behind her with the same hurt in her voice.

"Mr. Howell stood rocking back and forth, touching his white linen shirt with the scalloped ruffles down the front and the red apron. He was at a loss for words, Myrna said, which just about ended the whole story for me, Doreen. I mean, imagining that young man at a loss for words was like imagining Elizabeth Taylor at a loss for husbands. It just didn't seem possible. But Myrna testified to the fact anyway. Said it looked like he'd just been frozen there, his voice snatched away.

"'Jon,' Jane went on, 'we've been looking for you. We went to the address you gave us and there was nothing there except some place that had been closed up. What happened, Jon? Did you ever live there?'

"'Jane,' Myrna said, like she was cautioning her.

"'What are the two of you doing here?' Mr. Howell asked, finally.

"'It's a surprise. Isn't that right, Mother? We're surprising you. Jon, are you surprised?'

"'Quite,' the young man answered, and, as far as I was concerned, it was the most honest thing that ever came out of his mouth. Then he had to go on and spoil it. 'I was going to write you and let you know that I had moved.'

"'Oh I knew it!' Jane said, clapping her hands together and looking at Myrna with a child-like happiness. Myrna, however, did not share in the joy. All that love of the world she had experienced just a little bit before they arrived at Borne's Plenty sank out of sight, replaced by doubt.

"She said, 'Mr. Howell, are you really the son of the man who manufactures cod-liver oil here in Wicker? Is that really your father?'

"She said Jane just reeled back like she'd been struck at. 'Mother, what in the world kind of question is that?' she asked and laughed nervously.

"'Is he?' Myrna went on, just like nothing else had been said.

"'Mother!'

"Mr. Howell's face tensed up.

"'Jon, Mother's being awfully silly for some reason.'

"'Is he?'

"'No,' he answered and dropped his head.

"'No? What do you mean, no? Do you mean no, Mother is not being silly, or no, your father is not....' Then it hit her. 'Jon, what are you doing here in this place? Working? But, Jon, it's the Howell family reunion. You're supposed to be *there*, celebrating.'

"'Mr. Howell,' Myrna said, 'we drove out to the address you gave Jane this afternoon. We did not see a respectable apartment building as you described in your letters. We saw a hardware store and an old warehouse that's this close to falling in. How did you get my daughter's letters? Why weren't they sent back?'

"'I got them in care of the hardware store. I worked there, off and on, until last week. When I got this job.' His head still did not rise from his broad shoulders.

"'Mother, I'm not getting any of this. Jon, I'm not getting any of this. You and Mother are acting like I'm not even here. What are you saying? Are you telling me you've been lying to me?'

" Myrna said Mr. Howell was at his second loss for words. I told her it was a moment they should have immortalized on a plaque there in Wicker, Massachusetts.

"'Have you, Jon?'

"'Jane,' he began then stopped.

"'You know you didn't have to lie. I don't really know why you did. I mean, I'm not really impressed by wealth. It's nice, but it isn't the end-all, be-all of the world. I mean, we're not wealthy, and we're perfectly happy people, Mother and I, and…and…. And, Mother, I'll wait for you outside!' With a choke in her throat, Jane shot up at once from the table and hurried out of the restaurant, leaving candle flames waving goodbye. Myrna sat still and never took her eyes off Mr. Howell, or whatever his name was.

"She said, 'Is there a reason you lied to my daughter?'

"'I had no idea you would come up here.'

"'Obviously not! My daughter never lied to you. She was honest when said we don't care about money. We don't.

And never have.'

"'Jane was so nice to me when I was down there in South Carolina. She was the first girl in a long time to give me such kind attention. A lot of girls don't have anything to do with actors. Movie actors, yes, because girls know movie actors have money and cars and all that. But not part-time stage actors.'

"'My daughter's interest was in art. She thought it was yours also.'

"'It is! Oh it is! I've been working like a dog trying to raise money for my friend's play. I never lied about that.'

"'But all the rest about your family is a lie. Correct?'

"'I am from a different line of Howells, the branch not drenched in cod-liver oil. I thought I knew Jane's type, a young woman with an appetite for what is good in life, good and expensive. I knew she wouldn't be impressed by the son of a cabinet-maker trying to ape Olivier.'

"'My daughter is impressed with honesty!'

"'Yes, but I didn't know that at first, and by the time I'd realized it, the web had already gotten tangled.'

"'So you put on a little performance for us, didn't you? Very good. Excellent work. You had all of us fooled.'

"'Except me, Myrna!' I put in as she talked, but she didn't stop to acknowledge that.

"'Well, the charade is over,' she went on at Mr. Howell. 'We can all store away our costumes and clean off our make-up. You're free. Jane's free. We're all free.' With that,

Myrna stood and left, leaving Mr. Howell standing at the lonely table with the little pricks of white light dancing around him.

"Jane was standing outside by the lamp post looking into the dark. Myrna touched her arm. They headed back to their room.'

"'And well, Georgina,' Myrna said, 'that's really all there is to it.' She leaned back on the couch and let out a long sigh then covered her face with both her hands a moment before letting them drift down to her sides. She shrugged. 'The next morning I called Mr. McHenry and he picked us up. We spent that day back at the Cumberland boardinghouse. And the next day we hopped aboard another long, gray train packed with strangers and headed back to South Carolina. And here we are! Nothing to that, is there? Oh, but I do remember sitting on that train home and hearing, somehow, somewhere, maybe only in my head, the opening notes to the Mendelssohn violin concerto, just as plain as if Yehudi Menuhin were standing right in front of me playing it – it was the music we had heard when we came upon Mrs. Cumberland's establishment. It's a piece I've loved for more than fifty years! And you know, it turned my stomach. It made me all sick and sticky feeling, and I fought like the devil not to hear it. I don't know, but I kept thinking, This is a lie, you know? A great big ugly lie. It was the strangest feeling. It felt like the end of something that had been wonderful once.'

"Myrna sat quiet a moment, and the she looked at me and said, 'Well, Georgina, if you want to say "I told you so," go right ahead, my dear. Go right ahead.'

"Doreen, I wouldn't have said that to Myrna. Not that the temptation wasn't there, but…that was my aunt, my kin, and she'd just gone through a rough thing. Now in a day or two…maybe, but…."

The sun was almost down the whole way. Long shadows had taken hold of the room and crisscrossed the hardwood floor. Doreen went over and switched on a lamp near the window.

"Neither one of them was the same after it all, as you can probably imagine," Georgina continued. "Myrna took to gardening, something she'd never been good at before. (My mama was the one who'd gotten the green thumb among the girls in the family.) But she got right into it. Every time I'd come over here, she'd be in her garden, working away, busy as a beetle, hands and face just black with dirt. You remember all those prizes she won at the Compton fair for her tomatoes, don't you?"

Doreen nodded.

"And Jane moved even further into herself, I'm afraid. It took her years to break off and get on her own. She started painting, Doreen. Painting in the abstract style. All those slashes and curves and such that the viewer could make into anything he or she so pleased. Myrna said this was Jane's way of dealing with the hurt that still lingered. Oh well.

Better a paint brush than a pistol. The only thing that got hurt, I guess, was the canvas she had slashed up with her paints. And I hear that kind of nonsense sells right well if you can find the right fool to shell out money for it. Jane never did. You know, I have always thought the most harmful part of misery is that it brings out all these artistic leanings in the miserable that ought to stay shut up for good. And then the rest of us get almost as miserable looking at it as the one who created it."

Georgina leaned back deeply in her chair and touched her chin with an index finger.

"But you know what, Doreen? I've got to hand it to Myrna and Jane. At least they went out and did *something*, you know? It was a crazy something, but at least they tried. So many people don't, and they wind up at home painting in the abstract style. Oh, I despise to hear people talk about Myrna and Jane like they were oddballs. The things that have been said! I guess that's why I go on and tell this thing, to keep the record straight. For better or worse, they loved the world. They went out into the world with nothing but love in their hearts. God bless 'em."

Georgina smiled a wide smile and touched her hair. The room glowed in thickening yellow lamp light. Doreen stood again and moved to the chair with the dress in it. She hoisted it up against her own breast. "It sure is a pretty dress," she said. "Too bad it never had been used."

Vera Tera
Memoir & Requiem

Funeral by Committee

THAT IS WHAT THE LITTLE CONTINGENCY of Garden Club/Auxiliary regulars wanted when Vera Tuck died. After all, Vera was a Main Street resident, the same as they, and the very notion of the county handling her arrangements lacked a certain dignity. They came to me and offered me the "chairmanship" of this project.

"Her family," one of them said to me in supplication. They were seated in my parlor, spread in a semi-circle, in their bright summer dresses. "Such a fine old venerable name. You remember the Judge, don't you, Isolde? You are old enough? What a rock of a man. What a good man. He could have been governor of the state had things worked out differently. Is this the way the last of the line should be treated – like a pauper?"

I reminded them that Vera Tuck, at the time of her death, lacked family, not money, and that the Compton officials knew much more about this matter than I. It would therefore be best left to the "professionals."

"But it is the *idea* of it," another reminded me. "After

all, Isolde, you were her neighbor. You knew her best."

Hardly. Occasional conversations by the mailbox or over a honeysuckle-strangled steel fence dividing our properties did not constitute intimacy. I told them that. And then I reminded them that a certain indignity had already attached itself to Vera Tuck's demise. She had, after all, been found dead not in the luxurious trappings of her old family home, in a four poster bed shielded by silk curtains, but by the lake in city park with her gingham dress hiked to her thighs and a wicker hamper of spoiling food beside her. "Meeting her boyfriend," I added, but no one laughed. No one shook her head with bemusement the way ill-heeled, non-Main Street Comptonites did whenever Vera's phantasmagoric paramour was evoked.

One of them sighed. "Vera. My goodness. Some families are just marked for calamity, aren't they?" Then followed the list of Tuck losses: the Judge's early death of massive brain hemorrhage, the older brother's hunting accident, the sister's marriage to a disreputable poet manqué. All of sudden the six of us were young women again, transported to that time, some fifty years before, when the Tucks thrived in our imagination and clenched a permanent place in the local headlines for their charity work and academic achievements and elections to prestigious councils and committees for the betterment of one thing or another in South Carolina.

"Roman Tuck," one of them said presently, in the airy

intonation of a love-struck girl. She meant the brother, who, one winter morning in the thickets of Beaslap in the southern section of Compton County, had been mistaken by his fellow hunters for a deer and shot dead in the woods by his near-sighted uncle. Twenty-four years old. Duke graduate. Brilliant future. All gone in a puff of February gunshot.

"Golden hair," she went on.

"Like a girl's," joined in another.

"Do we dare say 'pretty'?"

"Oh say it! Say it! Just like a girl!"

"Like his father," one of them said with that same quality of dreaminess in her voice that suggested she might, at any time, just pick up and float right to the ceiling..

"No, no, no!" The five of them looked at me, mouths slightly agape, eyes hooded slightly, as though they expected me to rise and assault them physically. "You said you knew Judge Tuck. If you truly knew Judge Tuck, then you would remember that he had nothing of elegance about his features. He was *rough-hewn*." I balled my fists, made a face, to prove the point. Mr. Tuck had gone completely bald-headed by the time he was elected Compton County probate judge. His face had sharp distinct lines, not wrinkles exactly, just demarcations of character, sternness, avidity for truth that could leave a man looking scarred. Of course they didn't know him – other than from glances at newspaper friezes and glimpses at one function or another in town. Their kind did not deal with the probate judge other than to share mint juleps with him and stories of college boy rambunctiousness. (And even then, it was their fathers who had enjoyed such exchanges.) Only the riffraff had continuous contact with the judge and could discern him from any mythic evocation. Those people knew he was *not* pretty.

My guests moved on.

"When the news came that Roman was dead," one of them began with a sob in her throat which never fully rose, "well, it was as though *I* had died."

"Really?" They looked at me again.

"To be taken out that way in the very bloom of golden youth! To be mistaken for a deer!"

"And shot by one's own uncle! They said, the witnesses, I mean, that the woods had stood so unnaturally quiet for the longest, when all of a sudden there came this thrashing in the trees like an animal tearing through them. And well, Mr. Bud, bless his heart, couldn't see far enough to tell what it was and just...opened fire! They'd been there all day expecting something, and when it came, how else could they react?"

"When the gun smoke cleared it was Roman lying there."

"It's tragic."

"Awful."

"The stuff of classic tragedy."

"And almost comic if it weren't so terrible."

"Comic? Well, Isolde, you are the first person who has ever referred to this whole episode as *comic*."

"*If it weren't so terrible.* That was the rest of that particular sentence."

Then they let out a collective gasp, not at the morbidity of my particular observation however.

"Isolde!"

"Oh my dear!"

"Isolde, we are *so* sorry! Even to mention this. What were we thinking?"

They remembered the story that had circulated, right before Roman left for Durham, that he and I were a romantic tandem, when nothing could have been further from the truth. We had shared one dance at the Sadie Hawkins event in high school, and some alchemist had turned that bit of leaden dross into golden gossip. The story persisted even after I was *happily* married. I had not the energy to deflate it, not then, not now.

"It is fine. It is the past. It is long ago now."

"But still!"

"Then I guess mentioning Agnes would be…well…uncouth."

"And why would it be?"

"Well…."

I knew why. An even more fanciful tale involving Vera's sister and me had arisen after Roman's death. According to its prime teller, and the embellishers that followed, Agnes blamed me for her brother's demise. He was so distraught over my eventual "rejection" of him that he had, so to speak, manipulated his own death, been careless in the woods in hopes he would be mistaken for a deer and thus relieved of his melancholy (which I had produced). Soon after, Agnes, out of grief, had taken up with a poetaster from Charleston passing through Compton, a man whom we subsequently learned had charmed a string of women across the state with other poets' verses masqueraded as his own and whose poetic inspiration ran out once the ladies' bank accounts emptied.

"Mrs. Tuck had a fit!"

"She called the rascal a 'second rate verse-maker.' I thought she was being rather charitable."

"He was rather good-looking and had a marvelous speaking voice. I'm not sure I've ever heard 'Charge of the Light Brigade' rendered so *vigorously*."

"Don't give the scamp too much credit, dear. After all he took Agnes away from her mother for good! The only person Mrs. Tuck had left."

"Except for Vera," I added. They all looked.

"Only returned once. To bury Mrs. Tuck. She hasn't set foot back here since. But oh my goodness, we shouldn't be speaking of these things in front of *Isolde*."

"Speak away! Why shouldn't you? Agnes and I were always on the most cordial of terms. Up to the time she left for Baltimore. I told her I didn't blame her one bit for going.

I encouraged her to go." They looked again, stalled only a second, then resumed their chatter. But not word about Vera, not one, until the conversation wound down to its natural end and we sat around the parlor with the heat heavy and stiff on us like a newly-dried wool blanket.

Then, finally: "It's a gesture of grace, Isolde. An act of Christian charity."

"One you'll have to perform without me." They did not breathe. I stood. They knew what it meant. They made the first motions of exiting. "I'm too old to be a figurehead for anything. Call Agnes."

"We have. Every Schleppe in the Baltimore directory."

"Not a trace of her."

"Then leave her to the county." I made as though to walk away but didn't. They did, however, mumbling something about "disappointment." When they were vanished, I slumped back into my seat. Donzelle appeared from the kitchen, wiping her hands on her apron.

"Them *ladies* tire you out, Miss Izzy?" She knew. She didn't need confirmation. She came to me. "Why can't a busy body stay in one place and leave the rest of the world alone?" Her hand went under my left arm and lifted. "'Course, I reckon then they wouldn't be no busy body, now would they?"

"They want their names and their pictures in the paper – again – Donzelle. They must assure their immortality somehow. The poor dears."

"Uh-huh. Even in heaven, I reckon they'll find something to get into." She guided me to the first floor bedroom. "What you need, Miss Izzy, is you a good nap. And while you napping, ol' Donzelle will get out some of that ham from yesterday. Won't even heat it up. You can eat it cold the way you like to do. And I'll make some biscuits to wrap it in."

V e r a   T u c k

They found her dead by the lake at Veteran's Park, supine, staring up into the new sun with the avidity of a sunflower. Apparently she had been there all night. The geese hadn't touched her. No animals had touched her. She was intact. A hamper packed with cheese and ham and bread had begun to stink badly. She'd been seen the afternoon before making her usual trek to the park, taking the route from her Main Street home, past the High School, around Holland Boulevard, skirting Clement Elementary, singing that song she had made up, the one that had come to be known popularly as "The Song of the Lovesick Sailor":

Once I was a free man

Free as the seven seas.

 But then I chanced upon dry land

 And love dropped its chains around me

They said that school children picked up the song eventually, and some followed her down the road – it was a good two miles or more from her house to the park – singing it. There was no viciousness done to her, however, nothing physical anyway. She was too entertaining an oddity to stop with pranks or violence. And too it has always been my conviction that smaller places like Compton exhibit a far greater tolerance and sympathy for "eccentricity" than bigger ones. It has something to do largely with the Christian strictures which engird such a place. She told everyone who asked that she was going to the park to meet her boyfriend – a fine lad just out of the service with "hair like wheat and eyes like glass" who read German poetry and had a voice that "rang with the authority of a Beethoven sonata." He picked up such interests in Deutschland itself, fighting against Hitler. He came everyday to read and to sing to her, and then they had a meal from the food she brought before he went away. "She's deluded," the amateur psychologists on Main Street opined. "She confused this fantasy with Roman. She misses her brother. It is an expression of grief."

It was the gentlest expression of such. Others were not so mild. I was witness to many of them. There were the loud crying bouts at night, the piercing wails from the Tuck house that went on for hours at a time before suddenly expiring into low but still audible moans. Why no one, including myself, called the authorities to check on her is a mystery. It was as though the sheer suffering in her voice arrested all attempts at rescue – it was a pain that *must be*

got out this way and no other. There were the stories told
by Vera's girl to my girl (not Donzelle but an earlier girl,
now late, very late, and serving her Lord in Heaven) of
coming upon Vera fully undressed in her dining room,
denuded among one of the finest collections of Haviland
Limoge and Waterford in the country. Other stories
followed: of Vera's seeing a sorrel mare parked in her
mother's bedroom, standing with a regular chewing motion
of its blond jaw and refusing to move even when she pushed
it, and of the hairy Beelzebub that appeared from the attic
and took liberties with Vera's womanhood before
disappearing. Vera herself had told these last two with the
undisturbed matter of factness she might have used to relate
a tale of going to market.

So I would have nothing to do with her – other than a
stiff hello now and then, as I have already mentioned. I did
not want the taint of distasteful speculation on me that might
come merely from being her next door neighbor. After all I
had once been the subject of such talk myself years ago –
talk and derision and ill-founded pity. If you are from
Compton and are of a certain age, you remember it. You
remember the ridicule my mother suffered when she,
possessed by a Wagnerian fever shortly before my birth,
decided to name me for the distaff lead in *Tristan and Isolde*.
The name did not come trippingly to most of the tongues of
my contemporaries, unless they had some knowledge of
opera. You would not believe the unfortunate variations of

Isolde I was called (and still am). For years people believed I had arrived in South Carolina from Austria or Lithuania or some other foreign port and were stunned to hear me speak in the same language as their own. Then came the accounts, almost all of them fabricated, of my adventures in the flesh crowned by my marriage to a Yankee Jew with atheistic tendencies (oh he was the finest man I've ever known, with the manners and bearing of a saint) – an elopement that, according to the wags, nearly killed my music-loving mother. (Mr. Zorinsky and I were married in a Methodist church in Compton County. My parents were there. My mother afterwards said, "I now have the son I have always dreamed of having.") Mr. Zorinsky died young of a brain aneurism. We had no children but loved each other very deeply. Such a fact would surprise many people.

Donzelle came upon me in meditation.

"Miss Izzy, you crying?"

I looked up at her, the tears spilling into my mouth as I spoke. "I didn't hate Vera. I felt as sorry for her as anybody else. It is just…I was tired of the *talk*, Donzelle. Tired of not being able to leave this home without fear some new fantasy was being concocted. I just wanted some peace at last." This last I sobbed out with Garbo-like desperation. Donzelle's large, warm hand went to my forehead and stroked it. "If she had needed me, really needed me, I would have been there. I swear it. But if they had seen us together, well, you know what would have happened. You know what they would have said."

"Poor Miss Izzy. You ain't done a thing in the world to deserve this except live your life."

"I thought one time even of moving. When Vera's mother died and she lost her mind."

"You don't owe nobody nothing. No ma'am. You lived your life and minded your business, like anybody is supposed to do."

I looked up at her. "The county can take care of her funeral. Don't you think?"

"Yes ma'am. Let the vultures have her now. Ain't none of your business."

Still Life With Solitary Lady

You must be more careful with that piece! It's no plaything. It's been in the family for generations now. Armoire. Do you know what it is? Probably not, or else you wouldn't be so *rough* with it. I only hope those who wind up with it, the highest bidder I should say, will show it the care and the reverence it deserves. It came from New England, from the shop of a Vermont woodworker over a hundred years ago, or so that is what my grandmother told me. New England. I miss it so. I lived there almost twenty years until my husband died.   Have you been to Connecticut? Of course not. What a foolish question. You've probably never heard of it, couldn't spell it if your life depended on it. The young these days are so ignorant, so willfully, willfully ignorant. Please don't bang the armoire, young man! It's an exquisite piece still. All these years I've treated it, and everything else in this house, as though it were my own child....

The armoire is gone. Off to the auction block, like most everything else in this house. To pay back taxes. Oh, I shudder to think whose hands might come upon the armoire and the dinette set and the grandfather clock and those other beautiful, beautiful pieces. A family's things should remain in that family – even if the family has been reduced to one surviving person. I am the rightful owner! Watching you young men file past with what has been in my family all these years was like watching my spleen and liver and lungs removed and carried past me. My heart!

I don't mean to yell. I don't mean to be unkind. Really. If you were older, you would understand. One day perhaps you will understand, although I hold out no hopes for this. The barbarians have crashed the gates and taken over everything. The armoire will probably end up with a television set atop it. The love seat will go out in the yard for dirty children and animals to make a plaything of. And the grandfather clock will be broken by hands not used to its delicate machinery.

I have come to expect the worst....This is not my first encounter with loss.

No, no, I'm not faint. I don't need to sit. Where would I? The floor? You look at me, don't you, and see an old woman, and I am. You look and see a terrible snob, and I am that too, if a snob is someone who loves what is good better than what isn't, who prefers manners over beastliness. But it wasn't always this way with me. When I was young

I didn't give a hoot about antiques or family solidarity. I wanted out of this house in the worst way, out of South Carolina, which to me then was the absolute mud pit of the world. In some ways, it still is: I am in South Carolina, I tell myself in desperate times, not of it.

When I graduated college – oh yes a hundred years ago, you are thinking – right away I went to Greenville and took the civil service examination. Two years later I was in Washington, D.C., working at the Pentagon. 1961. Oh what a glorious time to be young and in a town like that one! The best years of my life in a place that reeked of elegance, that exuded style and taste from its every pore. Oh the parties in Georgetown! And that beautiful young president and his impeccable wife! I could cry right now remembering the excitement of that time. Camelot, indeed. It was a fairytale come true. Camelot? You don't know it, do you, young man? I can tell from the look in your eyes. If it's not on TV today, the young don't know a thing about it and don't care. My young friend, you have no idea what you've missed. And it will never come back.

Even on a secretary's salary I managed to keep up with other girls my age in Washington. We all wanted to look like Jackie. We all wanted that hair, that figure, and those clothes, and those things cost money. I ate frugally in those days, usually peanut butter sandwiches and apples, and stayed away from liquor and cigarettes. That way I could afford a good new wardrobe once or twice a month. I was still beautiful then, with a good shape and skin clear as glass. And I hid my South Carolina accent so as not to be made fun of. I'm sure other girls from the South recognized me as one of their own, but if I ever slipped I explained that only one of my parents was a Carolinian. It made a good ruse. I was popular. There were many parties and dances, and there were many interested young men. Oh the young men! If we girls wanted to be Jackie, then all the boys wanted to be JFK, and they made a good run at it. I declare they were prettier than storefront mannequins. Just immaculate.

At a friend's loft on Wisconsin Avenue I met a young attorney from Baltimore. As handsome as the President himself. In fact there was talk Paul would run for Congress. I am almost ashamed to admit how I threw myself at him, enthralled as I was by his looks and his ambition, but it worked. Soon we were an item around town. Indeed those not in the know mistook us for a congressional couple or as a member of the Cabinet and his wife. I didn't really know much about Paul even during the time we dated. I just loved going to parties and basking in the sheen of his promise and glamour. It was only after we were married, a year later, that I discovered his moodiness and his cruelty and his addiction to drink. It only took his striking me once to prompt me to walk out on him and file for divorce.

The ice in your glass is melting, young man. Would you like more? It would be no trouble at all. You're kind to stay and listen to the sad song of an old lady.

There was another husband a couple of years later and another divorce. By then I had left Washington. That vulgarian LBJ had taken over and turned the city into one big hoedown, and I couldn't take it. I ended up in Connecticut, where I worked for a manufacturing firm. One day a client came in to see Mr. Tunney. His name was Herbert Bodash. He was the most beautiful man I had ever laid my eyes on, tall and elegant, and his manners were flawless. I loved him right away and wasted no time ingratiating myself to him. He responded in kind. Soon we dated. He was very shy and reticent and did not speak much about himself unless I asked him questions. His shyness was like a small miracle to me. I had encountered too much phony bravado since leaving South Carolina. His modesty overwhelmed me so much that at dinner one evening I came right out and told him how I felt about him. A week later, with great, slow effort and build-up, he asked me to marry him.

I should have taken his laconic nature as a warning, as a sign that something was not quite right. History repeated itself. A few weeks into our marriage Herbert showed his true colors. And what odd colors they turned out to be! We were having dinner at home

– I am an excellent cook, by the way – when Herbert spoke up: "You're from the South, yet you don't speak as though you are. You speak as though you are from no place in particular."

I don't know what prompted him to say that or why it bothered him. After a minute to let the shock pass, I answered him, explaining that I had been out of the South for several years now and had lost my accent.

Herbert wrinkled his nose. "I know plenty of Southern people living up North who haven't changed the way they speak. They have lovely accents." He paused a moment. "I believe you are ashamed of where you come from. I don't know why. It's been my experience that Southerners are some of the finest people around."

I stood suddenly, exasperated. "Then why don't you have one come over, Herbert, and the two of you can have mint juleps and talk about the good old days under the magnolia branches with Mammy fanning you and the cotton growing high."

He laughed as I left the dining room.

From then on he came at me with one kind of insult or another. Everything I did reflected some personal flaw in his estimation, from the way I spoke on the telephone to the way I called him to the table for dinner.

"You're awfully vain," he said to me once out of nowhere. "I notice how you stop in front of any kind of reflective surface and stare at yourself. A mirror. A window. The hood of a car. Terribly vain, you are. Superficial really."

My skin crawled at his words. My temples pounded. When I could speak I asked him, "Then why did you marry me, if it bothers you so?"

He answered with a question of his own: "Why did you marry *me*? I know why." He ran his hand over his face and upper body. "Because of the way I look. You didn't know a thing about my inside, and it didn't matter. You said yes anyway. Terribly superficial, my dear!" He smiled.

"You're as vain as any woman if you think that!" I said and stood and left him, as I always did.

Herbert never hit me, as my first husband had. His verbal assaults were enough. He got to calling me The Peacock, which I despised, of course. "Here comes The Peacock," he would say, "with her feathers held high!" He said it at a party once, and everyone laughed, as though it were a common joke made about me behind my back which had now been brought into the open. At home, afterwards, I scolded him fiercely. He laughed himself into hysterics. I told him he was crazy and that I could no longer stand being married to him. He sobered up. He was a strict Catholic. Divorce was out of the question.

"I'll give you a baby instead," he said, staring at me unflinchingly.

I was thirty-four and had never had intentions of motherhood. Children always seemed to me such...a bother, an intrusion on a proper adult way of living. But when Phillip Massey Bodash appeared, well, it was like the announcement of some miracle. He was beautiful. He had the fortune of inheriting the best of my and Herbert's features. Right away I felt bonded to him, as I had nothing else before, and I believe Herbert felt more so. He seemed to stabilize. He no longer belittled me. He focused all his love and attention on our son, which was fine with me. Herbert had given me too much attention, all of it hostile. Well, I thought, life might not be exciting from now on, but maybe it will, at least, be pleasant.

I quit my job at Tunney's Manufacturing to raise Phillip. It seemed like the noble thing to do, and I resigned myself to it and didn't complain. But, oh, soon enough, I was climbing the walls, missing my job, my acquaintances, what social life I had had there in Connecticut. And I missed marital passion, physical passion. What passion Herbert could muster was directed entirely to our son. I am ashamed to say, but at thirty-five years old, I became a kind of New England Madame Bovary, thinking too much about romance and amorous adventures. So when Mr. Tunney, my former boss, showed up at the door one day in the middle of summer and confessed his feelings for me, I reciprocated. Douglas Tunney wasn't handsome and he had no glamour, but he spoke wonderfully well and told me how beautiful I was and how he missed me and had wanted a long time to tell me how he felt about me. We began our affair that afternoon.

We saw each other for the next few months, always at my home. Douglas would leave work and come over. Herbert was at the office, of course. Douglas spoke like a poet during our times together. I had no idea he had such a fount of feeling in him. Oh there's nothing finer than a well-spoken gentleman! Phillip was five at the time. I usually sat him in front of the television when Douglas was there or put him in the bonus room to play with his toys. He seemed preoccupied enough. Once, however, he walked in on Douglas and me. I threw on a housecoat and snatched the child up and took him outdoors, where I laid out a blanket in the backyard and set out some of his playthings and told him to stay there, that Mommy would be back soon.

A half hour later Douglas left and I went for Phillip, but he was not where I had put him. I searched around the yard, calling his name. I went into the small tract of woods behind our house and hunted. I went to the doors of neighbors and inquired, especially those with children with whom Phillip played. (All this in my housecoat.) No one had seen him. I panicked then, of course, and went back to the house and phoned Douglas.

"You must call Herbert," he told me. "Right away. And the police. I can't come back out there now, Helen. It would make for too much suspicion. God bless." And he hung up.

After he got off the phone with the police, Herbert turned to me with one of his steely stares. "What were you doing that you could not keep your eyes on my son?" I didn't answer. His eyes bore into me. A faint, humorless smile flickered over his mouth, as though he knew exactly what I had been doing, as though a scarlet A had appeared on my chest. Then he left me to go look for our son.

The sun was down when the news came, brought by policemen, that Phillip had been found, dead, at the bottom of an embankment some two miles from the house. His neck was broken. Obviously he had fallen from the road down the thirty or so feet of the grassy drop. There were wounds on his neck and arms, which could have been bruises caused by the fall or indications that Phillip had been carried off. Tests would have to be done. The officers went on with these details as though discussing an automobile theft. All the while I experienced tunnel vision; all I could see was my husband's face perched above the policemen's shoulders, pale, yes, very white and strained, but still composed, almost inhumanly so. When the officers left, bowing before us, full of condolences, Herbert closed the door after them and came over to me. "I know about you and Douglas Tunney." I shook my head furiously, so that my whole body shuddered. "You disgust me more than I can say." All the while his face remained calm as a statue's. A couple of days later Phillip's death was declared an accident.

After the funeral I thought, "If anything good can come from this grief, maybe Herbert will finally see that we need to be apart, that we can only fully heal separated." But Herbert would not divorce me. He no doubt saw our marriage as my penance for murder, my purgatory, and he played my tormentor, again, to the hilt. In public he made fun of me and spoke openly of my infidelity; he made jokes about it and called Douglas Tunney by name. People thought him odd, naturally, and they thought me horrendous, a woman who had sacrificed her child for pleasure. Invitations to dinners and to parties dried up. Herbert sold his business and retired at age forty-seven. He and I passed each other in the cool, quiet Connecticut house like a pair of shadows – or halves of the same shadow forever irreconcilable. Mostly Herbert sat in the den and looked at pictures of his son. Sometimes he spoke to them. Once, and for the only time, I heard him crying, the sobs so great and wracking I had to leave the house to escape them. I took to dwelling a good bit downtown and came upon some antique stores. New England is full of them, of course, wonderful places, entire new worlds one can enter and be lost in, and I wanted to be lost. I became an antique connoisseur. Here were these fine old things, these *solid* things, whose beauty would not go as mine was going, and I thought, "Maybe here is my peace, to be lost in what is fine and permanent." Herbert, of course, chastised me for such a hobby. "What good," he said, "is dwelling in the past?" When, of course that was all he did! Dwelling in the memory of a dead little boy. In any event, he would not allow any antiques in the house. I had to admire them in the stores and dream about their place in my home. And then, ten years after our son's burial, I was free: one morning Herbert got out of bed (by then we slept in separate rooms), took a couple of steps, and crashed to the floor from a massive, fatal coronary. He was fifty years old. I had no one then, no family, no friends, and looked South-ward, to the place I had begun, and suddenly it seemed like a good place to me, the best place, where there was grounding and permanence and ...*goodness*. That is why I came back. That is how I made peace with South Carolina. The child had become a woman.

I know you have to leave, young man. I see you're moving toward the door. I've talked too long, as the lonesome will. You have a job to do, of course. Again, I apologize for my earlier abruptness. If you only knew how much this house means to me! And the things in it. Those things have to be protected. Their beauty cannot be marred. They are all that is left of lives lived graciously. They have to live on to remind others that the beauty of *things*, if not people, is forever. If I had time I could tell you how I came to live with my mother in a stifling apartment, and how when this house went on the market, I begged her to pool her savings with mine to buy it and refurbish it with our family's things, with the beautiful old things that would not die, like that armoire, young man, when we shouldn't have, when we couldn't afford it. And how it has all come down to this. Me alone in a house full of summer heat. But I don't have the time, and neither do you.

I know the young well enough. They never have time for the foolishness of the old.

The Cold Front

IT WAS THE DAD BLAMED weather channel what drove me to it all. Day in, day out, hour after hour, she keeps the TV on that one channel, and they say the same thing in the same way, yet she is afraid if she turns it or blinks she will miss something. "But the weather changes!" she argues when I fuss at her. But not enough to where you got to keep your eyeballs glued to it twenty-four-seven. By now she knows enough to where I reckon she could stand up and give a forecast herself. She knows the highs in Denver, Colorado, and the lows in New York City. She knows who got the most rainfall in the month of July and who broke the record for drought. She knows the names of the hurricanes, men and women, from the last fifty years. I declare, sometimes I wonder if they ain't planted some signal in the television that turns women into zombies, like in that body snatchers movie.

Because it's not just the weather station. There's her soap operas too, her "stories," she calls them, which are the only thing during the day that have even a chance of interrupting the weather. Four hours a day she watches them

cry and holler and cheat on each other and this one going
with that one and that with this one and this one's been
married five times and that one eight and that one don't
know who her daddy is till she's done been to bed with him.
On and on like that. It's no wonder her nerves stay tore up.
She knows what's going on with these phony people better
than she does the people in the flesh around her. We'll be
sitting there eating supper, and she'll look up and say to me
or to our children (if they happen to be there that night),
"You know they had to take Doug's leg off today" or "Jack
and Phyllis have decided to finalize their divorce. They just
couldn't work things out." And me sitting there trying to
figure out whose side of the family Doug is on, mine or hers,
and feeling so sorry for Jack and Phyllis's younguns, whose
mama and daddy won't be together much longer. Then, be
durned, come to find out all them wounded and unhappy
folks are characters on the "stories," without a bit of blood
tie to her, me, or anybody else. It makes *me* feel like a fool.

Not that I don't watch TV. Don't get me wrong, for I
do. But not all day long. And I watch good stuff, stuff that
lifts you up, not brings you down. There's a TV in my
daughter's old room, and I watch the history station. Sports.
Old timey movies. I'll watch for a while, maybe a hour or
two at the most, no more than that, then shut it off. Just turn
the thing off. Snap off the remote and leave it be. See? That
one-eyed monster ain't got no kind of hold over me! I can
break the spell like that. Then I go off and leave it alone, do

something else. Might piddle in the yard some or take me a walk at City Park or visit my grandbaby or stop by The Club and shoot the bull with the boys there. I'm active. She's not. And it's beginning to show on her in not very flattering ways.

Once, oh once, she was so pretty, the prettiest thing you ever beheld with your two eyes – slim, with a good shape and lips like cherry maters and big dark eyes and hair black as night. She was the prettiest girl in all of southern Spartanburg County. Maybe the whole county. Maybe the whole state. She was the best looking woman I'd ever seen. She was nervous then, too, as she always has been, but she didn't let it stop her from getting out and doing. Oh man, we were on the go all the time back then – to the movies, to the skating rink, to the beach, to the mountains. She ate up life back then, grabbed handfuls of it up and just ate it, like I did. Now I am lucky if I can get her to move from one spot in the floor to another. "No, no," she says when I invite her to come walking with me. "My knee's hurting me too bad." Or "No, no, the arthritis is running too bad in my shoulder." "No, no," I mock her, all fumed up now, and point to the evil eye of the TV in the corner of the den. "It's your brain all melted by *that* that won't let you move." She doesn't like it when I say such as that, but I'm not the kind of man who holds back what I think from nobody.

All this is leading up to the day I decided that me and my wife should spend more time together. It is a thing she has talked a lot since I retired from the mill. That day she was in the bathroom. I had come in from a walk. The TV was playing. It was the weather station, of course. Had it been anything but the weather or a soap opera, I'd have had a stroke right then and there. But I was safe. It was the weather. Well, I pick up the remote and start flipping the channels and come upon this western on the classic movie channel. *Duel at Diablo*. I've seen it before, but then I've seen most every western ever made since 1970 many times over. It's a pretty good movie. I'm getting into it. Then the bathroom door opens. I hear her step up behind me.

"Oh no sir!" she bellows like a danged mountain lion. "You put that right back on Channel 11 where I had it!"

"Ma'am?" I says, feeling ambushed.

"I was watching the weather!"

"You been watching that all day. I thought you might like to see something different."

"I can't stand them old violent movies you watch. You know that. You know how nervous they get me."

"But, baby, I'm wanting to spend time with you. Don't you want to spend some time with your loving husband and something *he* likes for a change?"

"I want you to put it back on Channel 11 and go spend time watching *that* on your TV."

That was the moment I stopped trying to figure women out, after sixty-eight years of doing so. It was also the time I blew up something fierce at my wife, cussing her out, telling her I had bought that g.d. TV she watched the weather on and the g.d. power that run through it, and I could watch any g.d. thing on it I wanted to watch, g.d. it. But I didn't stop there. Years of built-up frustration came out of me that afternoon in language that, as a Sunday school teacher, should have embarrassed me, but, as a husband of forty-five years to one woman, seemed just right and fitting. By the time I was done, I left my wife standing in the middle of the den, the TV remote clenched in her hand, her face white as a sheet, those dark eyes, still pretty, all shocked and misted over.

I took off for City Park, where I walked round and round and round, hoping the repeated motion would get the heat out of me. But no deal. I was as mad as I'd been when I left the house. So I drove over to the Club, figuring a beer or two might cool me down. It was still early. The bar was nearly empty, except for a couple of regulars who always seemed to be drinking there, no matter what time of day. They said hey to me. I said hey back and looked around like I might find other folks to greet, better people, ones I'd really want to talk to, but they weren't to be found. A jukebox played in the far corner, real loud, "Boot Scootin' Boogie," but nobody was dancing to it. The low lights blinked off the chrome of the chair backs and the varnish of the tables. The video games against the far left wall burped and hiccupped and made other peculiar noises like they was inviting folks to come play them. The effect of it all was to make me feel really lonesome, really sad, a feeling I'm not used to and don't much care for.

So I turned away from it all, to the bar itself, to get me something good and cold. Anita stood behind the bar smiling. Anita is past fifty and keeps her hair dyed red. She wears big men's shirts to cover her big stomach, and she chain smokes worse than anybody else in the world. But she loves the Club. Lives for it. Spends every spare minute she's got there. She's got nothing else. Her children are grown up. Her husband has left her for a younger woman. She tends bar mostly and takes phone messages for folks, but if they're short in the kitchen, she'll help cook and do whatever else they need her to do.

"You here mighty early," she told me, tapping the ash off her cigarette into a glass tray. "This some special occasion?" She laughed a smoker's laugh, all hoarse and gritty. I didn't answer her, just placed my order. She drawed the beer off the tap and set it in front of me on a napkin. I drank it and watched the television that stood over Anita's head behind the bar, up among the min-bottles. She had it on sports, but it was dad blamed kayaking or some such foreign kind of sport and not worth a grown man's time to look at. I asked Anita if she couldn't find something else, or was the TV stuck on that particular channel? I said it real gruff like, with heat in my voice, and got the attention of the other two men there. It wasn't gentlemanly of me at all to talk to a woman like that, but I didn't care if I impressed Bob and Eddie, since I didn't much like either one of them much anyway.

"Yes sir. We'll try." Anita stuck her cigarette in the side of her mouth while she flipped the channels. She found a college baseball game on another sports station. That seemed to suit everybody.

It wasn't much longer, after maybe my third beer, that Bob and Eddie cleared out, both of them, saying they had to get home early for supper or their wives would skin them alive. When they were gone, I said, "Henpecked. Be durned if I'd let my wife dictate my comings and goings."

Anita took a drag off her cigarette and said, "Sounds like you got some trouble at the house."

Her statement was like an open door for me, and I walked on through, telling her everything that had gone on between me and my wife that day, everything that had gone on the last thirty years, when things began to disintegrate for us. At the end of it, I said, "Pull me another beer, Anita. My mouth's done gone dry from talking."

She did, with her cigarette dangling from her mouth, and when she set the mug in front of me, she said, "You know I been thinking a lot about this."

I looked up. "About me and my wife?"

"No," she said, laughing her gritty laugh. "About marriage. People getting married. You know we're supposed to do it. The Good Lord tells us to do it. Society says we have to do it. And we do, and look what happens."

"Right," I said. By then I was so foggy-headed from beer I would have gone "Right" if she had said right was left and backwards was forwards. I didn't care at that point.

Then she talked about her own marriage and how much she had loved Ken Stubblefield, her husband, and what wonderful children had come from them and how it all seemed so good and storybook-like till that morning when Ken came to her, her still in bed barely awake, and said, "I'm leaving you. I can't stand living with you anymore" and walked out the door, never to set foot in that house again. Left his clothes there. Left everything. This was after the children were grown and gone. He didn't have to worry about them. Wasn't long, of course, Anita found out Ken had gone to live with a younger woman, a blonde, with a little waist and big you-know-whats.

"I was pretty at one time myself," she finished and sucked long on her cigarette.

I stopped. That last statement nearly snapped me back sober. I tried to picture Anita pretty once, and it was hard, even drunk. Not that she was ugly now or anything. She was just…I don't know…run down, I reckon you would say. Of course I wouldn't have told her that for anything in the world, because, pretty or not, Anita is good as gold.

The bar filled up not long after that with good people I was glad to see. They offered me drinks. I accepted. Somebody brought in hot chicken wings and cheese sticks from the kitchen. I ate generously of them, thinking eating would balance out all the alcohol. Somebody cranked the jukebox back up. A redneck shuffle song appeared. Someone tapped my shoulder. It was Joyce Jarman, an old girlfriend of mine from a long time ago. She wanted to dance. We did. So did a couple of other gals I didn't know so good. I obliged them before going back to the bar and accepting a couple more drinks and standing and shooting the bull about this and that. The fool running for governor. The fool running for senator. The fall of the Gamecocks. Everything became a right pleasant blur for me, a mix of light and faces and noise, and the last thing I recall seeing was Anita's face, which she claimed at one time was pretty, and then there was nothing

When the lights came on again, I was looking up at a ceiling of uneven white mold with a ring of yellow light right in the middle of it. Lamplight. Opening my eyes was like lifting a ton of bricks. Then I heard this soft sound to my right, low, like a kitten's mewling. I looked to it, with some discomfort to my head, and seen it was Anita Stubblefield, seated in a leather chair, in her dress slip, with her face in her hand, just a-crying. The ashtray on the table next to her was piled high with ashy cigarette butts. She seen me look and tried to smile, but it was no use. It was then I realized we were in a motel room together.

"Anita," I says, real careful, like a house of cards stood near my lips.

"Oh!" she hollered out and bawled into her fist. "I

know I shouldn't have done it, Emory! I knew it was taking advantage of you. But...you were *so* nice to me tonight."

"I was?" I said, feeling suddenly even sicker than the hangover allowed.

She nodded. "Yes. At the bar. You were so kind to me. When everybody else was gone and it was just me and you, and you put your hands on my shoulders and said, 'You was pretty once, Anita. I do believe it. And you still are pretty.' It was the nicest thing anybody ever said to me since before Ken left me. I knew I should have taken you home, but...oh!" She cried, and while she did so, she lit herself another cigarette, and the smoke poured out of her mouth all shaky and uneven.

I was in a bed. I threw off the covers and was happy to see I was wearing my tee shirt and under shorts. I moved to the edge of the bed. The world moved with me and rocked unsteady a moment. But the reality of the situation killed off most of the effects of the drinking I had done. Things came into sober focus. I looked down for the rest of my clothes. "Anita," I said, "we didn't...?" Silence. I looked over my shoulder at her. "Did we?"

She shook her head. A veil of cigarette smoke covered her face. "My conscience got the better of me. I couldn't go through with it."

I stood slowly from the bed and bent carefully for my shirt. "You know that conscience is a good thing to have. It's a gift from the Good Lord. You got to heed it."

"I did," she said and sniffed. "If I hadn't you wouldn't have them undies on right now."

My pants laid near her feet. I went carefully and cautiously toward them, like a SLED agent approaching a live bomb. When I got to them and reached down for them, Anita did what I feared she'd do. She grabbed me and pressed herself against me.

"He just left! And me barely awake!" She gripped me hard and spoke muffled into my hip. "This kind of thing doesn't bother a man the way it does a woman. A woman needs reassurance about herself more than a man does. You know?" She looked up at me. Her makeup was all mixed up, red fighting blue, on her cheeks. I nodded and smiled and patted her back with the flats of my hands, careful not to touch her with my fingers, as though that might mean full-fledged adultery.

"Don't worry. You still pretty. And they are plenty of men in this town who'd be very happy to be your boyfriend."

"Oh, but I'm so weak!" she cried, pressing harder into my thigh. I just knew there would be a print of her face on my Fruit of the Looms when she raised up.

"We all are, Anita. We all are." After a few minutes more I pushed her gently away from me. "Now, young lady, we better get cleaned up and get dressed."

"Right," she said and moved to get her dress.

We left the motel light on. It was dark out, somewhere between late night and early morning. She drove, which was best, as I was still a little woozy. We pulled out of the motel parking lot and moved in the direction of the storm clouds ahead.

Second Sight
A Pastiche

For Miss O'Connor

REVIVAL WEEK AT COVENANT Baptist Church in Compton, South Carolina, was a time of great festivity. Some claimed it rivaled, in spectacle and variety, the state fair in Columbia. Indeed it had gotten to be such a large event, with ever increasing attendance year by year, that the church organizers, ten years before, moved the proceedings from the humble brick confines of Covenant itself to a nearby pasture, where, in a tent as cavernous as the jaws of the whale that held Jonah captive, all the traditional staples of revivalism could breathe and flourish. Fire and brimstone preachers, red-faced and hoarse, sweating and clutching handkerchiefs, were the mainstays, but also present, at one time or another, were snake handlers, fire-eaters, speakers in tongues, and the lame and afflicted who had been healed at previous such gatherings and were back to give witness to their miracles. Modern additions to the roster had been made to interest jaded young people in the event. A Christian rock band, however, had been vetoed by organizers who felt that, regardless of the well-meaning message of such groups, the medium was too closely allied with the forces they had gathered to fight, that the very rhythms of rock music had certain predictable influences over the behavior of young people, namely in their legs and hips. Instead a former assistant soundman with a minor country-rock ensemble from the 1970's had been brought in from Miami to inveigh against modern music and its attendant lifestyle. The highlight of his talk was a demonstration of the way certain famous rock and roll acts implanted satanic messages into their music using a nefarious process called "back masking." He even found an instance of such duplicity in a song by none other than the Captain and Tennille, whose "Muskrat Love" was surely an invitation to bestiality. And a couple of years later a young actress came to the revival to recreate the story of the woman at the well and to recount her own sad years as a teenage prostitute in New Orleans, Louisiana.

But by far Covenant's greatest coup, for young and old alike, was the Reverend Benny Troy Hoyt, an eleven-year-old minister from Birmingham, Alabama, who had won national acclaim for the intensity of his sermons. He had traveled and preached throughout the South and was venturing steadily northward following an appearance on the highly rated Manny Miller television talk show out of Chicago, Illinois, on which he claimed to have cured a young girl of the AIDS virus. That appearance made Benny

Troy more in demand and, according to his daddy, a minister himself who doubled as Benny Troy's manager, Benny Troy had been responsible in his three years of preaching for over a hundred thousand conversions nationwide.

"Looks like a little fireball to me," Maude Hutto observed to her younger sister Lilith as she studied a picture of the junior Reverend Hoyt on the back of a handbill she'd been given that day. She held the handbill in one hand and a spoonful of chocolate ice cream in the other. "Four feet high and bald as a butterbean. Isn't he precious?"

"Got close-set eyes," Lilith remarked after he own bite of ice cream. "He'll be hell for some woman some day with eyes that close. Can't trust a man whose eyes almost meet. It's a bad sign."

"Hush cussing a preacher, and what's his eyes have to do with anything?"

"See through a man in his eyes."

Maude made a disdainful face. "Oh my goodness. Well, it's too bad, isn't it, that you couldn't see through Briscoe in his? That would have saved you five years of grief and a divorce." Maude watched as Lilith touched the finger where a wedding band had been.

"At least I had a husband," Lilith remarked quietly, not aware that she was contradicting herself.

Ignoring that remark and still satisfied with her own put down, Maude turned back to the handbill. She'd been given it at the drugstore, where she and Lilith had stopped that afternoon for a box of Epsom salts to soak Lilith's callus-prone feet. Maude had been standing at a rack of paperback novels looking for a historical romance when someone had touched her arm. She'd turned, expecting her sister, and saw instead a small, slightly hunched, snuff-colored old woman in a white blouse and dark polyester slacks with a sweater tied around her shoulders. "Hon," the old woman had said in a croaking voice, "reading such trash as that ain't no good for you. It'll wind you up in the pits of hell. You ought to be reading this," and she gave Maude a red, matchbox sized copy of the New Testament and the handbill Maude was now studying. Sitting at the table in her home, she read it through again and tapped it positively. "We're going," she announced.

"To what?" Lilith asked, her mouth, like a child's, ringed with ice cream.

"To this. This revival. We're going tonight."

"To that?" Lilith asked with disbelief and anguish in her voice. When Maude nodded, she said, "Just when did you get religion?"

Maude answered in as clear and austere and pious a way as she could manage. "The impulse to be religious has always been there. I just need to get in touch with it again. Getting back to the church would do me good." When Lilith arched her dark eyebrows skeptically, Maude said with more force, "Well, it was the way we were raised."

This didn't appease Lilith. "I thought we was going to

the fish camp tonight." She referred to the plans they'd made earlier that day to eat at The Admiral's Fish Camp in Beasley, in lower Compton County, where Lilith could have all the boiled shrimp and hush puppies she craved so unreasonably.

"Your shrimp will wait another night," Maude replied, reading her sister's mind. "Little Benny Troy is here tonight, and the spirit is moving me to go see him."

Lilith cast her a resentful look and scowled at the handbill. "It's gas. That's what's moving you. You know you can't eat milk products without it bloating you. Besides, he's probably a crook. Do you know a preacher that ain't a crook?"

Maude looked again at the boy's picture. No, he wasn't "cute" in the usual sense a child could be. He did have those bunched-together eyes Lilith had remarked on which reminded Maude of a gangster, the kind Edward G. Robinson and James Cagney used to play in the movies when she was just a little girl. But the boy had character. She could see that in the serious, adult way he stared from the photograph, the way the photographer's gray light framed his blunt, plain, smooth features. He *knew* something, was confident of it, as though, young as he was, he had had some authentic glimpse at the empyrean truth of God. Why, he probably knew the Bible by heart, or big passages of it, and here he was only eleven-years-old. She liked him for that. She liked all children. She considered affection for children a mark of a stable disposition and the sign of a gentle heart. She made a fuss over children in public, pinching their cheeks and cooing aloud their names and remarking euphorically on their clothes. She loved their pink skin and enormous eyes, their little haircuts and their awkward attempts to express themselves. But they frightened her too with their restlessness, their irritability, their fits, their frankness. In the times she had babysat, she didn't know what to do with them in moments of crisis when they cried and stamped their little feet and made ugly faces. She would come close to hysterics herself.

Still she liked them, and it was, to some extent, her fondness for them that led her to rent out the front bedroom to that girl, Christine, and her baby, Lorrie. The room had been empty since her and Lilith's mother had passed, and she'd seen no reason why she shouldn't make some use of it, so she put an ad in the Compton newspaper announcing its vacancy. It wasn't a week later that Christine stood at her door, a pink suitcase in one hand and the child, Lorrie, in the other. It had been her inclination to refuse Christine when she had learned she was unmarried, that the daddy had run off to the army and left Christine to raise Lorrie alone. Maude wasn't sure she wanted such a stigma around her, the possibility that neighbors would find out and point and talk about her like she was running a house for moral reprobates. But Christine seemed modest enough and not a troublemaker, and she felt pity for Lorrie, who was a pretty little thing with her honey-blonde hair, crystal-blue eyes, and peach-bright smile. She gave in and rented the room to Christine. It hadn't been a mistake either, not so far. Christine wasn't delinquent in her monthly payments, though she had no job that Maude knew of, and the two of them, mother and child, kept mostly to themselves, cloistered like nuns (which concerned Maude; after all Christine was still young and should have been more outgoing) except when Maude could lure them out to have dinner with her or watch TV.

She regarded the Rev. Benny Troy Hoyt again. "He's a man and a child all at once," she commented, hoping Lilith, for whose benefit she had made the statement, would take it as a profound, even cryptic observation.

"More a child than a man though," Lilith returned. She grimaced wryly. "Children ain't nothing but trouble. They're God's punishment for grown people liking sex so much."

It angered Maude that Lilith had not appreciated her assessment of the Rev. Hoyt, and in vengeance she sang, which Lilith hated: "Red and yellow, black and white, they are precious in his sight! Jesus loves the little children of the world!"

Lilith made an even more terrible face than before and grabbed her ears. "I can't stand your singing! What are you trying to do, drive me nuts?" Then she stood with her bowl to go for more ice cream.

"When did you get religion?" Lilith had asked her. It was not an unfair question and had not bothered her. Indeed Maude pondered it thoughtfully as she dressed for the revival. But the question should not have been when did she *get* religion but when did she *lose* it. The both of them, Maude and Lilith, had been raised with religion. Their daddy had warned them early on, "You live in my house and you'll go to church," and since no other alternative existed at that time, they did it, they went, and even joined the choir and participated in the Christmas pageant every year until they were both out of their daddy's house; then they gradually dropped away from attendance, when it was no longer a parental mandate, till they stopped altogether. Lilith just wasn't interested. Maude claimed church was too political. Church people were always stabbing each other in the backs, sizing up each other's faith and commitment, and fighting over who would make the potato salad for church functions. She hated politics and used that for her excuse to stop. Then later, when she got sick with cancer, the disease that had stalked her family like a specter and had taken hold of her ovaries before she was forty years old, her indifference to religion turned to resentment. She turned away from it the way most people turn to it when they are sick. Christianity meant immortality, and she didn't want that. She wanted to be alive right here in this world, not in some place to come of golden walkways and stately mansions. She wanted envy, covetousness, hate, lust, all those emotions religion was supposed to dispel, as well as love and compassion and generosity. To feel such would mean she was alive, not dying, alive and wrestling with the world, still in the thick of things.

But cancer was behind her. She had won that fight. Now the idea of going to church didn't bother her. It would relieve her lonesomeness to be around other people regularly. After all she had nobody. Her mama and daddy were gone, and Lilith lived in North Carolina and did not visit all that much, which was a bad thing and a good thing at the same time. She would, however, have to choose another church. She couldn't go back to Mount of Glory. They would talk about her absence there behind her back, point to her, conjecture, and she couldn't have that. Covenant would be as good as any other. It had a good reputation. People weren't, according to what she'd heard, stuck up there; they didn't act like they were already sitting on God's right hand in heaven. She would see for herself tonight at the revival what kind of people they were and make her decision then. Then another idea hit her. She would ask Christine to go and to bring the baby. Christine needed to be out. She spent too much time isolated for a young woman, even though that was what she seemed to prefer. It was like pulling eyeteeth getting her to have a meal with Maude, and even when she agreed to, she'd sit at the table picking at her food, not saying a word, leaving it to Maude to fill in the silence with wandering chitchat. But

Maude would ask her anyway. It would make her something of a missionary, wouldn't it?

She looked at herself in her vanity mirror and judged herself presentable to the public. She had on a puce, calf-length dress and a nice velvet jacket with white shoes and a long white drop of pearls around her neck. To top it off she sat a nice pillbox hat with a climbing white feather on her head.

"You look like an ostrich," Lilith pronounced from the door. "Or an old prostitute."

"Hush!" Maude hissed. She noticed Lilith was still in her jeans and tee shirt. "And why aren't you dressed?"

"For what? I ain't going nowhere."

"You are! You're going with me!"

"No, I think I'll stay here and rent a movie. Where's your card at? They won't let me rent one without it."

"I've offered to buy your supper at the fish camp. The least you can do is go with me tonight."

Lilith sulked off, the grown child that she was, and Maude went to Christine's door. "Hello?" she called as she knocked. She heard a rustling before the door opened. There stood Christine already in her nightgown, very pretty in a shy, indirect way. Sometimes she would even look Maude in the eye when she spoke. Other times, if she were angry, she would scare Maude with her rage.

"Dressed for bed?" Maude asked in a musical voice. "It's still early!"

Christine stood back to let Maude in and said, eyes averted, "I've got a big day ahead of me tomorrow, Miz Hutto."

"Oh?"

"Yes ma'am. Jerry called. He thinks he may be on leave. If he is, he's coming down from Fayetteville tomorrow to talk."

Maude stood alarmed. The first thing she thought of was her utility bill and how nice it was to have a partner in payment. "You're not leaving me, are you?"

"I don't know yet. We're going to talk."

Maude started to ask another question, but there came a loud gurgling behind Christine. Christine stepped aside so that Maude could see Lorrie on the bed in her pajamas in one of those little fits of pleasure in which she would kick her heels wildly, throw her stubby arms over her head, and giggle just to beat the band. Maude watched her with mixed feelings: pity foremost for the poor, illegitimate little thing (the word *wedlock* almost always flashed in her mind when she saw the child) and, in some dark corner of herself, distaste but some delight too at Lorrie's joy and energy, so, in what she thought was the humane and decent thing to do, she went over and gently rubbed Lorrie's belly so that the little girl's arms and legs thrashed in even greater frenzy.

"Here," Christine said behind them, nudging Maude gently aside. "She'll make herself sick in a fuss like that." Maude put her hand to her mouth, ashamed, as though she had done something wrong. Then, to cover up her embarrassment, she rushed into her invitation. At its conclusion, Christine shook her head slowly, sadly, and said, "No ma'am. Thank you though. But I need to be here in case Jerry calls. He's not entirely sure about his leave. He *thinks* he's got one. He's *pretty* sure he does."

"Oh that's a shame!" Maude returned, embarrassed even further by the girl's rejection of her offer. To cover it she said, "Pretty young thing like you ought not to be so closed in. Why, if I were you, with all that young energy, there'd be no holding me down!"

Christine smiled as though in empathy and nodded at Lorrie. "But I got this child, Miz Hutto. It's different when you got children."

Maude, blushing, didn't push the point any further.

"I will melt in here," Lilith moaned after they'd taken their places on the bleachers inside the tent. They'd been directed there by a kindly man in a seersucker suit and were among the first to arrive, nearly an hour early, since Lilith couldn't have stood long on account of her chronically ailing feet. Maude didn't know why she had accommodated her. Lilith herself certainly wasn't thoughtful of others. She hadn't even bothered to change out of the raggedy tee shirt and jeans she'd been wearing all day. "I bet Jesus would let a humble soul like me into the pearly gates before he would the gaudy likes of you. I'm coming to Him *just as I am*." In fact Maude sat straighter, proud of each curious glance she earned from her fellow, incoming Comptonites, most of who were dressed casually like Lilith, some, just off the first shift at the cotton mills, in trousers and slacks dotted white with lint. If they looked hard enough at her, Maude would nod at them like a queen conferring recognition on her subjects. Suddenly she saw herself as the standard bearer there, the upholder of a certain dignity, and kept her head somewhat upturned as the tent filled, as Covenant's minister, a man with the demeanor and energy of a bloodhound, welcomed everyone, as he was followed by a succession of more animated, full-throated preachers who whipped up the crowd with their jumping cadences, as duos and trios and quartets from all over the South delivered their thumping, nasal renditions of songs Maude remembered as girl from revivals past. Then Covenant's slow speaking minister made his introduction of the Rev. Benny Troy Hoyt. Maude looked at the platform, anxious. Then she saw that everyone else was standing in a loud, excited ovation, and she stood too and got her first look at the Rev. Hoyt. He bounded out of nowhere in a gray, two-piece suit, stood on the edge of the platform smiling and holding up his arms, one small hand gripping a black Bible that looked nearly as big as he was, then hopped down and ran as far from the platform as his microphone would allow. He stood near Maude, close enough for her to see for sure the peculiar eyes Lilith had made fun of.

"He's a midget," Lilith hollered beside her, the most energy she had expended her whole visit so far. She hadn't bothered to stand. "He can't be no youngun. He's a dwarf. A munchkin straight out of Oz." Maude acted like she didn't know her and kept applauding along with everyone else.

"Hallelujah!" Rev. Hoyt shouted in a thin but firm voice that sounded like he'd just inhaled helium or were an adult imitating a child's voice. "I love to hear folks raising up the name of the Lord with proud hearts and strong voices! Keep a-shouting! Keep a-shouting!" The audience obeyed with an even louder surge of their voices and their clapping hands.

"Let the people of Compton, South Carolina, know we're not worshipping no dead god-ah. No Buddha. No Hare Krishna. No Mohammed-ah. No Rev. Moon-ah. But the one and only true and living God-ah, Jesus Christ of Nazareth-ah. The I am-ah! The Jehovah! The lily of the valley-ah! The bright and morning star-ah! The one what lifted me and you from the mirey clay and set us firm on the rock-ah! Let 'em know! Shout hallelujah!"

"Hallelujah!" the people cried.

Maude didn't shout, as she had never been a demonstrative person, but her eyes never left Benny Troy. He stood before her bouncing and gesturing like some sideshow oddity. "This is dark and unbelieving times, my friends," he went on after the crowd had settled again. "Times of doubt and disease, the AIDS and the Oldtimey's.

It's a time when folks puts more faith in their television sets and their telephones and their computers and their washer and dryers than they do the words of this holiest of books." He raised the Bible and it nearly upended him. "They go to liquor and sex and money and possessions trying to make up for what's right here." He shook the book, and it shook him. "If they would only realize that and turn to Him, they'd be filled to the brim with the peace and joy that's the Lord's bounty."

"That's right, little brother!" someone shouted from the bleachers.

"God can do anything! Says so right here! He raised the dead. He healed the lame. He cast the demons into the swine. Ain't no reason He can't touch you, every one of you, and fill up what's empty. He can heal them AIDS, brethren. He can wipe out that Oldtimey's with a flick of His wrist and give you the memory of an elephant. People have just got to believe in Him!" Calls of "Amen" and "Yes sir" followed his words. Maude sat and wondered what a child of eleven could know about emptiness. He wasn't even a teenager yet! What could he know about it? The words, the very idea behind them, didn't suit his little boy lips; it was like someone had cued him what to say, had rehearsed it with him. It rang such a false note to her that she started to reject him right then and there and just turn away. But, then again, he was so sweet-looking, dancing and prancing around in his little suit, saying his piece in that high voice Lilith had described so hatefully, that she forgave him this improbability and listened and was soon touched by his effort. Still, though, after a while, the monotony of his message – the same song of doom and redemption sung by the preceding preachers – made Maude drift off into daydreams.

Then her attention was brought back to the platform when Benny Troy's voice turned suddenly deep and unfamiliar and she saw that the boy's daddy, the senior Rev. Hoyt, had taken a microphone and was addressing the crowd while a three-piece combo, fronted by an electric guitarist, struck up a doleful accompaniment in three-fourths time behind him. The senior Rev. Hoyt wore a suit like his son's, was in his middle to late forties, silver-haired, smooth-complexioned, good-looking except for a little paunch, and had a nice, melodic voice. "You know, ladies and gentlemen," he began, "people have lost their faith in this day and age. There are skeptics all around us. Modern day Pharisees. Why there are some who do not believe that Benny Troy here, all of eleven years old, is actually doing what he is doing, spreading the message of God's eternal truth. They think he's too young. They reject the message because of the messenger. What do people have against miracles in this day and age, friends? Why is it hard for them to believe that a God that can part mighty waters and bring the dead to life and speak through a burning bush can set the voice of hope in an eleven year old boy, that Benny

Troy here is a living example of what God is capable of when they cast aside their doubt and just believe? Can I get an amen on that?"

"Amen!"

"Daddy's saying what's true," Benny Troy picked up from the ground, as though he and his father were a tag team. "People look at me like I'm crazy when I come out and do what I do. Why the folks at the TV station in Chicago stared at me like I'd just walked off a spaceship. They don't believe in the wondrous ways of the Lord. It was the Lord give me the gift a-preaching. It was Him come to me in a vision and pointed my path for me. I was standing outside in Birmingham in our backyard. I was six years old, brethren, when the sky growed black as night and I shook like a leaf I was so scared, just about to cry, when the blackness opened up into a peaceful golden ring and was Jesus's face in the middle of it saying, `I give you the gift, Benny Troy. I give you the Word.

Now go and take it to the people. Make the people listen and bring 'em to me.' Yes, he did-ah! Said them very words before the ring went black again and the sky cleared and I stood there-ah, His new servant and witness-ah, His messenger with the good news of His second coming-ah! Amen-ah! Amen-ah!"

He had roused the crowd so they stood again and shouted as one. Maude remained seated, debating whether to rise. Had she risen, it would have been more out of conformity than genuine excitement. Old doubts crept in, old skepticism, what the senior Rev. Hoyt had criticized so strongly, the feeling this was all a big put on. She couldn't swallow her pride and rise with the others nor could she shake the feeling – and didn't try very hard to – that she towered over all these other people intellectually.

When the ovation cooled, Benny Troy's daddy spoke next. He told of the Lord's blessings on the Hoyt family, how the Lord had let them travel all over the country spreading the good news, how He'd brought them many good and close friends during these travels. "And he has granted Benny Troy another gift," he concluded, "a special insight, a transparent vision, a second sight, so to speak. Benny can look at any of you, lay his hand upon you, and the Lord will give him a look inside of you, like your soul was nothing more than a hospital X-ray. He can see your misery, your loneliness, your want, your doubt, whatever it is that blocks you spiritually and keeps you from a fulfilling relationship with the Lord God Almighty. And then he can recommend a Bible verse for you that you can turn to for comfort and meditation."

"Oh God," Lilith moaned aloud upon hearing that, and an old man beside her patted her shoulder and said, "That's right, sister. Praise his name."

Maude frowned also and thought to herself, *Science fiction, voodoo, hoax,* and wondered how much the Hoyts would charge the audience to have such a feat performed in public. Again she thought of sideshows and was more embarrassed than ever to be there among all these dupes.

"This is no gimmick," the senior Rev. Hoyt continued, again as though reading Maude's thoughts. "It's no put on but a true example of the endless, boundless power of the Lord. And to prove it Benny Troy will go to some of you right now and lay hands on you and diagnose, so to speak, what it is that ails you spiritually. Now, please. Don't be afraid or ashamed if he comes to you. Be happy the Lord is looking through you. We're brothers and sisters here. No one will laugh at you. We will pray for you."

Then attention turned back to little Benny Troy, who stood in the middle of the tent quiet and deliberative, staring in front of him like he was meditating. Then he looked up and shouted, "With God all things are possible. The Book says so. Book don't lie for them that believes. Faith can move a mountain." He went silent again, like he'd been testing those words before making them public and found them unsatisfactory. Then suddenly he turned and was upon an elderly gentleman not far from Maude on the front row of the bleachers. Benny kept his Bible pressed to his chest with one hand and with the other touched the man's shoulder and spoke, telling the man that he was old and alone and beset by illness but that the soul was stronger than the body and if he trusted without doubt the Lord Jesus Christ his soul would outlive his flesh and he would be forever young in heaven. Then he named some Bible verses that referred to age and infirmity and clutched the old man's shoulder again reassuringly. The man nodded absently but gratefully.

"Wasn't nothing to that," Lilith said beside Maude. "Anybody could have looked at that coot and told he was old and sick. He should have smacked him on the head and made him fall backwards like they do on TV. I might like him if he did that."

Maude was too mortified to reply, too fascinated by the sight of Benny Troy moving along the front row, hunting faces with those close-set eyes, halting at one point in front of an over made teenage girl, whose promiscuity and yearning for peer acceptance he revealed to the crowd before moving on, hunting again, till he stopped at her, Maude, nodded, and said, simply, "Sister."

Something knotted in Maude's throat at his address of her, and when he touched her she flinched, afraid of what he might find and reveal. But he did not remove his hand, and a burning chill went through her like an arrow. He pinned his gaze on her, steadfast, penetrating, until all his charm, all the sweetness Maude had found in him earlier was gone, replaced by menace, an intent to do her harm. "Not me," she would have said had her jaws not been clamped shut by fear and humiliation. "I don't need your diagnosis. I have the healthiest soul here. I don't need your cures and recommendations. Not from a child. Go to someone who really needs you."

She was so lost in her silent defense that she almost

didn't hear his question to her: "What's your name, sister?" In the void Maude's silence left, Lilith said, loud enough to be caught by the microphones, "Gaudy Maudie! Call her Gaudy Maudie! Just look at that hat!"

Maude had expected an outbreak of titters and snickers in the tent and was surprised when none followed. She wouldn't look at anybody else for a moment, not even Benny Troy, and in the terrible silence that hemmed her in from all sides she nodded vaguely and said, almost hoarsely, "Maude...yes."

Benny Troy nodded in return and applied pressure to her shoulder with his small hand. His fingers bit into her like a weasel's jaws and held her still with surprising strength, and with corresponding power his small eyes held her attention completely. She should have fought him, squirmed free, gotten up and left, reclaiming the dignity he was stealing from her, but he she couldn't: Benny Troy had opened his mouth to speak and an odd part of herself wanted to hear what he had to say.

He spoke of Maude's loneliness, saying she was alone but too proud to seek other people's company, and that she had turned to food to fill up this emptiness she was feeling. She had given herself over to gluttony, which was a sin in the Lord's eyes. "And you have come here dressed in a bright and obvious way to draw the attention of others," he went on. "There's a sadness in you, sister, a need you cannot fill on your own, a great hole in your heart, but if you lay your pride down and embrace the word of God, proclaim it as true to them around you, acknowledge Christ as your Lord and Savior, as your true and only friend, He will fill you with a joy that surpass all understanding." He paused, bearing down on Maude with those small, hard eyes. "Do you believe, Maude? Do you believe me?" In her searing humiliation, Maude mumbled something that sounded vaguely affirmative. Benny Troy nodded like he understood her perfectly and made his Bible recommendations to her, but the only thing Maude heard right then was Lilith, who said, loud enough to be heard by everybody, "Smack her on the head, preacher. Make her go backwards like they do on TV."

"I didn't know I was staying with no hermit!" Lilith yelled through Maude's bedroom door the next night. "Fact of business, I believe I was promised shrimp tonight at the fish camp. Now get up and let's go. I'm hungry!"

But Maude was up, at her vanity, looking at her face in what stingy blue light twilight afforded her. She was looking at the face the Reverend Benny Troy Hoyt had stared into the night before when he had said, "There's a sadness in you, sister, a great hole in your heart." Emptiness he had meant. And pride too. He had remarked on her pride as well, and she owned up to that because pride could be a good thing after all – pride in your bearing, your way of dress, your behavior. Pride was a mark of distinction if you truly had something to be proud of, so she admitted to her pride. But emptiness? Was she empty, hollow, shallow just because she had come to the revival dressed nicely? She had turned the question over in her mind after they had gotten home from the revival the night before, after she had finally fought through the shame Benny Troy had netted her in. At first, when she'd found speech again, she wanted to curse the little preacher for implying such a thing about her. "I'm not shallow," she had told an indifferent Lilith. "I'm reserved. I'm dignified. I'm a lady."

"I don't know," Lilith had replied, treating it as a joke. "I think the reverend pegged you pretty good."

"He did not!" Maude had bellowed back. "He was jealous. They all were. The bumpkins."

"Of what? You?"

"Of my refinement. My intelligence."

"Honey, how could them people tell if you was smart or not, when all you done was sit there and get embarrassed by some dwarf? Didn't look too smart to me."

But Maude had continued to protest to the contrary to Lilith, and, later in bed, to herself. "I'm not shallow or hollow or empty. Proud, yes, but pride is a good thing. I'm dignified and refined. I have led an exemplary life as one could hope under the circumstances. I have made all decisions in my life intelligently. I have been prudent and chaste and considerate of others." She fought Benny Troy's "diagnosis" all night, sparred with it until her protests

themselves grew hollow, and, sleepless, she let the truth of
the boy's words wash over her and take her with their
inevitability. "Yes," she said aloud. "I am empty. So empty
I can almost hear my insides working away." The evidence
stood too solid, too insistent for her to refute it any longer,
so she did not. Then she thought of the source of her
emptiness, and, being an old maid, her thoughts turned
immediately to family, romance, and marriage. She had
wanted all of them, she really had, and she had never
considered herself too good for a man the way hateful Lilith
had insisted. The fact was she had never in her life been
approached by a man, as a teenager or as a grown woman.
Why not, she was not sure. She was not ugly at all, not a
beauty, but certainly not painful to look at. Maybe men
could see how smart she was, and maybe that had scared
them away from her. Maybe, when she got a little older, her
weight had put them off (although that had never been a
problem for other women she knew). Maybe men had
mistaken her natural shyness for snobbery. For whatever
reason, men didn't come to her, and she would never have
been presumptuous, even in a "liberated" age such as this
one, to approach them. (*It just wasn't done!*) It didn't matter
after a while. The cancer came and took away from her any
possibility of a family, and wasn't that what marriage was
for primarily? It was then she resigned herself to being the
confidante of married women and the doting, playful
"friend" of their children. That was to be her lot in life

obviously, and she owned up to it heroically.

"He knows me," she said of Benny Troy, her hatred of him melting into tender affection. He had revealed her and told her how to close up the emptiness. "Embrace the word of God as true to all around you and acknowledge Jesus Christ as your Lord and Savior," he'd said. There stood the snag for her in it all. It would be embarrassing to say those things to other people! She was afraid people would think her a fanatic, one of those bug-eyed believers that begged for money on television and picketed outside dirty movies. She didn't want that. She wanted a simple, dignified fate.

The fish camp sat far back from the highway behind a screen of pines. It was a ranch style building, brick and flat-roofed, and in its outside lights they could see tom turkeys and Chinese ducks and Canadian geese meandering in the dirt-and-gravel parking lot; and Maude picked up peacocks in her headlights, forlorn looking birds dragging their long, spear-like naked tails across the ground. There were only a couple of other cars there at that hour. Maude was disappointed. She wanted as many Comptonites as possible to see the new Maude Hutto, washed clean, revealed, full of love and Christian pride. She had dressed quite nicely in a blue polyester dress that was only somewhat tight on her and the same nice white shoes she had worn last night, but this time she had crowned the ensemble with a more conservative pillbox hat. She wanted everyone to know what dignity could come with belief in Jesus: that would be, as the preachers called it, her "witness" to the fallen world.

Maude and Lilith took a booth near the back of the restaurant. Their seats, of old pinewood with a very dark finish, were creaky and groaned if they moved the slightest bit. The whole place was done in hardwood, as was the tradition of Southern fish camps. It was buffet night, and Lilith went straight to the buffet bar, where she loaded her plate with boiled shrimp and deviled crab and hush puppies. Maude took more delicate portions so as not to seem a glutton. She picked at her food gently while Lilith attacked hers like a Hun, shucking shrimp shells so vehemently many of them ended up on the floor.

"I'm joining Covenant Baptist," Maude announced timidly, almost afraid she would be heard by her sister. "I spoke to Pastor Davis on the phone. He's very enthusiastic about it."

Lilith, her mouth smudged with cocktail sauce, said, "Why? Are you somebody special?"

"No. Just a new sheep in the flock."

"Well, sheep. Let me tell you something. If you had you a ram to give you an orgasm once in a while, you'd cut out all this nonsense."

"What nonsense? What do you mean? This is genuine."

"Yeah. Just like all the other things you've joined in your life. You get tired of 'em after a while and quit going. The book club. The history club. The music club. The garden club. It's just the same old thing with you."

Maude sat quietly resentful then scraped her plate with her fork. "Lilith will not spoil my joy," she promised herself. "Her negative attitude is a test for me, and I will not be defeated." So she drew in a breath and ate her flounder and scallops with more vigor and relish, as though she were Gabriel wielding a sword against rebel angels. It wasn't long before she heard a commotion at the door of people entering and looked up with heart-stopping, eye-blurring astonishment to see the Reverend Benny Troy Hoyt, his daddy, his mama, and another little boy coming towards her and Lilith, dressed in their revival best. She checked her watch and saw that, yes, it would be time for the service to let out. Maude smiled as the family passed their booth. The father nodded curtly, and she heard them fill up the creaking, popping booth directly behind them. She told Lilith, who had yet to look up from her plate, who had just come in and sat down behind them.

"You mean they didn't fall all over you, you being a new sheep and all?" Lilith replied and went right back to her food.

"It's a sign," Maude concluded to herself. "The Lord is confirming me, saying, 'Yes, Maude. You are my child. You are part of the flock now.'" She fidgeted nervously a second then said, "I'm going to speak to them" and stood before Lilith could make a wisecrack. She walked only a couple of steps before she was staring down at all of them as they studied their menus. They ignored her or were unaware of her presence until she cleared her throat. Then all their menus dropped simultaneously. Now she was left standing there with their eyes on her. She watched Benny Troy, hoping recognition would light in his face, but it remained blank and unmoved. She almost turned away in embarrassment until she remembered she didn't have to anymore: they were all related now, bound by love. She introduced herself and reminded them of what had happened at last night's gathering. "I just wanted to say...how much...Benny Troy's words meant to me...he was right about me...and his words were a Godsend...."

The senior Rev. Hoyt gave another curt nod, smiled with half his mouth, and said, "Thank you, Maude. Glad to hear it." He laid his hand on his menu to pick it up.

Maude blushed, feeling inadequate, and made a reflexive response. "And I want to show my appreciation by offering something to your ministry." She searched her purse, found a twenty dollar bill, and offered it to the senior Rev. Hoyt. "God bless you, Maude," he said with a third quick nod. Maude watched Benny Troy, disappointed he didn't recognize her and make fuss over her. (They had such kinship now!) He and the other boy were trading amused glances. She was struck at how plain, how ordinary Benny Troy looked sitting there in the booth. He'd lost the majesty and authority the trappings of the revival had given him. He was just a little boy now, and a very homely one at that.

"Benny Troy," she called in a voice nearing desperation, "I want to thank you for seeing through me last night. I'm going to try to get as close to the Lord as possible." Benny stared at her a second like she was speaking a foreign language then nodded sharply in imitation of his daddy and said, "Yes ma'am. You do that" and smiled with half his face to complete the mimic.

Maude stood there a moment longer, confused, before turning back to her own booth. Lillith sat there eating flaky peach cobbler and had even brought Maude a dish of it and asked Maude when she was seated again, "How much money did you give that man?"

Maude told her.

"All they'll do is buy their supper with it. If you was going to give money away like that, you should have give it to me. I need it worse than they do."

Maude picked at her dessert, distracted, wondering at Benny Troy's coldness towards her. "I'm his sister now," she protested to herself. But he sees so many people, another voice added. He's been all over the country, Maude. "Yes, but I should stand out," she countered.

"Gaudy Maudie!" another voice put in, hoarse, whispery. She looked up from her cobbler. This voice had come from outside her rather than within. "What did you say?" she asked Lillith, who reached over for a forkful of Maude's dessert.

"Nothing," Lilith replied with an ugly wrinkle of her

mouth.

"I thought you said something. Something ugly. As usual."

"You're hearing things. I'm going for more dessert." Lilith stood, upsetting her plate and knocking more shrimp hulls to the floor, and went back to the buffet line. At the same time the Rev. and Mrs. Hoyt stood and got in line themselves.

And shortly afterwards it came again. "Gaudy Maudie! Gaudy Maudie!" Those were Lilith's hateful words, but Lilith was several feet away and would have to have been quite a ventriloquist to throw her voice that far and that clearly. "Gaudy Maudie!" It came from above her. She looked up quickly and saw a small head blur away. It was that little boy who had come in with the Hoyts. Where had he heard that ugly phrase of Lilith's? "Little scamp!" she muttered under her breath but checked her anger against her newfound serenity and revised the barb to "Playful thing." Still she wondered where the boy got the name and was hurt he'd used it against a dignified woman like her. She thought she had made a very gracious presentation to the Hoyts, and had *she* been the recipient, she would have been quite impressed.

"Gaudy Maudie!" She ignored it this time. It would be undignified to look. Lillith was on the way back to the table and Maude snapped at her. "You've made a mess here."

"They pay people to clean it up," Lilith returned. She

stopped before sitting down, and a smile lifted her mouth. "Somebody's paging you, Maude." She nodded over Maude's head.

Despite herself, Maude glanced behind her and was shocked and saddened to see not only the other boy but Benny Troy himself peering at her over the booth and whispering, "Gaudy Maudie!" His plain face was fixed like a moon over the booth before it disappeared and he and the other boy slid down in their seats snickering.

"Jesus really loves you, doesn't He?" Lilith said with full mouth and crossed eyes.

"But he revealed me," Maude thought to herself. "He showed me who I am. He filled me up with true love." She decided to be staunch. She would ignore the nasty remark. She would eat peach cobbler and praise the name of the Lord. Hallelujah!

Then she felt something like a breeze pass above her, as though some bird had swooped over her. She took it for the ceiling fan, but Lilith looked up at her and burst out laughing. "Somebody's done borrowed your pillbox, Maude."

Maude reached up to her head and in shock found that her hat no longer sat there. She heard giggles and someone say, "Catch!" and she turned and saw that Benny Troy and the other child were in the middle of the floor playing with her hat. She stood at once. "Here now!" she hollered so that heads in the camp turned her way. "That doesn't belong to you!" Benny Troy had the hat and was ready to throw it back to the other boy. Benny grinned so hard at Maude his eyes narrowed. He seemed to be taunting her. Then he pitched the hat to the other boy. Maude grabbed the child, who had tried to sprint away, and shook him roundly. "You little devil!" she said, louder than she meant.

"What's the matter here, Miz Hutto?" It was Benny Troy's parents returned, their hands balanced with full plates. The senior Rev. Hoyt stared with a pointed, concerned look on his face. Maude explained and gestured to the anonymous child as proof: he was still clutching her hat.

"Yes ma'am! Yes ma'am!" Rev. Hoyt moaned. He set down his plate and with minimum effort had the hat out of the child's grip, smoothed it back into shape delicately and lovingly, and handed it to Maude like a boy giving his sweetheart a present. He apologized profusely.

Maude didn't hear him though. She stood, still dazed, and pointed at Benny Troy. "But he's a man of God," she mumbled.

"Yes, ma'am, but he's a boy too, and he's tired and irritated, the way a youngun gets. He's been working hard all week. Preaching really tuckers him out."

"He had a vision. He said he did."

Rev. Hoyt took her arm to reassure her further. "But don't worry, Miz Hutto, preacher or not, he's still my boy, and he's not too good to get his little hind end tanned. Ha!

Ha! I'll take care of him."

Maude snatched her arm way like the reverend had injured her and pointed again at Benny Troy. "He says he's a man of God with a vision and all, and this is how he acts! The undignified little scamp!"

"Quiet, harlot!"

Maude drew back some. Her pointing hand spread over her neck in defense. Benny Troy had assumed a stance almost martial. He was pointing back at Maude, his face red as a radish and indescribably ugly. "Quiet, Jezebel! Quiet, Bathe Sheba! Quiet, Salome! You mother of lies. I call on Jesus Christ to cast out the demons that make you run your big mouth!"

Maude veered back further, like she'd been struck, and she kept going back until she stepped in the pile of shrimp hulls her sister had knocked to the floor. Her foot twisted somewhat to the left then to the right, thanks to the shells' viscosity, and with all the fish camp watching, the world went out from beneath her and she lay straight out on the floor like some large catch just reeled in and left floundering.

"You can't trust a preacher in a three piece suit, Maude. How many times do I have to tell you?" Lilith asked on the way home from the fish camp. She was driving; Maude was on the passenger's side, moaning, "But he revealed me, I tell you, he revealed me!"

"Yes ma'am he sure did – as a durn fool."

But he had, she told herself again as she sat sickened in her seat. He'd come to her like some apostle, like Moses with the tablets, like some little burning bush on feet and showed her her emptiness, and she'd loved him for showing it to her; she loved him with a love that gripped her heart and made her feel like she marched in that long line of religious converts – Paul and Augustine and Charles Colson and Little Richard. That was why she had reached out to him in the fish camp – to requite what he had offered her first, to seal their pact as brother and sister. And what had he done in return? Stolen her hat and called her that distasteful name. Oh there was no greater despair than this! And everyone saw her too when she hit the fish camp floor. They gawked a full minute, like she was some sideshow freak, before Rev. Hoyt and the camp manager came to lift her –with Lilith sitting over her, laughing and saying, "Y'all don't mind her. She just can't hold her liquor." She'd been so ready to love too, to spread love all over the world like a blanket. Now love soured, turned to a black hate. Right then she could have taken Benny Troy into her hands and torn him to pieces like some graven idol.

A strange car sat in Maude's driveway. Maude didn't pay it much attention, though, as she strode slowly, funereally towards the front door. Lilith walked ahead of her, saying in mock concern, "Now watch your step, dearie. Don't fall again, or I will have to get you a walker." Inside they both stopped in their tracks because Christine stood in the den with a strange young man in a drab olive military uniform. Christine herself was dressed as though to go somewhere, and indeed her pink suitcase stood near her. For one of the few times Maude had known the girl, a smile came to her lips.

"Miz Hutto, this is Jerry. He's on leave from Fort Bragg. I think I told you about it. We're going to a motel for a few days to spend some time together and talk things out. I hope that doesn't bother you, what with you being a born again Christian and everything."

Lilith harrumphed off to her room, but Maude remained in place, staring at Christine and Jerry, and near Christine's suitcase sat little Lorrie, playing with wooden blocks. The tableau was complete: man, woman, child. The covenant that had been denied her, the love she could never have. For a moment she was filled with a quiet rage towards them, and she thought of striking out at them, physically even, for their equanimity. But it suddenly did not seem worth the effort. She hadn't the energy.

Maude shook her head slowly. "No, it doesn't matter," she said and turned and left the young people in the living room.

In her bedroom Maude went straight to her vanity and sat, as though to recover from some battle. She took off her hat and sat it down and stared into the mirror. She had left off the light, so she was looking at some apparition of herself, a woman who may or may not have been there. She had been denied all love, all chance for love, even love which transcended the ephemeral. Strangely enough the realization did not hurt her. If anything she found something comforting in it, something almost heroic. "I am resigned to it," she told her dark reflection. "I'm just like a monk, a nun, any great ascetic. How many people can say that?" She was distinct and dignified: the unloved woman in a world of women all too loved, all too attached, all too domestic.

She swelled up in the vanity's mirror. Her chest puffed out. Some color returned to her cheeks. She could discern bits of it even in the dark. The only embarrassment which now lingered in her was caused not by the events at the fish camp but by her attempt to fit in, her silly cries for love and acceptance. Who needed them, when one could be unique?

She embraced her emptiness like a child needing affection.

Hospitality

WHEN DUKE BRINKLEY TOOK my swollen left nut in his right hand and declared, "Goddamn, this sumbitch is big as a basketball!" I knew me and him would hit it off.

First of all, he was plain-spoken, which should be clear enough, said what he meant, didn't beat around no bushes. I like that quality in a man or woman about as much as I would good looks or riches. It lets you know where you stand with them. There are no questions and no mysteries about it. Lots of times folks will lie just so things will go more smooth and there will be no problems. Or so they think. Fact of business, if you are not honest but just hem and haw and hedge, it makes for more problems and worse ones on down the road than you started out with. Second, Duke cussed and done it with real ability and feeling as I hope I have demonstrated above. I do not trust people who are not honest, and I especially do not trust people that do not cuss. (There is a relation between the two things, I think, honesty and cussing.) Cussing is a good way to clean bad stuff out of your system, stuff that might otherwise clog up in you and go gangrene and kill you eventually. God made a way to keep that from happening. He give man language, and from that language man has made certain words that express his temper very well and keep him healthy. There ain't a thing in the Bible that says not to cuss, other than that part about taking the Lord's name in vain. There's not a mention of the F or the S or the D. Surely God saw them coming, and if He was against them, He would have said something about them in His book. And, besides, in those rare times I do say g.d., and it takes a lot of poisonous feeling to get me to do so, I am never thinking about God hisself but about god with the little g. Now I don't mean cuss just anyplace. Not in church and not around people who don't like it. There is a time and place for everything. But if you don't cuss, I'm afraid you may be laying up stuff inside yourself that will eventually come out hurtful and hateful and even dangerous than if you just said a simple four letter word and got done with it right then and there.

Anyway, Duke Brinkley had no qualms about cussing when he seen the size of my misshapen gonad. Fact of business, he got so excited about it he called for his nurse. "Linda, get in here and take a look at this baby doll! It's the biggest one I've ever seen, and it looks like it's about to pop!" Like I was some attraction in a county fair freak show and not a man in some serious damn pain. Sure enough, Linda rushed in and stooped down, and him and her went to oohing and aahing over my testicle like it was a prehistoric dinosaur egg in the Smithsonian museum.

While they made all their noises of disbelief and admiration, I stood there hurting so damn bad I thought I would pass out and wondering if coming to Dr. Duke Brinkley had been such a keen idea. He had been recommended to me by his own daddy, Old Paul Brinkley, who used to fix looms at Majestic Fabrics years ago. Old Paul belonged to the Compton Elks, just like me, and one time at a roast for the Elks Exalted Ruler, he told me about his son Duke and how smart he was and what a hell of a good urologist he turned out to be and if I ever had any plumbing problems be sure to go see him.

So when I woke up that morning and had the feeling somebody had done sneaked an air hose into my pajama bottom and proceeded to pump, pump, pump it full and looked and seen that sure enough my left nut could have been an NBA accessory, I give Duke's office a call to set up an appointment in Spartanburg, where he practiced. (Just about all urologists practice in Spartanburg, it seems like, and drive down to Compton at various times of the week to see folks. I couldn't wait for one of those times.) When it came time for my appointment I went back to one of the observation rooms. Duke was already there, at a table, sitting, talking on the phone. He was about fifty years old, with black and gray hair parted nearly in the middle but still smooth-faced, and wore his doctor's whites with black slacks underneath. He didn't see me or pretended not to anyway. I took a seat. He kept on talking. He had a Q-tip in the side of his mouth, chewing it like a match, and he talked and laughed through it and went on about what a damned good thing it was he had exercised those stock options when he'd had the chance or else he'd be eating that investment right then. He kept talking and never glanced my way. Was he blind? A blind urologist? Good God! I could just imagine where the finger of a blind urologist might end up. To let him know I was there (in case he didn't), I let out a series of moans – little ones, nothing too loud or showy, but they were sincerely meant. It was pure misery sitting there. My gonad *throbbed*. I couldn't get my two legs far enough apart to avoid the terrible hurting. Finally Duke barked into the receiver, "Ah, hell. Let me go. This fellow's sitting here acting like he's going to die if he doesn't get looked at right now" and hung up. He stood up and told me to stand too and to shuck my drawers and underpants. Then he seen the source of my pain and made the remark that began this whole account. And then he called his nurse in to see, and they stooped looking at my ball like they was waiting for it to hatch any minute. Duke didn't seem concerned. He seemed, well, almost happy to come upon something so deformed. Of course he could act like that. He wasn't the one hurting. I had to remind him of the fact.

"Ah, it will be all right," he said, standing up. "Infection is all. Bad infection for sure. You do take regular leaks, don't you? I mean, you don't hold back for long periods of time, do you? Sometimes that can activate bacteria."

I told him I went every chance I got.

He went back to his table, sat, and began scratching something in doctor-script on a pad. While he wrote, he said, "Daddy says you're a big wheel in the Elks down there in Compton."

"I'm on the board of trustees."

"You think you can help me get in? You know the Spartanburg Elks shut down a few years ago. Lack of interest. I miss it. I miss all the camaraderie."

I could and did get him in.

Duke loved the Elks Club and was there every day. He drove down thirty-five minutes from Spartanburg after his office closed just to have drinks at the club bar. He said he didn't realize how much he had missed Compton. He grew up there but hadn't been back much since he left thirty years ago to go to school. Hadn't been much of a reason to. His mama was dead, his daddy was about as much in Spartanburg as he was home, and he didn't have no brothers or sisters. It was like a reunion with all the folks he'd known when he was young. He bought everybody drinks and hot wings and even got their dinner when it was Family Night at the club. It was like seeing an old place through new eyes had opened up a big vein of generosity in him. He'd call me at the house and say, "Come on down, Emory. I'll spot you a beer or two. I need to talk to you." I'd joke and say I didn't like seeing him because it reminded me of when my nut got so big, and he'd come back with how I better stay on his good side in case I ever blowed up again. (Like they wasn't another ball doctor I could go to.) My wife didn't like me going back to the club so late in the day. I'd been gone all day doing one thing or another for the Elks or the Shriners. But I went. And Duke set me up for drinks like he said he would, and for a couple of hours he would talk to me about the plans he had for this thing or that. He wanted to include me in most of them. Going in halfers for a condominium in Myrtle Beach, for instance, or getting up a trip to Ireland so he could go and trace his ancestors. *Big* plans. I'd listen and nod my head, and when an hour was up, I told him I had to get back to the house. Doris had supper waiting, and she'd be mad as hell if I let it get cold and she had to reheat it.

"You know how a wife is," I told him as I stood to go.

He stared at me and kind of smiled but didn't say nothing.

"He don't know how a wife is," somebody told me later, when Duke wasn't around. "He lost his."

"She die?" I asked with instant sorrow growing from my stomach up into my chest.

"No. No. She left him. Divorced him. Took him to the cleaners, they said. Said she told him she couldn't stand living with him no more, him being such a asshole to her and all."

"Oh."

"Making fun of her in front of their friends and family. Supposedly he told her mama and daddy they had him to thank for taking their daughter out of the sticks of Roebuck and turning her into a lady, and if it wasn't for him she'd go right back down to them sticks."

"He said that?"

"Oh, Emory, you know how he goes on. Does it all the time down here at the Club. But not everybody takes it for a joke."

True. Duke did like to pester folks. One time he reached over to W.C. Poage and snatched off W.C.'s toupee and held it up for everybody to see and yelled in the bar how he had caught him a squirrel then set it back down on W.C.'s head so that it sat askew and covered up one of W.C.'s eyes. He done similar things to other folks. But what he most liked to do, especially if he was good and fueled by the bourbon he liked so well, was to put down Compton, his hometown. He was always talking about how Compton was nothing and never would be nothing, how it for all intents and purposes died when the cotton mills closed. He compared Compton to Spartanburg, which really wasn't fair, Spartanburg being much bigger and all, and went on about how stupid it was of the county not to let that interstate go through all them years ago when they had the chance.

"If it had," he said, "Compton today would be as least

as big as Gaffney. But it didn't. The fat cats and the big wigs weren't about to let any outsiders get a cut of this place. Well, they're dead now, and look at what kind of legacy they've left!"

He said this to men who had not left Compton for medical school or for anything else but had stayed and worked in them mills that was gone now and raised their families here and felt like maybe they done all right, all things added up.

"Now see why his wife left him?" my friend said not too long after that particular display. "And that daughter don't have nothing to do with him either."

Well, yeah, I reckon I could understand how Duke could get on folks' nerves. But at that point I was still willing to give him the benefit of the doubt. I felt sure the pressures of being a doctor, maybe especially a doctor who has to his hands all over strange men's plumbing, could make somebody act goofy now and then and say things in such a way that would relieve that pressure. But not everybody else was so generous-hearted as me. When Duke ran for board of trustees of the club, he got beat two to one.

He called me at the house after the vote sounding all blue and down in the dumps. I told him not to worry about it and reminded him he was a doctor in Spartanburg, a man who had done and seen lots of things, and some folks was apt to be jealous. I didn't mention the fact the club secretary was a chiropractor. Duke probably knew that anyway.

Anyway, my words seem to cheer him, and by the time we hung up, he was laughing and cutting up again.

I reckon I should have leveled with Duke and told him why the other Elks were so resistant to him. Goodness knows he would have told *me*. He didn't hold nothing back from nobody. But I hated to, I really did. I didn't want to discourage him. He was so open-fisted with his money and his time. He helped out so much and done more than some people that had been members for years who are too lazy or too indifferent to open a damned door for you. Duke helped set up for meetings and suppers. He cleaned up afterwards. He even cooked a time or two. When they was tickets to be sold for something, he sold his out quicker than anybody else and came back asking for more to sell. He had too much to offer to be discouraged. So I just kept quiet.

Every year, sometime between the end of January and beginning of February, the South Carolina Elks hold their state convention in Myrtle Beach. They reserve about three or four floors of the Landmark Hotel, and every county that has a chapter sends members down for a week of meetings and greetings and the big formal ball on Saturday night. The Grand Exalted Ruler shows up and takes his picture with folks. Every county opens a hospitality room in the central part of their floor, and there is lots of food and liquor to be had. The Compton chapter is famous for its hospitality. Folks even from Charleston and Aiken and such stop by to get some barbeque and Bud Light. Other chapters ain't so free-hearted. You'd be lucky to get a potato chip and a plastic cup of ginger ale from them. It is a good time. Since I retired from the mill I have not missed one convention. The younguns have abandoned the beach. The sea gulls have taken it over and made some room for the adults. The birds are quieter and nicer. And of course there is all kinds of good eating at the beach. We like The Captain's Table best and a couple of places in Conway. Even my wife looks forward to going, and she's not one to go much. She's usually satisfied to sit with a television or newspaper in front of her. But when the first of the year comes around, she says, "Emory, you done sent that deposit for the room down to Myrtle Beach?" It is a small miracle, I will have you know.

Well, this year Duke Brinkley also decided to go. He couldn't come down early because of his appointments during the week. But when Friday afternoon rolled around, he hopped in his car and made for the Landmark. He drove a 2004 Buick Cadillac the color of expensive beer. It was a long, sharp automobile that looked like it had been spit-shined by a giant. Once he arrived I didn't need my car no more that weekend till we got ready to go home. Duke done all the driving. Me and Doris and W.C. Poage and his wife piled in, and Duke took us every place we wanted to go. We went to the Pavilion and Broadway on the Beach and them good eating places I have mentioned. Duke drove us out to the place where the condominiums sat, the ones he wanted me and him to go in together for. He nudged me and said, "That could be us, bud." And he paid for just about everything too. Now I know there are people who criticized Duke for being a show dog with his money, and likely there is some truth to the accusation, but I know people good enough to know where they are phonies and put-ons, and Duke Brinkley was no such a-thing. He liked doing for people. He cared about them. Why else would he have become a doctor?

We got back to the hotel around ten, and Duke and W.C. and me sat around in my room and drank beer. Not for long though. Doris was tired and wanted to go to bed. So was W.C. So Duke and me moved our little two-man party to the Compton Hospitality Room, which would stay open till one that next morning. We had more drinks and talked about this Compton Elk and that one. We talked about Myrtle Beach. Duke said he liked it better in summer when all the girls were there in bathing suits. Somehow that led me to ask about his wife and daughter. I done it delicate-like, so as not to offend Duke. All he said was his wife didn't like the fact he was trying to take her and make something better out of her than what she started as. So she left him. He didn't miss her much, but he sure as hell missed his daughter. That's all he had to say about her. Then he mentioned he was dating a young woman, a very young woman, twenty-six years old. She made him happy, just for the fact she was so pretty. And she was. She'd been a runner-up for Miss Spartanburg a few years back. That is what he liked now, pretty young girls, and he didn't care what anybody thought about it. He was fifty years old. He had paid all his dues. He had earned his pleasures.

"Amen to that" was all I said. Then I pointed to the bar, where a Compton Elk served drinks. "That's me up yonder tomorrow night."

"Oh yeah?"

That's right. The House Committee had asked me to bartend in the Hospitality Room Saturday night during cocktail time right before the big dinner.

Duke said he sure hoped I knew how to make a screwdriver. That was his favorite.

Thank goodness he did not ask for a screwdriver that next night. I have never been good at mixing drinks that required another ingredient except water. Duke stuck to beer and whiskey, served neat. He drank a lot of both and was beginning to show some wear – and it was still early in the evening. There was the whole night ahead of us. He remained at the bar with me as I poured his drinks and others', talking about this thing or that as I tried to do my job. Finally I told him to go over to the hors d'oeuvres table right inside the door and get him a snack, else he would soon be on the floor. He obeyed and wandered off. The traffic in the Hospitality Room was pretty steady during my time bartending. It ebbed and flowed just like the ocean right outside. The regular faces showed and disappeared, and just like I predicted, lots of folks from other counties paid their respects and got their share of booze and eats. Someone said the Grand Exalted Ruler hisself was on his way to say hello to Compton, but he never showed. The room could hold maybe a hundred and fifty people, and at any given time there was maybe a third of that present. My wife Doris was one of them. Upholstered straight-back chairs had been placed all along the walls, and Doris sat in one in the far-most corner of the room talking with W.C. Poage's wife Donna and Nellie Mathis, the wife of a Compton city councilman.

At some point I noticed a couple of women standing in the middle of the room while others stood around them and talked and ate and drank. I didn't know them and for a moment wondered if they weren't part of some joke or prank or evening's entertainment I hadn't been told about. The reason I say that is because of the way they were dressed. They were old women. Well, not young anyway. In their sixties at least, I would guess, from the lines around their mouths and eyes. But they dressed so as to look younger. One was tall, the other short. One had a few more pounds on her than the other. They both wore these strange-looking pants suits (I guess you would call them). They were jet black, just pitch, with a deep V cut in the bosom-part and cuffs that flared out on all sides a good couple of inches. The backs were out too, and the sleeves, made of black fishnet, crawled down from the shoulders and ended at the wrists in wide, black ruffles. It was a queer kind of get-up to wear in winter, even if it was winter at the beach. Even more curious was their hair-dos. Wigs. Both of them. Jet black like their dresses and not at all lined up with the age of their faces. The short one's was short and ended with a pair of baloney curls flat against her rouged-up cheeks. The tall one's poofed out on top and at the back like somebody had planted a little explosive in it and she hadn't got it out in time. My first thought was that these gals belonged in some show from Broadway on the Beach and somehow had wandered into the Hospitality Room at The Landmark by mistake. They stood and looked around like a pair of blackbirds on the asphalt hunting their next meal. People passed them and did not speak but sure did stare. When there was a clearing and the women were plainly in view, I felt obligated to say something to them.

"Y'all ladies with the Compton Elks?" (When I knew better.)

"No," the short one said.

And that's all they said till I asked, "Y'all looking for something?"

The short one's make-up lit up with a smile. "Yessir. A drink. And it looks like you the man to get it from." The tall one hiccupped a laugh and nodded. Together they moved to the bar like they were joined at the hip.

Now I don't know how come, but my heart skipped a

beat or two and not for a good reason. It just flashed upon me as they settled on the swivel chairs at the bar how in the movies death is often portrayed dressed up all in black.

"I'll take a Manhattan," the short one said. Her friend asked for a Bloody Mary. I was afraid of that. Not many people from Compton ask for drinks named after cities or ladies. They have much simpler tastes. Thank goodness W.C. had left a bartender's manual near the refrigerator.

As I got out the vodka and tomato juice, I noticed Duke Brinkley shuffling back over to the bar from the hors d'oeuvres table. He took a seat at the bar next to the shorter woman. He was still good and plastered but seemed a bit steadier than before. He smiled at me then glanced around at the women, and I seen a kind of flinching in his right jaw like it got puffed up with air all of a sudden. And his eyes got wider too like they aimed to leave the sockets. His lips prissed up and he whistled and glanced back at me a second. I figured he knew them gals and recognized them and was about to say hey to them.

Instead he said, "Gah-ah-damn, if y'all ain't the ugliest two bitches I ever laid my eyes on!" He looked at me quick then back at them. "Y'all look like *shit*! Did somebody pay you to haunt this damn hotel?"

The women, for their part, just froze up and stared at Duke like he had dropped out of the sky onto his seat. They was like a pair of wax museum dummies. I swear.

"Emory," Duke said, "give me a double of the strongest

thing you got, son, 'cause I got to burn this picture off my eyeballs right now!"

Finally some color come back into the short woman's face. Her mouth got all pinched up, and her eyes nearly disappeared under her cheeks. "Why you son of a bitch. What the hell do you think you are, a beauty queen?"

"Come on, Margaret," her tall friend said, touching her elbow. "Let's go."

"Say!"

Duke swiveled on his seat away from them. "Emory, I can't look at 'em again, son! No! I'll go blind."

"Son of a bitch," Margaret said again but this time looking at me when she said it. "Does he think he'd win a beauty contest? Him?" Her eyes were hurt and angry and made it harder to look at her. But I looked and tried to say something to make all the tension go down some but couldn't find nothing.

Margaret's friend had a tight grip on her arm this time and got her off the barstool. She was still reluctant to leave, but her friend tugged hard enough and said, "Come on, he's nothing, come on" and they soon left the Hospitality Room in a quick, black huff.

"All right, Duke. They gone. You can look now."

Duke swiveled and stared after the door. He laughed. "Whew! You ought to call the Myrtle Beach dog pound and see if they're missing a couple of bitches!"

"You know them women?"

"No."

"I figured you might with the way you was talking to them."

"Nope. Don't know them, and don't want to know them."

"Then how come you said them things to them?"

He stared at me a second like he couldn't believe I could ask such a thing. Then he smiled and answered me. He raised his hand to count off fingers as reasons. "First off, they're not from Compton, so they didn't belong her...."

"Sure they did, Duke. It's the Hospitality Room. Anybody's welcome."

A second finger went down. "Second, they offended me. Their mere presence violated my aesthetic sense of things. I told you, Emory, I'm into young and pretty these days, and they were neither. They intruded upon my scenic enjoyment of Myrtle Beach. You understand?"

I poured the Bloody Mary down the sink.

I don't know how come, but for some reason Duke's behavior toward those two women at the beach soured me on him. Surely I have looked upon homely women and made remarks about them and even joked. What man hasn't? But not to their faces. Oh, I know that early on I commented on Duke's honesty and said it was the quality in him I liked best. And I don't take none of that back. I still mean it. But he crossed a line here, one between honesty and cruelty. I was raised, many years ago, to show women respect, even ones that are not exactly belles of the ball. Those two women at the beach hadn't done a thing to nobody except come into the Compton County Elks Hospitality Room and enjoy themselves a drink. They had as much right as anybody else.

I don't' know. It was like all the things other folks had said about Duke, about what a real s.o.b. he could be, finally became clear to me.

Anyway, it was never the same between me and him. The rest of that beach trip I didn't have much to say to him. And back home, whenever he called and wanted me to meet at the club for a drink, I always found an excuse not to go. I also switched to a urologist here in town, one I didn't socialize with. Duke was smart. He knew what was going on but, to my surprise, never mentioned it. It was the only time I ever knew him not to speak his mind.

A Song for
Mrs. Stratton

THIS OCCURRED MORE than thirty years ago in a small high school in the northwest upcountry of South Carolina. Chorus class was an elective option in those days, and an easy one, but not many people took advantage of it, at least not many people who moved in our circle of friends and acquaintances. (I'm not sure what the interest in the class is now; I haven't stepped foot in Compton High since I graduated in 1982. I suspect, however, participation has grown, what with American Idol the most popular television show in America and the notion afoot in the land that everybody is a star, regardless of the facility of his or her chops, and worthy of being heard on a mass basis.)

One very notable exception existed. This was Talmadge Pope, the de facto leader of our group, a position he pretty much took through force of will and because no one else vied for the post, not having Talmadge's interest in the military arrangements of all aspects of daily living, including lunch period and the order one spoke at study sessions. Talmadge was a good sort for the most part, at least possessing a sense of humor. He was slim and dark; one might say "exotic," and there was speculation that his mother and father, Mr. and Mrs. Jennings Pope, had been victims of a changeling, that their fair-haired, blue-eyed boy had been swapped for one who could have been mistaken as Samoan or Northern Italian.

Actually, Mrs. Pope had died giving birth to Talmadge, so it was Mr. Pope who raised him, helped by a trio of maiden aunts from a previous marriage. Mrs. Pope, at forty-six, proved too frail, too "delicate" for child-bearing, and soon after Talmadge's arrival had contracted a fatal blood infection. Mr. Pope, then in his late sixties, and a former infantryman in France during the first World War, as well as a leading cotton buying agent for the conservative Cook Textiles organization, had taken it upon himself to impose on his son a rigid standard of thought and behavior as one might take into combat or into high-level business negotiations. So it was no wonder to us that Talmadge could be a bit of a martinet who needed some collective standing down now and then.

What did baffle us was his signing up, in our sophomore high school year, the '79-'80 term for *chorus*. It seemed so, well, so fey for someone of Talmadge's iron-clad social and cultural (and, yes, eventual political) conservatism to study singing. (That same year he was an officer in the school's JROTC program and two years later would be its battalion commander.) Eventually he revealed to us that it had been his father's idea for him to take chorus. His father loved music. He spent countless hours of his retirement listening to records on an old-style phonograph player for which he had to send away for new styluses. Opera, jazz, and big band Mr. Pope especially loved. He regretted never having formally studied music or an instrument. He thought it the mark of a true gentleman to have more than a casual acquaintance with the musical arts. And he had convinced Talmadge of the same thing.

One bit of further intrigue, if not scandal, adhered itself to this whole episode. It had to do with the woman who taught chorus at Compton High, Mrs. Sylvia Stratton. She was an object of curiosity for us, even derision. First off, she was a Yankee. From where exactly – New York? Ohio? – we didn't know, and it didn't really matter. Being a Yankee, she might as well have just stepped off a hovering silver spacecraft and emerged with blue skin and waving tentacles attached to her head. So much alien behavior attached itself to the epithet and the notion of the Yankee for us lifelong Carolinians: their volubility, their brusqueness, their questionable morality. Did they even believe in God? Who knew? (Oh yes. Money. Money served as their deity. I'll never forget my grandmother's once saying, "All a Yankee studies about is money." In the years since I've discovered much truth in the statement, if not an entire ideology.) Worst of all, they had an unfortunate habit of coming south and doing their darnedest to get us to live as they lived or thought we should live. They even started a little war with that mind.

Wherever she had come – Cincinnati, Buffalo, Neptune – how did Mrs. Stratton end up in Compton, South Carolina, teaching music? Textiles. The god after Jehovah in which most Southerners placed their faith then. The eternal King Cotton. Talmadge told us Mr. Stratton had been transferred from a knitting plant up north to Majestic Fabrics in Compton as product quality manager. And naturally Mrs. Stratton had followed right along.

She certainly had the look of a classic schoolmarm – albeit no old maid of course – early middle-aged, with sharp, rigid nose and chin anchoring a face that in no way could have been described as pretty, though one would have a hard time forgetting it, silver-framed glasses with lenses nearly opaque, and a disciplined figure contained always in conservative skirts and blouses.

However it was neither her dubious origins nor her appearance which invited the greatest ridicule from those of us who did and did not study with her. It was her peculiar behavior, her overt theatricality, the unmistakable sense she gave that she really *cared* about this stuff, this choral singing, this presentation of music to the Compton High masses, which by her lights should approach the professional. That struck us as wholly eccentric. Music, after all was just – music, something to be enjoyed for a couple of minutes then discarded, forgotten, in favor of some other momentary preoccupation or diversion. It wasn't something one devoted one's life to, for goodness sake. It didn't really *matter*. Except it did to Mrs. Stratton. To her it mattered very much. A missed note would bring whitened fists to the sides of her head. An ignorance of correct lyrics would cause her to clutch her mortal breast and to breathe deeply a few moments as she attempted to regain composure. A flubbed bridge would have her turn from the entire group and stare into space for some melancholy moment while she readjusted the metronome of her own better sensibilities.

To us all that was just craziness. "She's crazy," someone declared simply and succinctly.

I had a front row seat, as it were, for these oddities for a whole week. As a sophomore writer for the school newspaper, *The Cougar*, I had been assigned to cover for a story Mrs. Stratton's sixth period choral class's rehearsal for their annual winter concert. With pad and pen I entered the choral hall, which also doubled as the band room, and sidled over to a corner so as not to be conspicuous. It was a large, airy room of green painted brick and slick, polished cement floor, and one easy to get lost in, even in plain sight. But Mrs. Stratton spotted me right away.

"Yes, young man?"

I told her who I was and why I was there, and she beckoned me closer with quick flexes of her long fingers, as though grabbing for me. I went to her. She placed her hand on my shoulder. I stared at her grey eyes swimming in the twin orbits of their thick lenses and concluded, with scant perceptiveness but plenty of silent self-congratulation, that she was indeed crazy.

"We are delighted to have you," she said with a smile perhaps not totally sincere, which pushed her round cheeks very nearly to the bottoms of her eyes. "Aren't we?" she went on, turning from me to the choristers, who were arranged neatly on the bandstand in plastic-backed, plastic-seated, metal-legged chairs almost too small for them. Talmadge Pope sat among them, of course, looking regal even in an Izod shirt and blue jeans. He smiled at me. He knew what I was thinking about the class and the teacher and wanted to show that he was impervious to such criticism, even unexpressed criticism .

"Aren't we?" Mrs. Stratton continued. Only a couple of students mumbled their agreement. And that was it as far as introductions. Then it was time for work. As if from nowhere, a young woman appeared and took her place at the upright grand piano situated diagonally from the bandstand. I sat behind Mrs. Stratton in one of the small chairs and opened my book of blank, wide-ruled paper to record impressions of the session and later to interview Mrs. Stratton. She led the group through the expected Christmas favorites before moving on to pop standards and even a few contemporary hits that lent themselves to choral arrangements. "Moon River" was one such standard,

"Everything is Beautiful" one such hit. She directed each of these pieces, even the most frivolous, with the fervor of a clairvoyant possessed. She paced back and forth in even measures, her eyes sometimes closed, her chin tilted heavenward or hell-bound. She chopped the air with short, quick beats of her hand. She leaned into the group as they sang, hands clasped tightly beneath her chin, as though trying to kiss them collectively. She grinned at notes achieved and grimaced at those abused. There was madness to her method, for sure, but to my surprise, and even dismay, I found myself unalarmed by her idiosyncrasies. Actually she fascinated me. I had always had a penchant for the dramatic myself. Indeed my career ambitions at the time involved the theatrical. But my chosen art wasn't drama or music. I wanted to be a movie director, and I caught myself framing the chorus class rehearsal as a scene from a film, with the languid camera moving, a la Hitchcock, a la Max Ophuls, panning the faces of the singing young, most of them without a musical gift, some wholly indifferent to what they sang, a few ardently involved, including my friend and classmate Talmadge Pope. The mind's camera retreated from the choristers, receding till the teacher came into view, pacing tirelessly, completely absorbed in the performance, regardless of its mediocrity.

Then came time for solo numbers. A solitary performer would step to the fore of the bandstand and sing his or her song to piano accompaniment. Talmadge Pope was the first male singer. His number was "The Impossible Dream" from *The Man of La Mancha*. This choice surprised me, as I had always associated that song with a bass or baritone (my first experience hearing it was on the old *Gomer Pyle Show*, when Gomer develops laryngitis right before he is supposed to sing the song at an enormous public event in Washington, D.C.) Talmadge was a tenor. But Mrs. Stratton directed him through the song with cautioning and beckoning motions of her long, pink hands. And to my further surprise, no, my astonishment, Talmadge did a damnably good job. The song fit him and vice versa. He was earnest without being comical and resisted any distracting movements of his hands. He kept his head slightly tilted up and his eyes fixed on the ceiling, as though it were there he espied the elusive chimera. When he was done, Mrs. Stratton remained still a moment, almost balled up within herself, her shoulders hunched, her head squeezed between them, her folded hands at her chin. Suddenly she burst into exclamation.

"You own that song, Talmadge Pope!" she said, now pointing at Talmadge with outreached fingers. "You have made it yours after all these weeks. Do you realize that?" Talmadge said nothing but nodded and flashed a weary smile, as though the effort of the song had depleted him.

That weekend a half dozen of us gathered at the home of our classmate Becky Ann Hobbs for a game of cards and hot apple cider. Talmadge had, other than his appearances at school, been quite the hermit lately, so his presence at

Becky Ann's was a novelty.

"Where in the world have you been?" Becky Ann asked coyly. Her romantic designs upon Talmadge had never been a secret.

Talmadge didn't answer but grinned quickly and dealt everyone his or her hand.

For some reason I felt uncharacteristically bold enough to answer for him. "Sorry, Becky Ann. There's a new apple perched in Talmadge's eye these days."

"Oh no!" Becky Ann responded with shock both feigned and real. "Who in the world could that be? I'm so envious!"

Thirty seconds passed before I answered. "Mrs. Stratton."

"Oh no!" Becky Ann repeated. "That dreadful woman?"

There was an outbreak of giggles.

"Will," Talmadge asked with low-key irritation. "What are you up to?"

"Talmadge is Mrs. Stratton's new protégé. Her latest songbird. She has him in a gilded cage." And I described the bars of such a contraption with all ten of my fingers. I don't know what made me go on thusly. Maybe something alcoholic had made its way into the cider courtesy of Becky Ann. (I had had two or three glasses by that time.) But probably not. More likely I had seen an opportunity to embarrass Talmadge, who over the years had been my friend and my enemy and always the recipient of attention and adoration, whether he deserved it or not. He had pretended humility in the face of such opprobrium, but I knew a flame of arrogance burned deeply within him, one that flared publically now and then but otherwise remained well-concealed. The truth was I envied to some extent his participation in the choral program. But I couldn't let anyone else know that. Instead I linked Talmadge to the most derided member of the Compton High School teaching staff.

And it worked. Right away each person there, excepting Talmadge of course, offered his or her less than laudatory opinion of Mrs. Stratton. The verdicts were harsh, owing to the adolescent rapacity for cruelty and exaggeration.

I chimed in again. "She has Talmadge here imitating Gomer Pyle. She says he owns the part. Talmadge Pope *is* Gomer Pyle!"

That was Talmadge's last straw. He flung down his hand of cards so they scattered the length of the portable table. He slammed his fist down hard afterward, and the table sagged some.

"Are you all human beings or what? Do you have any kind of heart beating away in your bodies, or is it just hollow there where a heart's supposed to be? Do you know anything about Mrs. Stratton, or do you only believe what you've heard or made up yourselves? No, you don't know anything. You're just pigs rolling around in filth."

No one else said anything until Becky Ann offered up timidly, "What are you talking about, Talmadge? What do you mean?"

Talmadge's face remained flush with anger as he explained. "What I mean is Sylvia Stratton's been through more than most folks have, so if she's crazy, by God she's earned the craziness." He paused a moment to let this sink in then went on. "You know her son died, don't you? Daniel Stratton. Her only child. No of course you don't know. You've never taken time out of your ridicule of the woman to find out any facts. Daniel Stratton died in a boating accident several years ago. Drowned when he capsized in Lake Erie. Fifteen years old. Her only child! That's what Mrs. Stratton has been living with all these years. That's what's made her crazy. It would make anybody crazy, don't you think? It's one of the reasons they moved down here, to be away from that house and that town without their son in it. And how do I know all of this? Because she told me. That's right. She's my friend as well as my teacher, and I don't care what you think of that. In fact, at this point, I don't care what you think about anything."

He didn't excuse himself or say goodbye. He just stood and left us, the new silence seared by his absence. All of us remaining could do was stare at each other and shrug.

Those of us at the card party could not elect out of the

choral presentation a few weeks later. If we could have we would have. It was mandatory – even though we had to pay a fifty cents admission – the other option was soporific study hall. We did not sit together but were spread throughout the auditorium. Yet we no doubt felt connected by the new knowledge of Mrs. Stratton's dead son Daniel and the probable influence it had on her peculiar behavior. We watched in a new if not favorable light the way she addressed the audience and directed each piece. And we felt an electric charge of nervous fascination when Talmadge Pope reappeared on stage by himself to render "The Impossible Dream." We watched the solicitous, even fawning way Mrs. Stratton introduced him and wondered about the extent of their bond and their friendship.

Then an odd thing happened. Talmadge smiled at Mrs. Stratton and shook his head. He said something to her. She wrinkled her brow, seemed to consider a moment, then shrugged. She announced to the audience that Talmadge had prepared a special number preceding "The Impossible Dream," if we would indulge him, and of course we would. We who knew Talmadge best attributed this change in program to his ego and his need to control everything around him, even the school Christmas musical. But we watched him on stage, solo, with a single spotlight trained on him, making him appear very small. He opened his mouth. The first words followed: "Oh Danny Boy, the pipes, the pipes are calling, from glen to glen and down the mountainside."

Those of us who knew better were stunned. It was the old Irish tearjerker, but Talmadge had taken it and turned it into some sort of tribute to his much-maligned choral teacher. Mrs. Stratton herself appeared overwhelmed. She did not move but remained in place with her hands joined, the index fingers pointed and resting against her pursed lips. Now and then a smile appeared there but did not last. Goodness knows what she thought hearing the familiarization of her deceased son's name repeated in the context of such a lilting melody. And Talmadge sang beautifully. There could be no denying it. His voice floated clear and sincere and convicted over the heads of his classmates and teachers. He was no longer Talmadge Pope, West Point aspirant and fledgling martinet. He was a bard, a troubadour, a man singing for something more than just his supper. And by the time he had finished his song, he had led some of us in the audience into the very heart of a confused woman's secret pain.

A Soldier for God

JERRY LEWIS.

Try as I might i couldn't help but think of Jerry Lewis whenever I regarded the boy, Jacob Lee, my student. Dustin Hoffman in *Rain Man* too, somewhat, in certain nervous affectations, but mainly Jerry Lewis. The young Jerry. Not today's Jerry, bloated with cortisone. The Jerry Lewis of Martin and Lewis, of *Scared Sti*ff, of *Hollywood or Bust*. And *The Nutty Professor*, of course, because Jacob wore the same vast-rimmed eyeglasses as the eponymous hero of that flick. He had young Jerry's gangling thinness also, his long limbs that seemed perpetually misdirected, and the habit of stuttering and elongating words in moments of urgency: "La-la-laaaaaaaaaady!"

I had been warned (for lack of a better term) by the university's chief admissions officer to expect a greater presence of "special needs" students in my classes that fall term. No explanation was given for such an increase in this type student. And indeed that one morning section of freshman composition contained three such individuals: a genial girl in a motorized wheelchair, a young man with hearing impairment, and Jacob Lee, whose disability had been termed, ambiguously, in the descriptive sheet sent to me, as of a "learning nature." I thought immediately of autism. I had known no one with that condition but had read enough about it to recognize certain signs. That first class, for instance, I noticed Jacob's rocking back and forth in his seat, just briefly, before stopping, and his staring off into a faraway corner of the room, a smile flitting for a moment over his long, pale face. The smile left, and one of his long white fingers found its way to his

mouth, as though to check any lingering evidence of the smile, then moved further up to his nose, into the right nostril, past the shadow of a moustache, turning, once, twice, three times before exiting, coming back down with whatever it had found. That's when I looked away. No official diagnosis of autism had been made according to the university's assistant dean for academic affairs.

Still Jacob must have lived in some sort of dream world. He *seemed* to be paying attention during class, but let me be done with one point and about to move on to another, and thirty seconds later this low growl would come from him and he would give one or two good rocks in his seat before halting at a downward dip to say, "Now you're saying…now you're telling us….well, what you're saying is" and then proceed to repeat what had just come from my mouth, almost verbatim, but as though it were an original insight on *his* part. The rest of the class would check with one another with narrowed eyes and stealth smiles. I wanted to check with them also and smile too and share with them the question they seemed to be passing around to each other almost telepathically: "Is this guy for real?"

He was from Spartanburg County and did not drive a car (his nerves were the reason). His mother brought him down to Compton each day so that he could attend classes; she drove a Winnebago that appeared to be an alumnus from the original class of Winnebagos way back from whence they first spawned. I learned much else about him from another student who knew a friend of his sister's. He was twenty-one, an astonishing fact, given his near-preadolescent visage (only the half-hearted moustache gave him away). He'd been quite a loner in high school, a fact not as astonishing to hear.

Once, in his senior year, he had urinated upon himself and refused to leave his seat to go clean up, until the teacher sought the assistance of a school vice-principal. An ugly row resulted. The aforementioned mother was diffident, almost to the point of non-existence. The father was a blue-collar drifter from job to job who complemented the mother's diffidence with indifference. Consequently Jacob sought his moral cues at a small fundamentalist Baptist church in Spartanburg presided over by a minister straight out of the Billy Sunday mode who had instructed Jacob, among other things, to steer clear of the company of both women and blacks, as, in this Christian gentleman's estimation, either could lead him to temptation. This same minister had left no doubt in Jacob's mind that he was an abject creature, eaten up with sinfulness, and that he would have to strive to atone until he drew his very last breath.

This puritanical influence made its way into Jacob's schoolwork. In fact the very first essay he wrote for me, a general self-assessment and statement of educational goals, ended with a single, stark line: "I aim to be a soldier for God." It also no doubt accounted for his nearly perfect, almost ridiculous honesty. For instance, if I passed him on campus and asked him how he was, he would reply with the standard "Fine." Then, later (it could be five minutes or five hours), he would seek me out, in the library or in my office, and confront me thusly:

"Um....Mr. McMillan...um...now do you remember earlier today when you asked me how I was and I said I was fine? Do you remember that?"

"Yes, Jacob. It was only a little while ago that I asked you."

"Hmmmmm. Well...." He halted, clicked his tongue a couple of times, lowered his head to show the long stalk of his pale, unblemished, translucent neck, spun around, dug his right sneaker into the carpet, then finally addressed me again. "Well, I lied to you."

"You did, Jacob?"

"Yes. I'm not fine."

After a pause, I said, "I'm sorry to hear that. If there's something you'd like to talk about, I'd be glad to listen."

Still averting his eyes, he wrinkled his mouth and said, "Ummmmm…no thank you" and turned and left.

There were times when I came upon him, in the student lounge, for instance, or perhaps outside in the hall, rocking, his eyes closed, his knees firmly clasped and his hands in front of him (if he were sitting; if here standing he would just stare at the ceiling as though waiting for one of the tiles to come loose and drop upon him). He was praying. If I came upon him in the act he might stop and bolt to the bathroom to finish or to an empty classroom, or he might continue the invocation regardless of who saw him. Other times I came upon him merely sitting and staring off with a pained expression on his long, pale face. He might exhale loudly, a sigh that said more than any essay he wrote for me that term. He was thinking, no doubt, of the life-long struggle described by his minister to be a good warrior for his Lord, and he realized, as we all do, that it was a battle he was doomed to lose. He was hurting. It was my instinct to stop and ask about his hurt and to try to assuage it in some way as I did with almost all my students. But I didn't, simply because I didn't want him to lie to me and then seek me out hours later to apologize for it. That seemed to me an incredible waste of time and energy.

I sought out the advice of colleagues who were also teaching him. They reported the same sort of aloofness. I thought the best tack was deference – not to push or to baby him, for he would surely resist that and retreat even further into himself, so that all that could be seen were those enormous glasses, as with the Cheshire cat and his ubiquitous grin. To encourage him in subtle ways would be best: I felt sorry for him frankly but was careful to remember that even young people of a certain defective temperament had access to cunning too and could take advantage just as well as the "straight" ones. So I directed questions to him in class and gave him all the time to hem and haw his way through an answer. I did not link, either physically or telepathically, with the not-so-subtle derision of his classmates. Outside class I was careful not to ask him "How are you today?" but to pose more specific questions of a non-personal nature, dealing with academics instead. That he answered at all, with a little less halting than usual, made me believe (or fooled me, to get right to the point) that I was gaining ground with him, winning his trust...

A trust that I quickly lost.

Two things happened, the first during mid-term examinations. As a "special needs" student, Jacob was entitled to time and a half to take his test. The test ran the usual class duration of an hour and fifteen minutes. That meant Jacob had an extra half hour to finish his exam. When that extra thirty minutes had elapsed and I asked Jacob, who was the last student there, for his essay, he looked up at me with his long pale face emotionless, and said, "The paper says I have three hours."

"No, Jacob. It says you have an extra half hour. I need your essay now."

He continued to write, oblivious. I sat at my desk, rambling through other student exams, growing miffed, thinking the thoughts that would have confirmed Jacob's pastor's no-doubt low opinion of college professors.

"Jacob?"

"I'm almost done."

"I need the test now."

"Time and a half."

I stood and walked to his desk and smoothly extricated the lined sheet of notebook paper from him.

"I hate you," he said, still looking down, presumably at the ghost of his now missing exam.

I turned from him and said, "That's fine, Jacob. I imagine you're not the only one of my students who feels that way," when what I really wanted to say was "Oh go in your closet and pray, soldier of God." I gathered his essay together with his classmates', slipped them into a manila envelope, and left him alone in the classroom.

The second incident occurred nearer the end of the term, when the freshman composition class were to turn in their short research papers on the meanings of modern popular cinema. Jacob, who had not turned in a paper, remained behind after the other students had left.

"I don't watch movies."

"You still owe me a paper."

"I don't watch them, so I can't write about them."

"What *do* you do?"

He didn't answer.

"You still owe me a paper. You are to have that paper to me, typed and double-spaced, no later than seven this evening. Otherwise you will fail the assignment and the course."

Later that day, in my office, I received a phone call from him. "Check your email." I found an attachment – a title page: "The Sin of Procrastination." Not even the topic. He called back shortly and asked if I'd received it. "That's a title page, Jacob. Not an essay." A half hour later another email from him appeared with another attachment – barely a half page of inchoate rumination on wasting time. A phone call followed quickly. "Ninety-two words!" Jacob hollered manically into the earpiece. "Ninety-two!"

"Keep going," I said calmly and hung up. But there were no more emails or phone calls, and at seven o'clock I entered a grade of "F:" beside Jacob Lee's name and washed my hands of him for good.

Knowing he had flunked, Jacob showed up at my office a few days later. He never entered the office itself but remained in the outside suite, within view, and performed his normal pacing, rocking, and stammering. "Now, Mr. McMillan….now what you don't know…what you don't understand…..there are things…now…that you don't know….Hmmmmmm." I was first inclined to go to him and strike him as I would an ill-performing clock or other piece of machinery to get it functioning again. That, however, would not look good come promotion time, so I decided on a peroration on discipline, duty, etc., virtues lauded in The Good Book, but as I opened my mouth to set forth, the door of the suite crashed open.

"Jacob!" someone bellowed like a bear. I stood and went to the door and found a middle-aged man there in a dirty tee-shirt and blue jeans. He was bald save for a fringe of white hair at the rim of his skull and a heavy moustache. At first I thought of the fabled reverend, the guardian of Jacob's spiritual life, but quickly realized otherwise. Surely a man of God would have greater sartorial self-awareness. The man nodded at me and pointed at his son. "He giving you trouble?" Then he looked exclusively at the boy. "Jacob, we waiting down yonder, son! Ain't you done yet? You think we got all day to wait on you?" As the man excoriated his son, I stared at him, the father, and left the specific dilemma unfolding right outside my office for a more general consideration of Mr. Lee, whom I had not met and did not know. Yet I did know him. He was a bully, one of the long line of that certain type of man and boy: cruel, humorless, hairy-knuckled, perpetually scowling, intellectually vacuous, sometimes hard-muscled and lean, sometimes corpulent: who had given obstacles to people like me: non-athletic, non-assuming, book-loving, introverted. They did us physical harm, of course, but worse: they turned what we loved and endeavored to do into general weakness and waste. We wilted under their muscles, their bulk, their sharp-toothed grimaces, their wild-eyed, loveless stares. It was an age-old tableaux – strong boy towering over weak boy in the schoolyard, with the eyes of the curious and inert looking on. They had bloodied me, yes, but I had wiped away the blood, stood up, walked on, carried on, till I was here, where I could give to young people what I had loved best and what Mr. Lee's kind had tried to take from me. Here the scene played out again, the old pattern, right in front of me, the father chastising the boy with a harshness out of proportion to the offense, the son absorbing it with tilted head. I didn't suddenly love Jacob Lee for enduring his father's tirade. I still, probably, did not even like him. But I knew him now, really knew him. We shared a kind of blood and were as much related as the son and father, in our own way.

I stepped out of my office, as though to referee, to put a stop to the one-sided verbal melee.

"Mr. Lee," I called into the maelstrom. The father stopped to watch me. *With those blank, loveless eyes – the eyes of a brute.* "It's all right, sir, really. Jacob's not taking up my time."

The blanks suddenly filled with disbelief. After a moment the man said, "Well, he's taking up mine. I don't keep the hours of no college professor." And he laughed his hollow, harsh laugh that described so eloquently his hatred of anything he did not understand. I looked at his son.

"Of course, Jacob. You may turn in your paper tomorrow. Take your time, son. Take all the time you need."

The Ghost in The Tower
An Exercise in the Fantastic
by Will McMillan

AT FIRST I WASN'T SURE if I dreamed it or if it was some food-or-caffeine-or-liquor induced hallucination. Maybe I drifted off. (Faculty meetings can be so soporific.) All I knew was, in the corporeal world or the phantasmagoric, the ghost of Tad Cafferty stood before my colleagues and me clear as day.

Mortality suited him. He looked good. It was the dead of winter, but he wore a bright-green, short sleeve polo shirt and cotton slacks. There was no gray in his hair or beard as there had been in the years before he died. He stood straight, giving no indication of the Marfan's we speculated about, the condition we were sure had led to the heart condition. He looked spry and as dapper as he had always aspired to be.

Dr. Shipley, chair of the Academic Affairs Committee,

had just commenced his report on the alarming rate of grade inflation at the college when Tad appeared in our midst.

"Tad!" Dr. Chambers, chair of the entire Faculty Organization, gasped at the sight of the man who had served longer at Compton U. than he had (and the only one with more wives and more divorces in that long academic trajectory).

It was as though Tad had come back to us after a long hiatus, and all we had to do was offer him up his old chair at the table to make things as they had once been.

All his former colleagues called Tad's name in tones of surprise, happiness, even relief. No one shuddered or backed away reflexively. But Tad had eyes for only one person in the room at the moment: me. He stared at me and shook his head with that opprobrious stare he always made by biting one side of his lower lip and allowing the other side of his mouth to remain still, as though he were trying to contain unendurable pain.

"Will McMillan!" was all he said at first. It was a question and an exclamation.

Tad Cafferty had been my colleague, my mentor, my friend, my enemy. In a way he had been a brother to me and a father as well, although my own daddy had been (and still is) alive and kicking and very much a force for good in my life. Tad it was who had suggested my looking into teaching at CU upon my unemployed return from Washington, D.C., as an assistant to a retiring South Carolina congressman.

Tad it was who took me into his confidence and, in the deep dark hours of weekend nights in his home, clutching tumblers of Glenlivet and stogies the size of babies' arms, regaled me with tales of our colleagues' peccadilloes:

Chambers and his lechery
Shipley and his pedantry
Delaney and his booze
Blitch and her girlfriends
Laughlin and his parsimony
Hayes and his gambling
Deal and his pettiness
Hall and his pornography

It was Cafferty who brought authors unknown to me – Powell and Hamsun and Green and Hanley – and made me view the world less with the benefit of my rose-colored spectacles and gave me a cynicism from which I am still trying to recover. And it was Tad who, when I brought out my own small book of stories and had a modest local success with it, went around telling anyone who would listen that he had edited the book from a mass of inchoate prose into something publishable. When I went in behind him refuting the claim as best I could, he grew vicious and belittled me and even went to Dean Poshard to complain of my indifference in the classroom.

That was shortly before the aneurysm that came in the night and took him away.

Now, weeks later, he stood facing his old colleagues

with an accusatory finger pointed at me.

"Will McMillan?" he repeated in agonized tones. "You're still here? You shouldn't be. You're young. Go now while you can. If you stay, you'll die. You'll up end like these." The finger shook at everyone else. "Bitter, petty, irrelevant. Hating the thing you profess to love. Hating those you are professing to. Hating those with whom you profess. Look around you, Will. Look at each face here. It is a mask of bile hiding fear and jealously and despair. They hate each other. They hate you. They hate the young ones who come to them everyday expecting erudition and enlightenment and go away laughing at what fools they just wasted their time with. They hate Shakespeare and Copernicus and Jefferson and Plato and any other soul lucky enough not to have been trapped in this Ivory Tower. They wake up every morning full of contempt, the greatest reserved for themselves. It's the repetition of routine that's done it to them. The pursuit of the irrelevant and the ephemeral. It's the obsession with red tape. The reducing of everything, even the simplest human impulse, to theory. I don't have to give you examples now of how they tricked and bad mouthed each other and tried to sabotage each other's projects and tarnish their reputations. You know. You have been the target of it yourself with that little book came out.

"But if you get away now, it won't infect you. You can heal. You can keep something of your soul. If you go now!"

He said no more but remained standing staring at me imploringly, and I stared back, just as agonized, before I could say, "But it's easy! It's all so easy!"

But Tad was gone, and I had spoken the words to my colleagues who watched me closely, with concern, even alarm, which again made me believe I had dreamed all this in the midst of our gathering and had ended the whole thing with my cry of protest. I blushed deeply then saw them stare at each other with the same perplexity with which they had just regarded me. Had we then, really, truly shared the vision?

No one spoke to confirm such a thing. No one said anything. After another moment of silence, during which I couldn't help but feel that we had been frozen out of some moment in time, Dr. Shipley cleared his throat, made the pretense of shuffling the papers before him, and resumed his report.

II

"Do you ever dream of Tad Cafferty?"

This was Vince Delaney, professor of economics at the school. After the faculty organization meeting he and I had convened to a small sandwich shop a couple of blocks down from CU.

Of course the question startled me.

"Why do you ask?"

He chuckled. "Well, two reasons. First it seems like

almost everyone else on faculty has been visited by the man's revenant. Being a man of numbers, I took a poll. You're the last one I've asked."

"Everyone else said yes?"

"I suppose it's natural. He hasn't been gone that long. And goodness knows when he was alive he was certainly a powerful force on campus. For good and bad. I guess we haven't quite cleansed him out of our systems yet." Delaney took a moment to recount instances of Tad Cafferty's famous temper, his impish humor, his genuine brilliance.

Our food arrived shortly afterwards, and I still had not answer Delaney's initial question. Instead I asked one of my own. "You said there were two reasons you asked me if I have dreamed about Tad. What's the second?"

Delaney stirred sweetener in his coffee then shook out a paper napkin and made a bib from it to hide his silk blue tie.

"You started at the meeting today. Like you had come out of some kind of trance. Automatically my Tad Cafferty Dream Radar started blipping."

I still didn't answer him. "Have the others told you what they've dreamed?"

"Yes. Most of them are what you expect. Grinning, leering appearances. Tad expressing his jealousy of those of us who actually finished our Ph.Ds and made reputations for ourselves beyond Compton."

"He was jealous?"

"Well, not ostensibly. But that is how we have all interpreted the dreams. It's no secret what Tad felt about most of us. It came out of his resentment at not having been promoted because of his lack of a doctorate degree." He stopped and eyed me briefly with quiet concern. I too, of course, held no terminal degree. When he saw I was unscathed, he went on.

"Apparently Irma Blitch's dream was the most traumatic. She seemed truly shaken by it. She said Tad visited her in the library of her home – I'm talking about Irma's dream now – and proceeded to tear down all the volumes from the shelves, yelling 'Fraud! Fraud!' He turned to her and kept repeating 'Fraud! They'll soon find you out!' She didn't tell me what she thought he meant by that. But she was certainly shaken up by it, whatever it was. Visibly so. Pales as a ..a…well, as a ghost."

We ate without speaking for a while. Then Delaney put down his sandwich and smiled at me, as though he knew I was trying to avoid something.

"So you never answered me."

"Hm?"

"I asked if you'd dreamed about Cafferty, and you never answered me."

I thought only a moment before I said, "No. I haven't dreamed about Tad. He and I were close. At least until the end. He's still too much a part of my conscious life to haunt my dreams."

III

My lie to Delaney bothered me. It followed me from lunch to my office to my late afternoon freshman studies class back to my office and then home. In its irritating way it seemed prophetic of what Cafferty had warned me of in his "visitation" that morning. I was becoming one of *them*, my colleagues, duplicitous at the drop of a hat, with their low regard for the truth. It was a slippery slope. Soon all the other moral and intellectual failings would crowd behind, the bitterness, the envy, the resentment, the growing distaste for the subject I had proclaimed to love, the poisonous contempt for my students.

I thought of my rejoinder to Cafferty's entreaty – "But it's so easy!" – which made it all the worse. This was moral and intellectual laxity at its most pitiful to allow myself to be swept along in something because it required only a minimum of exertion. But it was true. I had wedged myself into a nice little sinecure there at the school and by that time could practically run the classes by rote. The routine was set, it could be – and often was – performed on autopilot: find a theme, I'd tell them semester after semester, discover your thesis, introduction, body, conclusion. In the literature class the syllabus was set in stone, with the same authors, the same selections, the same discussions and little or no variation. And the freshman studies class? What a joke! We could easily spend an hour and fifteen minutes talking about anything else but freshmen or studies and usually did.

So, I thought presently, what happens when all this repetition becomes much too unbearable? What will I do then for my jollies? Lie about my colleagues? Lie about myself to my students about my place in the literary pantheon? Make up war exploits? Take heavily to the bottle? Inveigle coeds into licentious assignations?

Like you, Cafferty.

It suddenly dawned on me and made me furious, so much so I spoke aloud.

"Who do you think you are, Tad Cafferty, coming back here to accuse others of your own sins? Four wives. Years wasted on drugs and alcohol you could have spent writing your poems and editing the little magazines you wanted to edit. A penchant for the pettiness you've accused others of. What nerve, even for a dead man! You're a hypocrite, Tad! A hypocrite!" I banged my desk hard with fist, one, two, three good times.

On any tableaux representing the Seven Deadly Sins, it would be easy to fit Tad Cafferty's likeness. Sloth, gluttony, envy....Tad could have been the poster child for any of them.

My wife appeared at the door. "Will, are you all right? Who are you talking to?"

I smiled at her, and I can only imagine how diabolic my grin looked.

"He couldn't become a decent human being even after

he died," I told her. "Can you believe that?"

IV

That next morning we got news of Irma Blitch's suicide. She asphyxiated in her garage.

To our greater shock we discovered a long note explaining her action which she had emailed to all the faculty simultaneously. In it she admitted that much of her forthcoming book-length study on "gender-switching" in the fiction of Virginia Woolf, to be published with much fanfare by a prestigious university press up north, had been largely cribbed from the work of other scholars she had found in obscure feminist and literary journals. Much of it had been lifted verbatim. She knew that when she had been found out for such dishonesty, it would mean the end of her career. "And my work," she wrote, "is all I have." The shame, she concluded, was already to great too bear.

Only one of my colleagues ventured forth with a cynical response. This was Laughlin, a fellow English instructor. "Gender-switching? Virginia Woolf?" he wrote me in a private note. "Good God! Maybe ol' Irma did us all a favor when she sucked down that carbon monoxide."

I called Delaney right away. It sounded as though he had been drinking but had been sobered by the news. "Well, Irma always griped about getting out of Compton. Looks like she finally did it. Not sure *this* is the way she intended to do it. But, hey, now she has all the fame she craved all these years."

I asked him about the other faculty's dreams of Tad Cafferty, for specific renderings of them. His own, he admitted, involved Tad's challenging him to a drinking contests with interminable rows of shot glasses lined up on a non-ending table in an endless, single-lit hall. The winner was in no doubt. He, Delaney, the loser, suffered an ignominious, ugly defeat that featured disfiguring bloating.

"And you mean to say, Will, you haven't had your Tad Cafferty nightmare?"

I wanted to say yes, I really did. He was now my best friend at the university. I didn't want to prevaricate and one day lose his trust. But I did, because I was afraid admission would make the dream, and all it implied, come to pass.

"No."

Delaney paused a moment. "Well, then. You're lucky. You must have escaped the curse." Then he laughed so hard he made himself choke.

Dreadful news followed tragic, two-fold.

Three days after Irma Blitch's suicide, Dr. George Hall, professor of comparative religion at the school, was arrested at his home for possession of child pornography. A week before he had taken his personal computer in for repair. The technician inspecting the machine found a massive number of files containing such material. And that afternoon a CU student, a sophomore and student government president, filed a complaint with Dean Poshard accusing Dr. Hector Chambers, history professor, of sexual harassment, claiming he had made a lewd suggestion to her following class and had even placed his hand on her buttocks. When she attempted to refuse his advances, the student continued, Chambers became even more aggressive.

At once news organs from around the area and as far away as Charleston descended upon the school in regards to these sequential tragedies. Dean Poshard appeared on television amidst a small battalion of microphones jabbed into his face, pale and haggard. He nevertheless put on a good front for the media, assuring them that the CU community was coherent and united and ready to face the challenges posed by these unfortunate occurrences. It helped, I suppose, that Poshard was a biology doctorate; such background, and his own ill-concealed atheism, gave him the necessary, convincing dispassion. At the emergency faculty meeting, however, held at the end of the week, he seemed anything but confident about what had transpired. He looked as confused and bewildered as the rest of us and stuttered through his brief speech about "faculty perseverance" and the "tenets of the Enlightenment" being more relevant than ever at this moment. He also mentioned the need not to read anything into the proximity of Blitch's suicide and Hall's arrest and the accusation against Chambers. His attempt at rationalizing did not work. The feeling stood palpable in the room that we, the remaining faculty, shared a terrible secret among ourselves, the secret of the simultaneous dreams, the nightmares starring our departed colleague, Tad Cafferty, and what those dreams might mean for our very survival.

When the meeting broke, Atkinson, economics, approached me and leaned in with a whisper almost anguished. "Vince says you haven't dreamed of Cafferty. Is that true? If so, how can that be?"

I didn't answer him. I left to find Delaney in his office.

"What did Hall dream?" I asked him. "And Chambers? Did they tell you?"

Delaney nodded with a brief laugh. "God, I need a drink!" He removed his wire-rim glasses, ran his hand over his face, and stared at me a moment. "Hall said Cafferty came into his bedroom dressed in a cassock and surplice. Cafferty? The consummate atheist? Dressed as a priest? Anyway Hall was in bed, and Cafferty sat down beside him with a stack of unidentifiable objects in his laps, and he suddenly began to pelt Hall with them."

"Hall didn't say what they were?"

"Not until I kept at him."

"And what were they?"

"Pictures."

"Pictures?"

"Yes."

"Of what?"

Delaney laughed again and bent toward the lower

drawer on the right-hand side of his desk where, I knew, he had hidden away a flask of Wild Turkey. "Come on, Will. You know what Hall was into. And it just got him arrested."

"And Chambers?"

"Hector said in his dream Tad met him in a very elegant restaurant for supper. And he brought with him a pair of unexpected guests. An elderly man and a teenage girl that he held by the hand."

My quiet, persistent stare asked the question for me.

Delaney went on. "Nabokov."

"The author of *Lolita*?"

"Well, then, you know who the girl was."

V

Later in the evening, at home, at supper with my wife I broached the subject of leaving academia for at least the time being.

Paula laughed. "To do what? No, I don't mean to make fun. But what else are you cut out to do? Hm? Go back into the political thicket? I don't think so. There's not much promise these days for a Yellow Dog Democrat in Washington or South Carolina. No. You are where you belong."

Paula was neither a Compton native nor a native Carolinian, but she had come to love both. Perhaps she had prematurely taken my notion as a suggestion we leave the area altogether. Her calm patronizing more than irritated me; it was alarming, another totem of Cafferty's predictions. I didn't speak or eat for a while. Paula watched me.

"You're spooked by the awful things that have been happening on campus, aren't you? You think you're the 'next in line.'" She quoted the phrase with her fingers.

That is when I came out to her with the dream of Tad Cafferty and the fact my colleagues had had their own Cafferty dreams, and to some extent three of the dreams had materialized into tragedy for the dreamers. Then I sat back and waited for Paula's response.

She took her time, still eating, and didn't speak until she had wiped her mouth with her napkin. "There's a lot of negative energy up there at the school right now. For whatever reason. It happens to every place. It's cyclical. It's like money markets. Up and down. Back and forth. Good and bad. Things are stable for a while. Then they destabilize then get stable again eventually. It's natural. It happens in any sort of enterprise, business or academic. You can't blame these things on dreams or signs or portents or visitations by the dead. You all have just entered a mutual period of negative energy. It will pass. It always does." Paula prided herself on her rationalism. This time, however, I wasn't so sure about her.

When I insisted that, real or not, the Cafferty dream might contain a fair share of wisdom about my situation, she lost her rationality and bristled. She accused me of wanting to "mooch" off her again, as I had when I'd been in between jobs.

"Nonsense" was all I said.

Then she said I was trying to "sabotage" the good set up she had in town – her job, her social circle, her community responsibilities which had brought her recognition in the local papers. (*Sabotage*. Wasn't it a word Tad had used in admonishing me in the dream? The very thought sent a buckling chill over me.)

"I didn't say we had to leave Compton!" I tried to interject, but she would not relent. Instead she stormed on, rehashing old instances of my sloth and indifference in all the years she had known me – the job opportunities I had let get past, the manuscripts I had begun and not finished, blaming this non-productiveness on writer's block and the despair that everything had been said before, that the world did not need another novel limning Deep South. "You can't imagine," she said, "how your discouragement affected me. It took me years to recover and regain my own sense of initiative." All I could do was sit and listen until she gave out, and her peroration ended in a series of low sobs and staccato sniffles. Then she was quiet and eventually stood and left me for the upstairs and bed.

I remained alone in the dark in the den. I had had a few glasses of wine at supper. Even in the heat emanating from the argument with Paula, I was exhausted and near-sleep. Still a succession of wild ideas fell over themselves in my brain. I would leave, get up and go, without even packing.

I wouldn't even tender my resignation from the school. Let them panic over who would finish out my classes for the term? But where would I go? Atlanta was three hours down the road. Charlotte an hour northeast. Florida eight south. I had loved the mountains of eastern Tennessee since boyhood. There was D.C. Or New York. There was a great big wide world of possibilities for any man with the guts to look into them. Any of these places would be ideal locations for weeks, even months of leisurely dissipation until diminishment of income necessitated employment.

In the middle of these ruminations Tad Cafferty appeared and took a place beside me on the couch.

"Defeated already" was all he said.

"No."

"Yes. She's beaten you down as she always does."

"No. If you're in my dreams, you're in my thoughts, and you know what I was thinking."

"Idle thoughts. You've thought them before and not done a thing to realize them."

"This time!"

He laughed and shook his head. "This time. Next year. Next week. In ten years. Maybe twenty. And pretty soon time is out, and you have no more options." There was silence for a moment; then he resumed. "If your wife is the obstacle to your living the life you should be living…" He stopped again, prompting me to watch him full on, to stare into his dead, glittering eyes. "…then you must get rid of your wife." From his right flank, as though from the couch itself, he produced a stainless steel blade, twelve inches long, with half that width and with a dazzlingly bright reflection that showed my wide, sad, disbelieving eyes. The tip of the blade was no bigger than a teardrop, but my oh my, how *sharp* it must have been! As I watched my eyes in the knife's surface, Cafferty reminded me of the dead ends that awaited me if I did not act: the creative and the emotional cul-de sacs. He spoke with such inevitability and authority that to refute or refuse him would be fatal folly. He passed the blade, handle first, into my hand.

"But I'll be like Blitch. Like Hall. Like Chambers," I said through tears.

"You'll be *free*," he hissed. "They're free. No longer prisoners in the Ivory Tower."

Paula lay sleeping on her back. An outside streetlight showed her face clearly. At nearly forty she still retained the angular beauty, highlighted by her high cheekbones and red, rose-full lips, that had attracted me to her more than fifteen years before. There was no gray in her long blond hair. It took only a few minutes to remember all the joys and the angst that had followed us in the years since college, the kinds of scenes similar to the one that had unfolded between us that evening usually followed by the sweetest sort of reconciliation.

"Don't worry!" Tad Cafferty said behind me, with no attempt to whisper or hide the fact he was there. "Do it. Get it over with then get out. Be free."

I raised the blade slowly, wondering whether to deliver it into that beautiful face or to go lower and plant it between her neck and clavicle bone. I decided on randomness and brought the blade down quickly. Paula's eyes opened. She caught my hand. The knife was not there. Her hands went to my face. She rose and took me into her arms.

"It's all right, Will. It's okay. I'm not mad. We'll work it out. We always do."

The Unlikely Bridegroom

For Geraldine Page, in memory and gratitude

ONCE, MANY YEARS AGO, there lived in Compton County a wealthy farmer named Angus Henshawe. He had lived almost his whole grown-up life alone, tending his peach crop and raising his livestock, in a house in the country several miles from the county seat. He had no friends to speak of and not many acquaintances save for the serious and sullen-faced men who came into his home and drew up contracts for his peaches and made all his financial transactions. He did not go to church or attend the theatre and was not invited into the homes of others, for while his money made him well-known to everyone in Compton, he was considered aloof and miserly and not at all suitable for social functions or even simple friendship. "All he cares about is peaches and profits" was the assessment made of him by most folks there, and it was true: peaches and livestock and the tending of his finances had been his whole life for as long as he could remember.

One morning, however, as the sun began to insinuate

itself into the mud-gray sky, Mr. Henshawe rose from his bed, went to his bedroom window, and in the blue darkness of the new day said to himself, out loud, "I believe it is time I found me a wife."

He made the decision the same way he would have decided to buy a new coat to work in or a ploughshare, with great deference to practicality. His problem was that his cook, Miss Ada Jennings, was getting older and less conscientious in doing her job; in the past few weeks Mr. Henshawe had discovered strange objects in his food: eggshells in his okra, feathers in his mince pie, and a thimble in his soup. Also, his home had fallen into disrepair; dust had mounted the furniture in a fine white wave, cobwebs hung from the ceiling like lacey gauze, and the wallpaper was slipping from the walls. Mr. Henshawe, after all was a businessman, and could hardly be expected to look after the upkeep of his home, since he spent the greater part of the day out in the fields overseeing his hands or shut away in an office dealing with distributors. And being frugal, to the point of stinginess, over money, he would not, could not, be persuaded to hire someone else to do it and instead let it all hang as it was, so to speak.

He reasoned then that what he needed was a sturdy, steady, tireless woman, a lover of cooking and cleaning who would be as dedicated a penny-pincher as he. But he knew, busy as he was, that he could not take the natural route to courtship. That would mean making the acquaintance of a woman, wooing her for the customary and proper year and a half, and making extensive wedding arrangements. For none of these steps could he take the time. After all, it was the middle of summer and his peach crop was shortly to come in. There was no question that he would have to be there through the harvesting. So, as many men and women had done before him, he decided to hire the services of what in those days was referred to by the elegant term *marriage broker* but which today is more commonly known as a matchmaker. In this case the marriage broker was Miss Eleanor Pickle, who, despite her profession, lived alone in a large house in town. Mr. Henshawe had seen her discreet advertisement in the newspaper and had once heard one of his field-hands praise her services to the moon for the woman with which she had paired him.

So that afternoon Mr. Henshawe bathed, shaved, and dressed carefully (he had trimmed his own hair the night before), and leaving instructions with his foreman, Jack Weston, he set out for Miss Pickle's home. Along the way he hardened within himself the resolve that Miss Pickle find for him a woman of practical mindset, one suited to work and of small ambitions when it came to spending money. "I want her to work like a horse," he rehearsed to himself as his pick-up truck moved toward Compton. "To care only for the upkeep of my home and farm so that it will be easy for me to harvest my peaches and raise my livestock." She must not care for glamour or be enamored of glamorous things, he went on, nor must she be given to fits of anger or demands for passion. Work, and work alone, must be the thing for which she lives.

At her door, Miss Pickle regarded the gentleman-bachelor with unmasked surprise.

"Mr. Henshawe, is that you? Well, yes, it is Mr. Henshawe! Mr. Angus Henshawe! Well, hello there! Is there anything I can do for you? Are you having automobile trouble? Need to use my telephone?" She was a short, plump woman of fifty years or thereabouts with a fair complexion made lighter by her choice of dark garments. She had a wrinkleless face and hair that, through some kindness of time or trick of beautician's hand, had remained rusty brown.

Being a man as frugal with words as he was with money, he took a moment to answer her. "I've come for your services," he said finally and left it at that.

The woman started again and leaned closer to him. "Come again," she said.

Mr. Henshawe, irritated now that he would have to repeat himself, stalled another long moment, then raising his head and in a very long, unmistakable voice, said, "I want you to find me a wife!"

"Of course," the woman replied and invited him into her home.

"I must admit," she told him once she had him seated in her brocaded and brightly carpeted parlor and had set tea and a plate of sugar cookies before him on a table of blinding cherry finish, "that you, Mr. Henhawe, would have been about the last person in the world I would have expected to turn up on my doorstep seeking assistance in the, uh, the *marital* sphere."

"A time comes for everything," Mr. Henshawe replied.

"Indeed it does. What a wise thing to have said. Well, let us cut to the chase, as they say, Mr. Henshawe. Just what sort of woman are you seeking?"

The question startled Mr. Henshawe, although he knew it was coming. He had a rehearsed reply that for some reason would not rise to his lips. He took another cookie and chewed it. He was stalling. Something was happening in him, something strange and unwelcome. He wished the question had not occurred, that it would disappear from the room just like smoke, but Miss Pickle stood above him, kindly waiting, face polite but firm. So he calmed himself, set down his tea cup, and as simply and quietly as he could, he told her, "I would like somebody young and pretty."

Now this rejoinder startled Mr. Henshawe as much as it did Miss Pickle – perhaps more. It was not the answer he had prepared on his way to town, and indeed he had not thought until that very moment to say such a thing. It was as though another voice had interceded his own and made the request. He started to correct himself, to say, "I meant, somebody strong and sturdy and practical," but his voice would not allow a sequel. A clamp had been placed on his vocal chords.

"Young and pretty?" Miss Pickle asked above him.

"Young and pretty," Mr. Henshawe returned.

"Young and pretty," Miss Pickle said again as though in final confirmation. "Of course. It is what most men want. But do you have a specific type in mind? After all, young is young, but beauty is in the eye of the beholder. Is there a certain kind of prettiness you fancy? Blonde or brunette? Short or tall? Thin or big-boned?"

"No. Just young and pretty."

"Should she be college-educated or play a musical instrument? Should she know how to cook and make her own clothes? Should she come from a good family and speak a foreign language?"

Mr. Henshawe shook his head back and forth, back and forth. "Young and pretty, young and pretty."

"Good enough," Miss Pickle replied. "You have given me a large canvas on which to work. Which is a good thing, Mr. Henshawe. I thank you for that." She asked him to sit where he was while she went upstairs to check on what she referred to as her "records."

He continued to eat cookies and drink tea while she was away, and when she returned, only a few minutes later, she was carrying an elegant, cream-colored portfolio the size of a portmanteau which sat on the floor near the coffee table. From this satchel she fetched out an endless number of manila folders and stacked them on the coffee table like sets of dirty dishes.

"As you can see, Mr. Henshawe, I have quite a selection of candidates to choose from. Women from every walk of life, with every conceivable background." She opened the first folder on top of the stack.

"Miss Paulette Broaderman. Isn't she pretty? Look at those eyes. You can look into those eyes and see right into her pretty soul. She attends business school at night in Spartanburg and works at a dry good store during the day. Think about it. Good looks and industry all in one woman. It seems she would be highly compatible with a hard-working man like yourself –"

"No," Mr. Henshawe replied.

"No?"

Mr. Henshawe shook his head.

"Well, let's look at another." She opened a neighboring folder.

"Miss Mildred Sartor. She's a seamstress, an apprentice to Miss Lynette Haven. You don't know her, do you? No? She's not as pretty as the other one, but she is young and she works hard. I do know that. In fact, she made the dress I am wearing this very moment, and I have felt nothing but joy all day long, happiness I attribute in great part to this dress and its masterful – " She stopped, for she saw that Mr. Henshawe was expressing his disinterest with a glare. "Let's try another," she said.

She opened a third folder. Mr. Henshawe glanced

down at the revealed photograph and felt something stir immediately within him. The photograph showed a pert young face, small-mouthed, bright-eyed, and fresh – with a tiny nose and delicately cut chin and glowing blonde hair that curled at the shoulders. His heart, which up to that moment had been filled with peach fuzz and pig mud and banknotes and summer heat and winter cold, broke in two.

"Miss Mary Elizabeth Frances Jenkins," Miss Pickle announced, with such regality of tone that for a moment Mr. Henshawe expected – or halfheartedly hoped – that the girl herself would walk into the room.

"She is a voice student, or was one. I'm a little fuzzy about her occupation. Her mother teaches piano. *That* I know. They live in town. But they are not from here originally. They came to Compton from Bantam, Georgia, just southeast of Atlanta. They've lived in Compton for two years. That's how long they have been coming to me too, seeking a spouse for young Mary Elizabeth. They are terribly precise in their requirements. Very steadfast and resolute. I have to say – "

"This one," Mr. Henshawe said, looking up from the photograph with bright and glassy eyes.

"What's that, Mr. Henshawe?"

"This girl here. This is the one I want to meet." He spoke with a muted joy, an emotion unfamiliar to him and one which he had some problem controlling.

"Mr. Henshawe? Mr. Henshawe, are you sure?"

He nodded.

"Well, I was just going to tell you that these women are terribly straightforward in what they require from a potential — "

"This is the one," Mr. Henshawe broke in.

"Now, Mr. Henshawe. This is a very important decision you are making. Are you sure you would not like to look at another record? I have many others."

Mr. Henshawe glanced once more at Mary Elizabeth Frances Jenkins's photograph and shook his head. This was the one. Her name had already inscribed itself on his heart.

"I'm sure," he answered. "When can I see her?"

"Oh not for a few days, I'm afraid. After all, I must inform the other party of your interest. She must be given time to consider it. I'll be in touch with you as soon as they make a decision."

And then Miss Pickle asked Mr. Henshawe if he would be good enough to answer some questions about himself and his business. She would need to keep a file on him as well, now that he was one of her clients. Mr. Henshawe was not a man anxious to talk about himself and gave in only after Miss Pickle insisted, saying that negotiations between himself and Miss Jenkins would be impossible without a record. But he absolutely refused to have his picture taken.

It was another week before Mr. Henshawe heard from Miss Pickle, as she had assured him. She told him that the

Jenkinses had looked over his record, had listened with pleasure about his interest in Mary Elizabeth, and said they would be delighted to meet with him in Miss Pickle's home.

"Can I come today?" Mr. Henshawe had asked eagerly.

"Oh no. Quite impossible. I have many things to do before the meeting. Many details to attend to. Let's count on tomorrow evening, around suppertime. What do you say?"

After hanging up with Miss Pickle that afternoon, Mr. Henshawe did something he rarely ever did: he went into town and splurged on a professional haircut and shave. Then, even more astoundingly, he bought himself a new suit of clothes. That evening he sat in the bathtub for two hours, hoping to rid himself unquestionably of the smells of peaches and dirt and sweat; when he got out he dried off, dressed for bed, and went into his room, where the light was out and moonlight streamed through the window. There, on a hanger near the window stood the coat, moving slightly from side to side as though someone had grazed it. He moved towards it and stood in the moonlight to stop its rocking, and when he touched the cuff of the left sleeve, he felt suddenly very ashamed of the idea of the enterprise upon which he had just embarked with Miss Pickle and of the swift and irrational changes which had overcome his normally practical heart and mind. It was as though some neglected part of himself, some hidden impulse of which he had not even been aware, had gained control of his vocal apparatus in Miss Pickle's parlor and made him say, "Young and pretty" when he'd actually meant "Stout and frugal." He was a businessman and a man of deliberation who weighed the values of things, the advantages of one thing over another, and their disadvantages too, until he could think about them clearly and come to a decision. But in Miss Pickle's parlor last week he had done no such thing. He had seen Mary Elizabeth Jenkins's picture and immediately said, "That one. That is the one I want to meet." And what was a man like him, a man who had known nothing for more than fifty years but work and sweat and worry doing chasing a girl like this one? A girl young enough to be his daughter! Why had he not told Miss Pickle the kind of woman he wanted would be plain and work-loving? He was a farmer, not some Romeo. What would a young and pretty face do him in harvesting peaches?

Then he thought about his life – all fifty-six years of it – and the hardships and the deprivations and the struggles and the swindlings by distributors and the peach-killing winters and the runaway horses that had to be caught and brought home and the blue and pink bloody ugliness of pig birth and the discovery of wolf-ravaged cowhides and the prevalence everywhere of mud and dirt, everywhere, everywhere, everywhere, as though the whole world had obtained that same dispiriting gray hue. And it was as though that same hidden impulse which had made him say "Young and pretty" to Miss Pickle had told him, "Enough of this is enough. You need some beauty now in your life. Some sweetness. You need a play-pretty for once instead of a plough." Mary Elizabeth had come to him as something strange but wonderful. There had been no paradigm of such beauty in his life before this. He was unacquainted with movie stars. He did not go to movies. Movies were an unnecessary expense and not crucial to the operation of Henshawe Farms. So when he saw Mary Elizabeth he thought he might have had the same sensation Adam felt in the Garden of Eden at the arrival of Eve: she was wondrous and new and indefinable in any language common to him. The world had just begun for him.

He couldn't help it: when he thought of Mary Elizabeth and how beautiful that photograph made her out to be, how purely, simply beautiful, and then thought what his life had been before he saw that picture, he felt something rise slowly in him, rise until it caught in his throat and chest and hung there for a while; then it fled him, this new emotion, this hungering for beauty, as quickly as it had come. Indeed Mr. Henshawe would have sworn he could see it tearing across the moon-bright yard into the woods.

Miss Pickle opened the door of her home. "Mr. Henshawe, you made it!" she exclaimed. "You are here!" she went on, clapping her hands near her throat and letting out an audible sigh, as though there had been some question as to whether or not Mr. Henshawe would show for his appointment. "And don't you smell good too!"

That afternoon Mr. Henshawe had soaked himself again in the tub and then dusted himself with talcum powder, sprinkling it on his arms, neck, even his legs and feet. He had stood in front of the bathroom mirror and slicked down his hair with a thick white gel he had got from the barbershop, hoping to make it glint when touched by light (he thought such a display would impress a young girl); then he took a large-toothed comb and drew a long white line down the side of his head so deep that he swore he had felt the wind whistle through it on his way to Miss Pickle's.

Miss Pickle took him by the arm and gently guided him into the foyer. "This could be a big night for you," she whispered, edging closer to him with the familiarity of a sister. Mr. Henshawe, anxious as a child, glanced in the direction of the parlor – he could see only the corner of its left wall where a hutch closet stood bright with porcelain bric-a-brac.

"I think we should go and say hello to the others," Miss Pickle suggested, nudging him forward.

He turned to face the room fully, and when he looked straight ahead, his vision blurred at once, as though he had looked right into the face of the sun, and it seemed to take forever for his eyes to clear. When they did, when he was sure he was seeing what he was seeing, he broke into a chilly sweat that made the talcum go rancid. Sitting before him, not more than a few feet, was the girl from the photograph, Mary Elizabeth Frances Jenkins. When he first spotted her he had not recognized her, indeed had mistook her for some painting or sculpture, so arranged in her chair she seemed, so well she blended in with the tasteful luxury of Miss Pickle's parlor. But then she had made a small movement, turned her head to her shoulder ever so slightly, and all her features came into familiar and stunning focus.

She was not alone, however. Another woman stood almost directly behind her. But Mr. Henshawe paid her no attention. It was as though all the light in that room from all the lamps reflected in all the mirrors and off all the shiny surfaces had been drawn about Mary Elizabeth's face to the exclusion of everything else. She positively glowed, as had her photograph.

"Mr. Angus Henshawe," Miss Pickle called behind him. He felt her hand on his back, urging him forward into the parlor. Then she stepped in front of him, as though on second thought, so that she was standing in the middle of the floor, a point of neutrality between two gravitational forces. "Mr. Henshawe, it gives me the deepest pleasure to introduce to you to Miss Mary Elizabeth Frances Jenkins and her mother, Miss Veronica Roseanne Latham Jenkins, formerly of Bantam, Georgia, now residents of Compton."

The air stood stiff. Mr. Henshawe nodded feebly and smiled awkwardly and immediately felt himself go red to the scalp. The Jenkins woman, the mother that is, standing behind her daughter, smiled broadly and gave a proud kind of nod which Mr. Henshawe found queenly. The mother was a tall woman in a long black dress of mute design with her dark hair tied behind her head in a bun. Mary Elizabeth sat below her, unmoving and quiet, and merely stared at her own shoes, a pair of dainty, silver slippers.

Miss Pickle seemed pleased with the introduction and told them she would not bother with statistics, as everyone was familiar with everyone else's record. "Now I am going into the kitchen for tea, and while I'm gone I'd like for all of you to take the first, most crucial and sometimes the most difficult step in a prospective courtship: getting acquainted. I want you to stir up a conversation between yourselves, get to know each other and find out what you have in common. It is the only way to begin." She headed for the door but stopped and turned. "Now talk," she cooed and went on her way.

Mr. Henshawe remained standing and stared at the girl, who sat and stared at nothing in the room. He yearned for her to be the one who spoke first, to stir up the conversation; that way he could hear her voice and see her face at the same time, and it would also be a sign that she was really, truly interested in him.

"Mr. Henshawe."

Mr. Henshawe awoke from his thoughts. It was the mother, however, not the daughter, who had called his name. She was moving, coming around the daughter's chair, smiling that queenly smile again, with her long arms extended toward him as though she were going to hug him.

She clasped his hands and heaved a long breath.

"Mr. Henshawe, you have made Mrs. Jenkins's night by coming. Lord yes, you have! She didn't know whether or not she was ever going to marry off this pretty little thing. Yes Lord! Poor old Mrs. Jenkins has been coming to Miss Pickle's agency for two years now, and Miss Pickle's tried to set her little girl up with all kinds of young, good-looking wet ears. Yes Lord! Poets and students and adventurers and what not. All charm, all looks, but no experience, no bank accounts, nothing that really matters. Nothing that shows the mark of a real man of the world, a man in control of all that is around him." She stopped, sighed, gave indication she might faint, then rallied again, all ablaze, eyes and arms spread wide. "Oh Miss Jenkins was beginning to give up all hoping of matching her precious girl with a man of practical mind and heart and means. Yes. Then you came along: Mr. Angus Petit Henshawe: *en-tre-pe-nuer*, established businessman, a cog in the Compton industry, and a leading peach ven-dor in the state of South Carolina. Why, when Mrs. Jenkins saw your profile, she just dropped to her old knees and thanked the Lord Jesus Christ! She did! Didn't she, Miss Pickle?"

Miss Pickle had returned, laden with the tea service. She went to the coffee table and set it down. "What's that?"

"Didn't Mrs. Jenkins say *hallelujah*! when she saw Mr. Henshawe's record?"

Miss Pickle nodded. "Yes, dear. For a moment I

thought you were having a stroke."

"Oh a stroke of luck is what it was! A stroke of fortune, delivered from the hand of the good and the gracious and the almighty Lord himself!"

Mrs. Jenkins broke her grip on Mr. Henshawe and returned to the spot where her daughter sat.

"Just look here," she said, placing her hand on the girl's white-blond head. "Isn't she the prettiest thing? Tell us, Mr. Henshawe, don't you think so? She's like a pic-ture on the wall of a museum, yes. If this were a perfect world, she should walk about framed, she should glide from place to place on a pedestal, such is her deserving. And she knows it too, which is the problem."

"Problem? Why don't you explain to Mr. Henshawe what you mean, dear?" Miss Pickle asked.

"Yes! There isn't a practical bone in this child's body. Why if she could not live off her looks or charm, the poor dear might well starve. That is why it is *im-per-a-tive* that she fall under the tutelage and example of a wise and industrious man such as yourself, Mr. Henshawe. She must learn that nothing is free. She must appreciate the value of the hard-earned coin, the sweat-bought greenback. You are the very man to teach this to her, so that, oh Lord, when she no longer has either you, Mr. Henshawe, or her loving but exasperated mother, she will be able to fend for herself in this treacherous and uncertain world."

"What you're saying, dear," Miss Pickle continued as

she poured tea into small white cups, "is that Mary Elizabeth here has been spoiled by gracious living."

"Oh yes Lord! Spoiled rot-ten! Handed everything. She was a banker's daughter, after all, a child of affluence. But we're not going to talk about the past. We're not going to talk about how Mr. Jenkins got himself mixed up in a bad business deal, how he lost everything and drank himself onto a mortuary slab, how he left his poor wife and daughter nearly destitute, while the daughter still craved the life of a debutante without the necessary means. No, it is too sad a story to be recounted here, in this lovely parlor, at the threshold of this momentous meeting of two perfectly matched people. The past is the past."

Mrs. Jenkins snatched up one of the tea cups from the table, tossed its contents down her throat, then looked again to the ceiling, shaking her head slightly. "Poor old Mrs. Jenkins. Poor, poor thing. What's she has come down to now! Teaching piano to a bunch of fidgety chim-pan-zees! They come in thinking they know EVERYthing in the world about music and bang on those keys like there is no tomorrow. Poor Mrs. Jenkins goes to bed every night with a headache. Oh, Beethoven in the hands of barbarians! But she must do it! She must! To satisfy the material cravings of her only child! But no more! If Mrs. Jenkins cannot instill in this profligate girl the value of hard work, then the job lies with a man such as yourself, Mr. Henshawe." She bowed to him, her arm out and lifted at her side.

"Mr. Henshawe," Miss Pickle said, handing him his tea, "why don't you sit down? You must be tired just standing there." Mr. Henshawe moved to the chair opposite the couch on which Miss Pickle and Mrs. Jenkins had been sitting. He had not, the whole time Mrs. Jenkins had conducted her peroration, taken his eyes off Mary Elizabeth, who was now staring down into her tea.

Miss Pickle lowered her cup. "Mrs. Jenkins, tell Mr. Henshawe how you sang in the Atlanta Opera when you were a girl. Tell him how you sang lead in *Aida* and how they wrote about your performance in the *Constitution* and called you the 'Jenny Lind of Bantam.'"

"Oh, it was quite a time for Mrs. Jenkins," said Mrs. Jenkins, taking the bait. "And the only reason she gave up her musical career was for hearth and home and the raising of this pretty little thing." She indicated her daughter.

"Mr. Henshawe," Miss Pickle said, startling him. "The Jenkinses have agreed to provide us with a bit of musical entertainment this evening. It serves the dual purpose of showing you what a well-rounded girl Mary Elizabeth is. Right, Mrs. Jenkins?"

"Oh, she is a fount of talent and deep feeling, that girl? But so much sensitivity has been lost to the pursuit of material things and ephemeral pleasures."

The girl kept her head down a moment longer then raised it and looked straight at Mr. Henshawe. He had not expected the look and it seared him deeply. Was she saying something to him? It seemed so, but he could not tell for sure.

Both mother and daughter, without further prelude, moved to a small piano perched near a window.

"This will be a treat," Miss Pickle exclaimed, smiling broadly.

"Mr. Henshawe," said the mother, seating herself on the bench, "tonight we will present for your listening pleasure a selection from Verdi's immortal depiction in music of love and loss *Aida*. It is Aida's aria 'O cieli azzuri,' which, translated into English, means 'O blue sky.' In it Aida yearns for her homeland after being captured by the Babylonians. Do you know the opera, Mr. Henshawe? It will break your heart, sir. Yes!" She turned around on the bench to face the keys then glanced back at her daughter standing near her. "Ready, Mary Elizabeth, to let the song possess you?"

The girl nodded and her mother lightly laid her hands upon the keys to begin.

Mr. Henshawe knew nothing about music – any kind of music: opera, hillbilly, big band, jazz, blues, comb and tissue, knee and spoon: music was another of those ornaments of the idle, a luxury for which a workingman/businessman like himself could spare no time. He had a radio in his house, but it was rarely played except for occasional news, and there were no records or a record player. The idea of opera frightened him, made him think of enormous men and women garbed in armor, holding spears and shields, wailing and moaning and hollering at each other as though they were all in great pain. But he tolerated opera *that* night for Mary Elizabeth's sake, because he knew, no matter the *sound* of it, the *sight* of opera would be quite lovely indeed that night.

Mary Elizabeth, as she was wont to do, paid no attention to anyone else while she sang. Her eyes remained fixed on the ceiling, one part of the ceiling, and she would reach her arms out to that section of the ceiling, as though she were drawing her voice from that one spot. Her small body remained still in the long white gown, but her voice moved. It rose and fell, it shivered and shook and trembled perilously, as though there were danger of its toppling over altogether. And the mother stayed right in behind her, hunched over the keyboard like a blacksmith at his anvil, her arms and shoulders bobbing on even the softest notes.

It was a sad song. Mr. Henshawe did not need to know Italian to know that. He could feel the sadness of the song. Near the end of it Mary Elizabeth's voice softened and calmed, pulled back, like a wave on the beach drawing back to the ocean and disappearing. Her upraised arms fell to her sides and she lowered her eyes, and it was over.

Everyone sat still. Then the mother turned on the bench, half-laughing, half-crying, and said, "Now, wasn't that something? If that didn't move you, then you are made of stone for sure!"

"Splendid!" Miss Pickle remarked and turned to Mr. Henshawe. "Didn't you think so, Mr. Henshawe?"

He stammered to respond but could only say, "I think it's probably the prettiest opera song I ever heard. I really wouldn't mind hearing the rest of that opera sometime." He reddened immediately.

Miss Pickle then mentioned that she had a chocolate cake in the kitchen that had yet to be cut and asked Mrs. Jenkins to help her in cutting it. Obviously this was a ploy to leave Mr. Henshawe and Mary Elizabeth alone. Mrs. Jenkins appeared reluctant to do this. She hemmed and hawed a moment and stood frozen in indecision then agreed and disappeared from the parlor behind Miss Pickle, looking behind her at her daughter and Mr. Henshawe with something approaching barely suppressed agony.

They were alone. An enormous silence filled the room, one that threatened to smother Mr. Henshawe. With shyness he regarded the girl. She did not regard him at all but sat and stirred her tea instead.

"I meant what I said about your song," Mr. Henshawe offered finally, before the silence choked him. "It is awful pretty, and I wouldn't mind hearing the rest of it sometime. With you singing it, I mean." Again he went scarlet and looked away a moment.

Mary Elizabeth continued stirring. Mr. Henshawe heard her clear her throat. He looked back. She was watching him, without fear or diffidence.

"I'm afraid you won't get to hear the rest from me because that's the only song I know."

"I'm surprised to hear that. I thought a singer would know lots of songs."

The girl shook her head sadly. A lock of her blonde hair hung loose in the lamplight. "That's the only one I know. Mama says I should pick a song that people will remember, one that will make them cry. I picked that one and worked on it. I don't know any others. I don't care to learn another because I don't care to be a singer." There came another of those painful pauses which had punctuated the evening. The girl ended it. "Sir, do you really want to marry me? Really, deep, deep down?"

The question struck Mr. Henshawe like a cannonball. He fidgeted for an answer, but the girl didn't wait for one.

"What if I said I could never love you? Could you stand it? What if I said I hate peaches and dirt and hogs and would rather be dead than live among them. Could you stand that too? But I hadn't said none of that, have I? Tell me, Mr. Farmer Man, do you really love me? Could you put up with me for long?"

After a moment's hesitation, he answered, "You the prettiest thing I ever laid my eye son."

"That's not an answer. Miss Pickle says you're a clear-headed gentleman, but are you thinking so clearly now?"

She held him with that piercing look that would not allow him to answer her, and frankly, since the first time he had seen the girl's picture a week ago, he did not know what he felt. She marched upon him like a troop of soldiers and seemed to defy him to know what he felt."

"Yes ma'am. I believe so."

"Well, I hope you're right," she replied and laid her soft white head on her hand.

They met in Miss Pickle's parlor a third time and a fourth, and at the end of the fourth Miss Pickle declared, "I believe, my friends, we have come to the point where you no longer need me to steer you along."

"What do you mean, Miss Pickle?" asked Mrs. Jenkins with no small look of concern.

"I mean that I think it is time for Mr. Henshawe and Mary Elizabeth to take off on their own."

And they did. Mr. Henshawe began stopping by the Jenkins' apartment in town to take the girl for a ride in his truck. The mother insisted on riding with them. Fortunately Mr. Henshawe was so happy to be in the presence of the girl, he did not mind this arrangement, even when Mrs. Jenkins insisted on sitting in the front seat with him and leaving Mary Elizabeth in the flatbed with Mr. Henshawe's coat underneath her to keep her from getting soiled. He could still see, by turn of the rearview mirror, Mary Elizabeth's blond curls blown by the wind, and the sight gave him great pleasure.

They rode from sunset to sunrise, up and down the

southeastern wing of Compton County, skirting the town of Selden on the Chester County line; down old dirt roads they went, past old farms and farmhouses, past old sawmills and long stretches of wheatstraw and goldenrod and stark displays of sorry brown soil put to no use at all. And of course they drove past his peach crop. Once he had his supervisor, Jack Weston, line up all his workers on both sides of the road so that when Mr. Henshawe and the Jenkins women went past, they could wave and call to Mary Elizabeth. "Hey, Miss May-ry, how you?" they called out, but she did not wave or call back.

Mr. Henshawe could have gone on like they were going forever. He had the two things he cared about most, the land and Mary Elizabeth, with him simultaneously, and he loved their country drives and country visits. He already felt close to the girl, already considered himself her kin of some sort. But after a week of such excursions, the mother, sitting beside Mr. Henshawe in the truck, said, "Mr. Henshawe, you will pardon Mrs. Jenkins's frankness, but, sir, she believes it is well-nigh time to become serious about things. Now Mrs. Jenkins and Mary Elizabeth love riding in your truck. It is a very nice truck and a very fine truck, the very finest truck of its kind they have so far encountered in Compton County, and your peaches have a kind of celestial loveliness to them lying there in the sun. If time permitted, Mrs. Jenkins would not mind everyday coming out to stare at your peaches. Time does not permit, however. Mary Elizabeth is young, her mother is old, and both the old and the young share the same impatience with things. They want things to happen. Now. If things do not happen in one place, they want to move on to someplace else where things will happen. Do you understand, sir? So," she concluded with a brief sigh, "Mrs. Jenkins must ask you a very crucial question: are you going to marry Mary Elizabeth or not?"

Mr. Henshawe was startled. He slowed his truck a bit. He thought it was a foregone conclusion that he and Mary Elizabeth were going to marry. They had been getting on so well now for over a month. There had been no arguments or misunderstandings between them. Everything had been so *pleasant*.

"Because if you are not," Mrs. Jenkins continued, "then Miss Pickle must be notified of the fact. She will have to bring out the old drawing board. Mrs. Jenkins and Mary Elizabeth will have to bid you a most reluctant farewell and — "

At those words, Mr. Henshawe slammed on the brakes, sending Mrs. Jenkins lurching forward. She glared at him when they were stopped and she had recovered. She opened her mouth to reprimand him for such a jolting reflex.

"Mr. Henshawe," she began with a note of alarm.

"What's wrong up there?" Mary Elizabeth yelled from the back. "What you trying to do, give me whiplash?"

Mr. Henshawe threw open his door and hopped out.

Mrs. Jenkins followed him. "Do not touch that child!

Do not lay a rough hand upon her! It was merely a question!"

Mr. Henshawe had made it to the back of the truck and was lifting himself onto the flatbed. Then he slowed and approached Mary Elizabeth gingerly. He crouched on one knee in front of her.

"Miss Jenkins," he began.

"Who taught you how to drive a truck, a drunk man?"

"Miss Jenkins, I'm not good at all with words, but I will tell you right now – " He stopped again. Mary Elizabeth slid a fist under her chin and watched him speculatively. He wished she had not. Looking at him that way, directly, face to face, she reminded him of the photograph Miss Pickle had shown him that first day. This is the girl in the picture, he thought, and hobbled a bit on his knee.

"What's that?" she asked. "You were going to say something?"

"It's just that I've never….When I saw you that first day at Miss Pickle's, I knew in my heart…oh…I don't have much experience at all in these things and it is hard to come out with what I need to say, but – "

"What are you trying to say? Do you want to marry me or not? If you do, say so. Just come out and say it. If not, say that. Don't worry about being all poetic. Just say it!"

"Will you marry me?"

"I don't know." She glanced away a moment then

looked back. "Depends...."

"Mr. Henshawe! Mr. Henshawe!" Mrs. Jenkins, who had heard this exchange, stood at the back of the truck, pounding on the tailgate. "Mr. Henshawe, Mrs. Jenkins and her daughter have talked it over, and we concluded that before they are able to commit themselves to anything, you should agree to certain terms."

"Like what?" Mr. Henshawe remained on one knee.

"Well, a list has been compiled," and from out of nowhere she produced a long sheet of white foolscap and held it in front of her like a public notice.

He stood and went to her and took the paper. It was written like a letter and said

Mr. Henshawe,

You have made your decision, now we must make ours. It will not be

easy. It is never easy for a mother to turn loose her flesh and blood into

the world. It will be much easier, however, if we can secure from you

certain promises. First, that you will be so gracious as to pay our half

of Miss Eleanor Pickle's commission fee. Second, that you will allow

Mary Elizabeth to have a wedding dress made to her specifications and cost of said dress will be no object. Third, and finally, that the wedding

ceremony itself will not be an isolated affair. We demand, Mr. Henshawe,

that you prepare a long and extensive (not to mention highly inclusive)

guest list, including the names of the following....

And the Jenkins list of demands closed with a roll call of prominent town denizens, including various well-heeled doctors, businessmen, city councilmen, the mayor, and three state senators from Georgia.

"But I don't know any of these people," Mr. Henshawe confessed earnestly.

"Oh it doesn't matter," Mrs. Jenkins replied. "You're all rich, aren't you? Money builds quick bridges between people, Mr. Henshawe. In a way you all belong to the same club. You're like fraternity brothers, and they would not want to miss the wedding of one of their brethren."

Mr. Henshawe glanced at the list again, still skeptical.

"What do you say, Mr. Henshawe? Is this agreeable to you?"

"Well, I don't guess it would be too much to ask to...."

There was silence in the air suddenly rent by a handclap. "Well, Mr. Henshawe, it looks as if you have yourself a young and pretty briiiiiiiiiiide!!!!!"

Miss Pickle was the next to learn of their decision. Mr.

Henshawe told her when he came to pay his and Mary Elizabeth's fees.

"Now are you sure?" Miss Pickle asked him, her hand firm on his arm, her eyes unrelenting in their search of his face. "After all, I have many other files."

"Oh, yes. I'm sure. Ever since I saw that picture of Mary Elizabeth the first day here I've been sure." And before he turned to go he handed Miss Pickle her invitation to the ceremony.

It was as though some plague had invaded the town of Compton. When they had all been made out, the wedding invitations were lugged in several peach baskets to the post office to be mailed. Mr. Henshawe paid three of his field hands overtime to go into town with the delivery. Home after prominent home received the white and gold, hand-lettered requests of their presence at the betrothal of Ernest Angus Henshawe and Mary Elizabeth Frances Jenkins. And on the day of the ceremony, the church was almost entirely full. Mr. Henshawe, peeking around the altar door, recognized only three or four faces among the invited and wondered aloud at the attendance.

"Everybody loves a wedding," Mrs. Jenkins answered just before she left to join her daughter. "And everyone wants to see a good man like yourself get his happiness."

The ceremony itself passed like a dream for Mr. Henshawe. His best man, who was also his stockbroker, wanted to talk about business and next year's prospect for the peach crop, as they stood with the minister awaiting Mary Elizabeth. Then he glanced up and saw her, his bride, on her way down the aisle. She had not the vaguest hint of a smile on her face, looked, almost, as if she would wished to be anywhere else in the world but there in that church at that hour. Her mother walked beside her. Mr. Henshawe heard her voice above the organ-swell. "Lift up your veil, my dear," she whispered. "Lift it up and let them see Mrs. Jenkins's beautiful, beautiful baby on the happiest day of her life."

A reception in the high school gym followed. Mr. Henshawe sat in one corner with Mary Elizabeth beside him and drank pink punch. A long, cloth-draped table stood in the middle of the gym floor loaded with all manner of food – great big hams and golden pheasants, turkeys and Cornish hens, plates of green beans and squash, boiled potatoes the size of softballs, black olives, and rolls, sugar cookies and cakes, and peaches, of course – peaches fresh and candied, ice-creamed and cobblered. A dance band from Charleston played. A girl sang. Some folks danced, unsure at first if they should be enjoying themselves. Mrs. Jenkins milled about everyone, shaking hands, speaking in the excited way only she could employ. One would have thought she was running for political office. Mr. Henshawe watched everything for a moment before tuning it out, replacing the scene of the reception with a vision of the future – his future with Mary Elizabeth. "I feel whole now," he told himself as he imagined. "I feel I have everything in the world a man need have. I've got a business and now somebody to share it with." Mary Elizabeth was his partner now, as well as his wife. It had been her mother's ambition to make an honest, practical woman out of her daughter. This he would do. He would teach her to love the farm. He would take her out every day and let her become acquainted with his world – its cool mornings, its reddening sunrises, its feel of dirt, its wrestling with the unexpectedness of nature. He had never been more proud to be Angus Henshawe than he was right at that moment.

But it did not take long at all for Mrs. Jenkins to thwart this vision of domestic contentment.

First of all she would not allow him to share a bedroom with his wife until at least a goodly and respectable amount of time had passed. "Oh, six months I would say," she had replied when asked about such a limit. Mr. Henshawe settled into the extra room right off the kitchen. Mrs. Jenkins shared the master bedroom with her daughter.

Secondly, Mrs. Jenkins announced that neither she nor Mary Elizabeth would do the cooking. "Mrs. Jenkins and her daughter have spent almost all their lives learning the vocal and performing arts. There has been no time to master the culinary arts as well." So Mr. Henshawe was forced to hire a new woman to cook, a competent woman with good eyesight and a talent for more high-bred kinds of meals.

Thirdly, Mrs. Jenkins was hell-bent on the idea of turning Mr. Henshawe's modest home – the home of a practical businessman – into some roost for society women. She decided, solely with her own counsel and no one else's, to renovate the house. They took everything off the wall, moved all of Mr. Henshawe's furniture out onto the lawn so the house could air out, and rolled up the green worn rug which had covered the living room floor the very first day he had moved in himself all those years ago. Then with the frankness and determination with which her entire being seemed composed, Mrs. Jenkins asked Mr. Henshawe to sign a blank check which would allow her to buy the "elegant replacements" for the house. Bewildered, but nevertheless feeling it was his duty to give Mary Elizabeth's mother free reign in such matters, he reluctantly agreed. This shopping spree did not occur in Spartanburg or Charlotte or even Columbia. No local establishments would do. They spent a whole day, mother and daughter, in Atlanta, a more than four hour drive from Compton, and returned with three flatbed pickups weighed down with all kinds of things from all kinds of places. There were enormous wing-backed chairs with damask with gnarled arms and legs, a divan, wide as a hog, draped in a gold coverlet, several gilt-edged mirrors for the halls and bathrooms, and a gigantic carpet with a red and gold spiral design, which, Mrs. Jenkins claimed, was "handsome enough for a pasha's den." She bought oak end tables and a marble coffee table and coal-black Victrola with a small mermaid for a needle. She put a stone water fountain in the yard with Cupid aiming his arrow toward heaven and dressed the front yard with exotic, heavy scented plants and flowers whose lavish tendrils overflowed their pots and boxes in bright floods of green and red and yellow.

As a final touch she took from the attic three full-length portraits, kept wrapped, all the way from Bantam, Georgia, in oilcloth, of three men who, according to Mrs. Jenkins, were the "closet things to gods to walk this earth since the Savior himself." And she named them, one by one, in a voice of thundering reverence – Wolfgang Amadeus Mozart, Giuseppe Verdi, and Richard Wagner (pronounced by the lady as *Ree-card Vag-ner*). The pictures startled Mr. Henshawe, the first showing a boy-like man with a soft white face and powdered wig, the second an older man with a black beard and wide-brimmed hat, and the third, the most frightening of the three, a stern-faced man with a high forehead, piercing blue eyes, and beard which ran under his chin like wild moss. Mrs. Jenkins hung the portraits in three different places in the parlor. "They will look down like guardian angels," she claimed. She had not lied about her passion for music. It was as strong as a fisherman's net. Almost as soon as she and her daughter moved in with Mr. Henshawe, she kept the house filled with those strange orchestral sounds. She played records all day long, and sometimes she sang herself, took right to the little stand-up piano they had brought along with them and played and warbled until she had herself twisted into emotional knots and let the particular aria trail off with her own deep weeping. No matter where he was or what he happened to be doing in the house, Mr. Henshawe heard the sob, the whisper, the wail of opera. The plaintive melodies haunted him outside the house too, in his peach field, a tool shed, a barn; the memory of music became as pervasive as the music itself.

Mrs. Jenkins had brought her grand world into Mr. Henshawe's modest world with such thundering finality, he felt displaced, as though *he* had been the one to move. He wanted to express this concern to her and decided to do so one morning at breakfast. Both mother and daughter had taken chairs across from him. He wasted no time in broaching the subject.

"But, Mr. Henshawe," Mrs. Jenkins answered, laughing and clapping her hands simultaneously. "You *are* teaching Mary Elizabeth the value of practicality and hard work. She is getting a first-class lesson in all the wonderful things that are available to men such as yourself who have dedicated themselves to toil and thrift and industry. You are a marvelous teacher. Now Mary Elizabeth sees that when one works hard and saves and puts away, one will, at some point, be able to enjoy the fruits of one's labor in very grand style. Thank you, Mr. Henshawe! Thank you so much for such a bright and brilliant lesson on the benefits of the free

market system that has made this great country what it is!"
Her peroration nearly brought Mrs. Jenkins out of her chair.

Mr. Henshawe scratched his chin slowly in preparation
for a mild protest, no more than a question really, about the
nature of this "lesson," when his mother-in-law cut him off
abruptly.

"Mrs. Jenkins has decided that we are going to have our
first *soiree*," she announced simply and stood and went to
the kitchen counter where stood a pile of white, business-
sized envelopes. She lifted them into the air and held them
aloft like one of the antiques she had purchased in Atlanta.
They contained, she said, invitations, made out, by hand, to
a group of the wealthiest, best known men and women in
town and the surrounding area. "We're going to debut in
brilliant style!"

"Soiree? Here?" Mr. Henshawe inquired with no little
alarm.

"Of course *here*. Where else?" Mrs. Jenkins laughed.
"Do you think one would spend so much time and expense
remodeling a home with such care and attention only to let
it sit unutilized in the way it was meant to be utilized? No!
We are bound and determined, dear Mr. Henshawe, to make
this house the very show piece of the county!"

Mr. Henshawe scratched his chin again and thought a
moment then said, "Well, I reckon I could drive into town
that night. Have supper there. Leave you to your soiree. Be
out of your way."

"Oh no sir! You are going to be right in the thick of things! Sitting in the chair of honor. After all, you are the man of the house. We've got to show you off, haven't we?"

"It's not the best idea I've ever heard. No ma'am."

Not surprisingly, Mrs. Jenkins went about planning her get-together with great relish and enthusiasm, and on the very night of the event itself, she blazed with pride like a forest set a-fire. There was plenty of champagne, and a large suckling pig sat in the middle of the elegantly-set dinner table. She even hired a violinist from a restaurant in Atlanta to come and serenade. He would play all Mozart, she insisted; Mozart, according to Mrs. Jenkins, was the very soul of joy.

The guests arrived as it began to darken outside. Mr. Henshawe, who was still protesting his presence at the party that very afternoon, stood at the door and greeted everyone stiffly. He did not have more than two words to say to any of them, most of them being strangers to him, but it was all right, because once Mrs. Jenkins took over, no one else could get a word in edgewise. She was like a thunderstorm: she broke out all over at once and did not let up. She flooded the room with charm and electric magnetism. As each man and woman made his and her way into the house she caught hold of them by the arm or shoulder and greeted them like old friends, hugging them and staring into their faces with maternal solicitude. They were taken aback at first by such an insistent show of affection from this stranger but soon melted and were smiling and laughing right along with her.

Supper was served, and while the guests ate and the violinist limned an aria from *Cosi Fan Tutti*, "Un bella serenata," Mrs. Jenkins regaled them with stories of her operatic youth. She told them how the governor of Georgia had come to see her once when she sang in *La Boheme* in Savannah. He visited her backstage and told her – and these were, most assuredly, his own words – that she was the single most talented individual he had ever encountered and that he would soon issue a citation in honor of her great gift, which he did and had presented before the state legislature. She told them how, on a rainy day in Atlanta, a woman, a total stranger, had stopped her in the middle of a sidewalk on Peachtree Street, having recognized her from a performance of *Aida*, and begged her to sing her signature aria, 'O cieli azzuri." After some initial hesitation, Mrs. Jenkins had complied, and to a gathering crowd of passersby sang the song a cappella, leaving them all soaked in rain and tears.

"I would love to hear it," one of the guests said diffidently.

"What did you say, my dear?"

"I would love to hear that song you sang on the sidewalk in Atlanta."

Mrs. Jenkins laughed and feigned girlish embarrassment. "Oh no! That is a young woman's song. Mrs. Jenkins is too old to sing it now."

There was a polite protest to the point, after which Mrs. Jenkins, smoothing down her skirt with continued modesty, rose and went to the middle of the parlor. Her guests followed her. She cleared her throat and began.

Mr. Henshawe did not listen to the song but watched at how rapt Mrs. Jenkins's guests seemed to be at the sound of her voice. He remembered their earlier laughter and calls of amazement at Mrs. Jenkins's stories. He knew many of the men there, not personally, but as fellow professionals, and could not recall, as he had casual encounters with them on the street or business meetings with them in their offices or places of business, seeing them laugh with such abandon or taking an interest in "high culture."

When Mrs. Jenkins had finished, concluding her song with a slow, dramatic bow of her head, there was hesitation on the part of her guests, as though everyone waited for directions on what to do next, but once one person began to clap, others followed, and the room was soon filled with the sound of a vigorous rainfall of handclaps. Mrs. Jenkins accepted the applause with long bows, clasping her hands in front of her as though gasping for something. "Oh there is music in the air tonight! Mrs. Jenkins just feels it!" she exclaimed with a smile. She calmed a moment, her arms slipping to her sides and her smile fading, but almost at once she perked up again. "Let's waltz!" she cried. No one responded, and silence hung in the air.

"Waltz? We don't know that dance," someone offered.

"Oh, don't worry about steps. Steps are not the secret of the dance. It is joy! Joy is the secret of the dance! Joy is the great motivator. Let's go! Let's go!" Everyone stood and pushed back his chair so that the floor was cleared. Mrs. Jenkins moved into the middle of it and turned to the violinist. "Give us Strauss, Alfredo!" she commanded him, and he bowed in obeisance. Mrs. Jenkins began the dance solo, one jeweled arm arced above her head, the other held out in front of her waist in a half-circle. She moved slowly with majestic turns of her head and seemed, at once, to be lost in some languid and graceful dream of Vienna.

These bankers, these businessmen, these lawyers and doctors and all their stiff wives, who had lived so long in a small town and had hardly known a wild, abandoned happiness such as possessed this woman, watched Mrs. Jenkins turn herself loose, waltzing with herself, and were shocked and delighted at the same time. "Let's go!" she called again, and a few took the first, tentative steps; their audacity impressed still others who, after the first round, joined in. They did not worry about the formal steps of the waltz, although one or two of them had some experience and acted as models for the others. Most, however, moved as their spirits commanded. They whirled and pranced and kicked up their heels. They stumbled into furniture and into each other and moved so quickly that Mr. Henshawe swore he could hear the change rattle in their pants pockets.

"Dance! Dance! Live! Live!" Mrs. Jenkins

admonished above the din, and they obeyed.

"Why don't you go out yonder and join them?" Mr. Henshawe asked Mary Elizabeth. "You'd look right pretty doing that dance."

Mary Elizabeth glared at him. "What, and have another old man chasing after me?"
The waltzing did not last much longer. After all, these were not young people. Many of them bailed out after only a couple of rounds, felled by coughing fits and wiping their red faces with handkerchiefs. Others clutched uncooperative backs and knees.

The evening ended soon after. Before that, however, there was coffee and another story from Mrs. Jenkins, who told her audience about the time she had been mistaken for the Princess de Maintaigne by the viscount of Barfar. Then the guests lined up at the door to embrace their hostess and to thank her for such a splendid evening. "You made me feel like a youngun again," one of them confessed to her and hugged her urgently.

A few days later an item appeared in the society section of the Compton newspaper. The writer of the piece had been one of Mrs. Jenkins's guests. It read: "Spent Monday evening in the home of Mr. and Mrs. Angus Henshawe. Mr. Henshawe, of course, grows peaches. His mother-in-law, Mrs. Veronica Latham Jenkins, entertained all present with her superlative sense of culture and gracious manners."

"'Superlative sense of culture,'" Mrs. Jenkins read and

slammed the paper down on the breakfast table. "How splendid!" She stood and strolled about the dining room. "It's a triumph! That is what Mrs. Jenkins thinks it is! A veritable triumph! Mrs. Jenkins will have this town buzzing, just you wait and see." She grabbed up the paper and thrust it in the direction of her daughter and son-in-law. "Oh, all you have to do is tell them a story. That's what people want. A simple story. You might have to paint over the truth just a bit, but that's all right as long as you win your audience."

And from then on, once a week, Angus Henshawe's house swelled with the wealthiest and finest men and women of Compton and Spartanburg and Gaffney and Newberry, who came and drank his liquor and ate his food and danced with his mother-in-law until the early hours of the morning. There were even attendants from Charlotte and Columbia. Mr. Henshawe tolerated it all because he thought by appeasing Mrs. Jenkins he would win the affection of her daughter. But Mary Elizabeth had very little to do with the parties and seemed unimpressed by her mother's new-found celebrity (and with everything else, for that matter). Mary Elizabeth passed the first several months of her marriage in a hard, silk cocoon of sadness, surrounded by luxury but no more happy for the fact. She picked at her meals. She sat in one corner of the parlor during the day and sulked the whole time and at night went to bed early. She hardly spoke a word to either her mother or her husband, which pained Mr. Henshawe especially, who since that fateful day in Miss

Pickle's house months ago, the day he had seen Mary Elizabeth's picture for the first time, had come to have a strong belief in the power of love to change and transform a person – it had certainly changed him – and had hoped that the mere fact he loved the girl would sway her to him.

He expressed this concern to Mrs. Jenkins.

"Oh, don't worry yourself, sir. You are not aware of these things, but when a girl is coming into her womanhood, she cannot help but feel some measure of sadness. It is, after all, an enormous change. *Tres difficile*! Not like a young boy coming into his manhood. Oh no! He's all ready and raring to go. But a girl is more cautious about these things."

Then something happened. It was a day in early fall, and Mrs. Jenkins was out with one of her new-made friends, leaving Mr. Henshawe and Mary Elizabeth to lunch alone. Mr. Henshawe was reading over a letter from a banking associate in Columbia when, all of a sudden, there was a sharp crash of porcelain. He looked up quickly. Mary Elizabeth was staring at him in only the way she could – with cold relentlessness. He looked down at the floor beside her chair. She had picked up her plate and dropped it intentionally. Mashed potatoes and salted ham covered that spot on the floor.

"You don't want me to live!" Mary Elizabeth said, never taking her eyes off him. "You want me in this house like a caged bird to be looked at all the time. Well, I'm tired of being stared at by you. I'm not a fair freak. You think

I'm some old lady ready to be shut up in this house for good. But I'm not! I'm young and I want to act young and be young. And I want a young boyfriend."

The announcement came as a severe blow to Mr. Henshawe. "But can't you see," he whispered out of his pain, "you're everything I ever wanted."

Mary Elizabeth's look scorched him. "You don't know what you want."

When Mrs. Jenkins returned later that afternoon, Mr. Henshawe informed her of the conversation, and Mrs. Jenkins went straight up to Mary Elizabeth's room where she sat on the bed staring out the window and said, "What's this all about? Why are you behaving like a child?"

"Because that's what I am!"

"You better cease this foolishness. You better look around and see what you have. You are living like a queen. A queen, I tell you. And so is your mother. Your mother has earned all this. She has! All those years of deprivation and humiliation! You want it all taken away?"

"It's not enough! It's not enough! It's not enough!" Mary Elizabeth wailed, covering her face with her arms.

Mrs. Jenkins went to the bed and yanked the girl's hair hard. "Stop this foolishness now, I tell you, before you ruin everything!"

"Oh, a child's ingratitude," she told Mr. Henshawe a few moments later. "Nothing pierces one more deeply than a child who does not appreciate that which she has been given. Here she has a fine home and a fine man like you for a husband, and she behaves in such a way. Oh! Mrs. Jenkins's heart breaks to think about it!"

"Maybe she's got a point," Mr. Henshawe offered quietly. "Maybe she needs to be around other young people."

"Oh no sir! The *last* thing she needs is to be around young people. That will ruin all of Mrs. Jenkins's training, all the years of careful breeding and refinement. Mary Elizabeth is special. You know that. Groomed for the finer things, that's what she is."

And before leaving him, Mrs. Jenkins told Mr. Henshawe that she was planning to throw a grand Halloween party at the end of the month, which, she felt sure, would help cure the girl's ills. Mr. Henshawe, however, did not feel so encouraged.

One morning, the day of Mrs. Jenkins's Halloween party, he heard her and Mary Elizabeth arguing with each other in their bedroom. It was a familiar verbal tussle. "You're not ruining all this, do you hear?" the mother yelled. "If you do not reform your behavior this instant, I'll find some way to get you thrown out of here. I'll say you're not really my daughter. I'll say you're touched in the head. Yes ma'am! Just try me!" It was a startling exchange, not the least for the fact that Mrs. Jenkins finally referred to herself in the subjective. Then a crash followed and the thundering sound of footsteps, and before Mr. Henshawe knew it the girl had flown down the steps and flung herself onto the couch, face down, wailing like a banshee. Her mother followed calmly behind her, taking each step cautiously, and when Mr. Henshawe went to his young wife to comfort her, the mother said, "Don't touch her! She's just showing herself again. If you say anything to her, it will only encourage her insolence."

Mr. Henshawe watched Mary Elizabeth on the couch shaking with her sobs and felt deeply sorry for her and for himself too, but he felt more angry towards himself than anything else because, for the first time, he wondered if he were not some villain in a conspiracy against the girl, a plot to rob her of what rightfully belonged to her, her youth, her mobility, her right to live and laugh among her contemporaries.

"We've got a lot of things to do today," Mrs. Jenkins announced, oblivious to the drama proceeding around her. She told husband and wife, man and girl, how she expected them to behave at that evening's festivities.

She had gotten the notion into her head that Mr. Henshawe and Mary Elizabeth would attend the party garbed as two of her favorite characters from grand opera – Siegfried and Gutrune – from the epic Wagnerian *Ring* cycle. "Mr. Henshawe, since in so many ways you are a hero," Mrs. Jenkins had told him shortly after she conceived the idea, "and a hero especially to Mrs. Jenkins, she has decided that you should come attired as the chief figure in

The Ring of Nibelung. Oh, you'll make a handsome, Siegfried, sir! Mrs. Jenkins just knows it! And, Mary Elizabeth, since you are Mr. Henshawe's beloved, and therefore Siegfried's beloved, you shall go as Gurtrune."

"No, ma'am," Mr. Henshawe had said quietly.

"What's that?"

"I must refuse you."

"Refuse?"

"I cannot prance around this house in front of other people dressed like some clown."

"A clown? Mr. Henshawe, Siegfried is most certainly not a clown but one of the noblest, most dignified personages in all of musical drama."

"I don't doubt that for a minute. But I still must say no to you this time."

Mr. Henshawe had said nothing further then and rose and left the kitchen.

"Mr. Henshawe, where are you going? Mary Elizabeth, go after him!"

Mr. Henshawe had gone to his room and sat on his bed, as though to wait for some storm cloud to blow over. He knew he had to be firm this time. He had seen pictures of men singers in Mrs. Jenkins's opera books. They usually wore makeup and tight pantaloons, and one sight of him in Compton in that get-up would ruin his reputation. He would be a laughing stock.

There came a tiny knock at his door. He opened it.

Mary Elizabeth stood there with her head down.

"I would like you to go to my mama's party," she began in a low, meandering voice, "in the costume she has selected for you. She plans to work hard on this whole affair, and if you are not there, it will seem empty." She stopped a moment, as though to remember the next lines in her script, then resumed. "After all, you are the head of this household."

"Do you mean that?" he asked. "Is this what you want? You. Not your mama."

She had stared at him with bright eyes that could have been saying anything. "Yes," she said then turned.

"I'll go," he had said after her, almost beseechingly. "For you."

Now, weeks later, hours before the actual event, Mrs. Jenkins stood choreographing Mr. Henshawe and Mary Elizabeth's entrance into the party. "You are to come down together, Siegfried and Gurtrune, hand in hand, while Siegfried's Rhine Journey music plays behind you. You are to walk slowly, *slowly now*, to give the impression of gracefulness and stateliness. Oh, there won't be a back in the room free of shivers when the two of you arrive! Yes!" She clapped her hands, smiling and swollen with pride.

The guests began to arrive near six that evening. There was Mr. Hudgens, president of Compton Federal Bank, dressed as Don Giovanni's father, in a black coat and cape, with a black cravat and a black scarf flaring at his throat; his son came as Don Giovanni himself, and his wife was Donna Elvira, one of Giovanni's scorned lovers. There were three other Giovannis present in the first batch of guests – a dry goods merchant, a state house representative, and an attorney, who, despite the October chill and their own redoubtable paunches, came attired in silk shirts open at the throat, thin singlets, and thigh-clenching pantaloons.

Later, other Giovannis showed, along with two or three Figaros and at least one Idomeneo. G.V. Gibbons, the much-revered principal of Compton High School, tall and gangly and over eighty years old by then, came as Othello, in blackface and sporting a huge gold earring in his convoluted right ear; his wife Kathleen, also octogenarian, was Desdemon, with a black wig that reached the small of her back and bony shoulders which protruded from her diaphanous gown. The three Pope sisters and the Rivers boys were the gypsies from *Il Travatore*; they even entered the house humming "The Anvil Song" in happy unison. There was Claudette Applesteep as Madame Butterfly and her daughter Isolde as, well Isolde. There were a handful of Carmens, one Boris Gudenov, and even a Faust with Mephistopheles in tow.

And in the midst of all of them stood, like the ringmaster in the middle of a human menagerie, Veronica Jenkins, as Aida, of course. There was a certain grace in her appearance: her makeup had been applied to highlight her hard blue eyes, so her face looked both tender and powerful.

She greeted each guest in the manner she had assumed at her regular soirees, one of passionate homecoming, as though the house had been suddenly filled with prodigals begging return. She hugged and kissed everyone and made extravagant fuss over his or her costume. "Oh Mrs. Jenkins feels like she has died and gone to La Scala! She does! It's like a dream come true."

Meldrin Hubbard, the mayor of Compton, dressed as Pagliacci, turned the tables on her right away and proposed a toast in her honor, saying she had brought color and glamour and life to Compton. Glasses clinked, everyone cheered.

Through a cracked door, Mr. Henshawe watched it all from his room off the kitchen. Mrs. Jenkins had given him his final instructions. "You will wait until Mrs. Jenkins has completed singing 'O cieli azzuri.' Then she will put on the Siegfried music, and you will proceed."

His costume lay behind him on his bed, and he stayed as far away from it as he was able. It felt like a second person in the room, a stranger, a villain, a menace. Mrs. Jenkins had procured it at her Atlanta opera shop (after asking Mr. Henshawe, ever so nicely, for another blank check). It consisted of a short silk skirt, bearskin cap, sheepskin boots which tied about the shins in gold laces, a scimitar which fastened to a braided belt at the waist, and a blond wig and beard. He didn't give a hoot about opera, and the only reason he agreed to dress up was because Mary

Elizabeth had come softly into his room and asked him to, so softly, with such a gentle look on her face. And, Lord, he loved her – he really did – even though he barely knew her, barely knew who she was or what she wanted. He only knew her name and how beautiful she was, that was all, but he loved her and he was supposed to love her. It was one of those things that was meant to be. Some things are decided without our consultation or consent, and it had been decided, by someone, that he love this girl no matter what.

Mr. Henshawe closed the door all the way and went to his bed where the alien garment lay. He picked up the blond wig. It was stiff as a bird's nest and made him grimace. But he would wear it, and he would wear the beard and the skirt and he would carry the little knife, because Mary Elizabeth had asked him to.

Then a bold thought occurred to him, one that both frightened and thrilled him: Tomorrow I will take her out of here. Away from this that hurts her so much. That's right. We will leave this house, her and me, every board and brick of it to her mother, and she and her fine friends can prance about in it like fools all they please. Yes. Mary says she is a caged bird. Well, I will free her. She'll be free, and I'll be with her. I'll be free right along with her. That will make her love me. The fact I let her go. We'll go somewhere else and make a home. Just us. She'll be young. I'll see to it. I will fill our new place with young people. I have plenty of money. We'll make a good life for ourselves.

There was a roar from behind the wall, followed by applause and laughter. Someone had called for the waltz, and the music struck up and sent the dancers to the floor. A whole other hour came and ended in applause.

Mr. Henshawe's door opened, and Mrs. Jenkins stuck her head in. "You're not dressed yet? Mr. Henshawe, Mrs. Jenkins is about to sing her song! Yes! Now you get dressed and go up and get Mary Elizabeth. Mrs. Jenkins hasn't had a chance to check on her all evening."

The door closed, and Mr. Henshawe set about changing into his costume. He had wanted to say to Mrs. Jenkins, "You had better sure enjoy seeing us tonight, because you won't see us again. We're going. Far away."

Once dressed, he went to his door, refusing to look into the mirror as he passed it. He opened the door, peeked out, making sure no one was in the hall, then hurried from his room to the stairs. He chanced to look in on the event unfolding in his home as he went past and saw everyone gathered around Mrs. Jenkins, who was standing on a chair. The guests were toasting her with upraised glasses of champagne.

He climbed the dark steps, thinking, "Tonight I will free her. And she will love me for it. It will be me and her from now on. Nobody else."

The upstairs hall light was on, and Mr. Henshawe went straight to Mary Elizabeth's door and tapped gingerly on it.

"Are you dressed yet?" he called. "It's time to go." He

tapped again. No one answered. "Mary Elizabeth? Dear?" He blushed to say it. "Are you dressed?" When he got no response this time he tried the door slowly. "Excuse me if I'm...." He stopped. The room, lit by a red-shaded lamp by the window, was empty. The lamp threw out enough light on the bed so that he could see Mary Elizabeth's costume out on top of it, deflated. He switched on the ceiling lamp. There was a sheet of paper pinned to the dress. He took it and opened it. It read

Mama and Mr. Henshawe,

I don't mean to spoil your evening, and I'm sorry if I have, but I cannot go

on living this lie. I am not a singer or a society lady or anything else but a plain

girl with a plain girl's heart and mind and I have to live like one. I cannot

do this in this house because you two expect strange things from me that

I cannot do. I WANT TO LIVE. I'm going back to Atlanta to see if I can

pick up some kind of life there. Don't come after me. I don't want to be

found. Mr. Henshawe, I don't have anything against you. You probably

have a good heart deep down. But I don't love you and you don't love me,

Just that picture of me. I truly believe that to be so.

271

The note ended and Mr. Henshawe closed it.

He did not wonder how she had left the house or when; he did not feel sad or angry; he felt only regret that it had not been he who had set her freed as he had recently promised himself he would do. If she had stood there and asked him for permission to leave, he would have said, "Go on. Be free. I love you. I wouldn't stop you for the world."

He left the room and walked slowly to the top of the stairs. He heard, from the parlor, Mrs. Jenkins's announcing that she was going to sing, which provoked handclaps and cheers from her guests. Then there was silence followed by piano notes.

Mr. Henshawe started down the steps but stopped half way. Something had flashed beside him. He turned abruptly and saw himself staring into one of Mrs. Jenkins's gilt-edged mirrors.

Lord, there he is. Yes, that's Angus Henshawe in that mirror. That's what he has come to, the lovesick old fool. Made a fool of himself for a girl. Where's your bride now, Angus, the one you dressed up for? Where'd she go? She in the peach field? Better go get her! No, she's gone, she's gone, she's way too far gone for fetching.

He raised the letter and was going to read it again in the dim light from the parlor, but he didn't. Instead, for truly the first time, he listened to Mrs. Jenkins's singing as her voice floated up the stairwell, like some ghost haunting his once-peaceful, once-quiet house. He could not help but be impressed by it. It was an old woman's voice for sure: it shook at times and threatened to break, but the thing was it didn't; it persisted, bell-clear and happy somehow, though the message of the song was very sad. The voice singing it seemed glad to be holding such sadness. And right then, to Mr. Henshawe anyway, it seemed the only happiness in the world that night was in that old lady's voice.

Snake in the Grass

For Julian Ivey

THE BLACKSNAKE NEATLY SLID into place in the short grass very near Emory McMillan's left leg. And there it stayed, as though it had finally found the place for which it had been looking all his short blacksnake life.

Mr. McMillan had been working in the yard that summer day, mowing the lawn, tending to the small tomato and cucumber garden he had cultivated in his backyard. He had just returned a small hand shovel to its place in the aluminum work shed that sat a few feet from his house.

Now, as a rule, Mr. McMillan did not fear snakes. His had been a rural boyhood and young manhood, and he had encountered all manner of reptiles through the years, from moccasins and rattlers to snakes that had to this day probably not been properly classified and named. He had come upon nests of them in the woods while hunting. He had walked right past a rattler once, ringed quietly in the sedge, mistaking it for a pile of horse dung. He had even eaten rattler once at the behest of a zealous cousin who had dared him but could not go along with his cousin's assessment that rattler was every bit as good as a piece of medium rare sirloin.

Still he was good enough of a Southern Baptist that some degree of uneasiness and distrust attached itself to the idea of the snake. It all went back to the Garden of Eden.

The blacksnake continued to lie peacefully near him, immobile as a piece of black thread or strand of licorice.

"Mister, you best get along now if you wish to stay intact," Mr. McMillan said quietly, as though the snake would be intimidated merely by the sound of his voice.

Leave him be, something told him. Blacksnakes are good to eat rats.

He had killed animals in his time and not merely hunting. He'd bludgeoned rodents with axe handles and dissected snakes with axe heads. He had done none of this for sport but for protection against injury and disease. Of course there had been the time, when he was twelve years old or thereabouts, when he had stuffed a pile of mewling, new-born kittens into an old army gunny sack, tied the mouth tightly closed, took the noisy contents to a pond in the grassy bottoms, and threw it into the water, where it sank without a trace or a sound. The kittens had posed no harm to him other than as potential mouths to be fed. A small, nagging guilt over that incident had followed him fifty years down the road.

The blacksnake lay in the grass as though it were too happy ever to move again.

They eat rats, the same voice told him.

Another voice followed directly behind the first: "Man

is master of the lowly creature."

The snake seemed so content where it was, so comfortable around human beings, that it occurred to Mr. McMillan that maybe it was somebody's pet that had gotten away from whatever confinement held it and somehow had made it to his yard and his left leg and saw no reason to turn around and go back. Maybe if he left it there, in time it would find its own way back home and in the meantime clear the area of whatever scourge lived there.

Then Mr. McMillan thought of his grandson, whom he and Mrs. McMillan were to tend to later that day. The boy loved to roam the boundaries of the yard.

He unlocked the shed and found the hoe. It was dusted nearly orange from so much contact with the raw ground. The snake did not move at the approach of the man.

"I told you," Mr. McMillan said before raising the blade.

He brought it down hard and afterwards took comfort in the fact that he had been so lightning-quick in the strike, the snake could not have felt a thing.

About the Author

RANDALL IVEY is a native of Upcountry South Carolina and senior instructor in English at the University of South Carolina-Union where he has seven times been named Distinguished Teacher of the Year. Besides short stories, which have received numerous prizes, he is the author of a children's book, *Jay and the Bounty of Books,* an entertaining tale of the triumph of books over television. Ivey is the founder and director of the Upcountry Literary Festival, which has featured readings by noted writers.

Available from Shotwell Publishing

Non-Fiction

Nullification: Reclaiming Consent of the Governed (The Wilson Files) by Clyde N. Wilson

The Yankee Problem: An American Dilemma (The Wilson Files) by Clyde N. Wilson

Maryland, My Maryland: The Cultural Cleansing of a Small Southern State by Joyce Bennett.

Washington's KKK: The Union League During Southern Reconstruction by John Chodes.

When the Yankees Come: Former South Carolina Slaves Remember Sherman's Invasion. (Voices From the Dust) Edited with Introduction by Paul C. Graham

Southerner, Take Your Stand! by John Vinson

Lies My Teacher Told Me: The True History of the War for Southern Independence by Clyde N. Wilson

Emancipation Hell: The Tragedy Wrought By Lincoln's Emancipation Proclamation by Kirkpatrick Sale

Southern Independence. Why War? - The War to Prevent Southern Independence by Dr. Charles T. Pace

IF YOU ENJOYED THIS BOOK, we'd be very grateful if you would post a brief review of it on the retailer's website, GoodReads, Facebook, Twitter, or anywhere else you think might help us get the word out about this and other titles from Shotwell.

In the current political and cultural climate, it is important that we get accurate Southern-friendly material into the hands of our friends and neighbours.

Your support can really make a difference in helping us unapologetically celebrate, honour, and defend our Southern heritage, culture, history, and home!

Join the Revolution! To Sign-up for New Releases Notifications and get a FREE eBook, please visit us at

www.ShotwellPublishing.com